Lee Mackenzie, [illegible] pseudonym, is the author of a series of tough thrillers. She started her career as assistant editor in a paperback company, then spent ten years working on various magazines. Now a full-time writer, she is an active member of the Crime Writers' Association and will be its Vice Chairman in the coming year.

Also available from Sphere Books by Janice James

THE BROTHERS Volume 1
THE BROTHERS Volume 2

The Brothers

Book 3

LEE MACKENZIE

SPHERE BOOKS LIMITED
30/32 Grays Inn Road, London WC1X 8JL

First published in Great Britain by Sphere Books Ltd 1974

TRADE
MARK

Set in Intertype Times

Printed in Great Britain by
Hazell Watson & Viney Ltd
Aylesbury, Bucks

ISBN 0 7221 5696 0

CHAPTER ONE

David Hammond felt inclined to turn up the collar of his jacket. The wind across the parking bays was bitter. But the corpulent Mr. Rogers might misread the action: 'Poor devil, can't afford a decent overcoat,' or 'They haven't the money to build a proper wall to cut that bloody breeze short.'

No, no – nonsense, of course. Mustn't let himself get jittery about Rogers. If they didn't hook his contract, there were other fish to land. David glanced at his eldest brother who, with that confident calm he always showed in his natural surroundings, was leading the way across the asphalt.

'The warehouse is this way, Mr. Rogers.' Edward glanced over his shoulder, to find their prospective client eyeing a collection of wine casks at Bay No. 4.

'What's in them?'

'Wine. From France.' Edward was rather pleased; there was something sophisticated and international about being able to toss off a phrase like that. Damn good thing he didn't ask about the load of crates on the lorry just pulling out which held, as far as he was aware, kitchen towels. 'We'd bring your goods down in bulk from Leeds,' he went on as he ushered Rogers into the busy warehouse. 'Store 'em here till we receive your schedule of deliveries.'

'Then we'd distribute them according to your instructions,' David took it up. 'We cover all retail outlets in the South East. I think I mentioned that in my follow-up letter . . .'

Edward gave him his head. He had a gift for the medium-hard sell, had our David. It never ceased to amaze him, the change that had come over the family playboy since he joined Hammond Transport's board of directors. Or was it since he married Jill?

Edward was sometimes a little uneasy when he thought about David's marriage. Had they pushed him into it? Certainly you couldn't wish a better wife for a footloose younger brother, and he seemed to love her – but had it been the kind of love that ends up in church or had they, his family, more or less marched him there with a shotgun at his back?

The shotgun had been the need of a big injection of money

into Hammond Transport. A fine mess they'd nearly landed themselves in, what with buying that expensive parcel of land to extend the depot, and the strike, and the tie-up with Carter Express. Like a good angel, Jill had appeared with a very large inheritance in her hand and the light of undying devotion in her eye. Luckily for them, it was David Hammond she was devoted to.

Right. Wedding-bells and orange blossom. Nobody had actually said, 'Damn it, you like her and she adores you and she's *rich*' but it had been in all their minds. It had been so loud an idea in Edward's brain at the ceremony that he wouldn't have been surprised to hear the parson say: 'Wilt thou have this woman and her one hundred thousand pounds . . .?'

Somewhere around that time, David had taken a real grip on himself. No more discos and gaming clubs, no more racing power boats in the choppy Solent waters. Almost overnight, he turned over a new leaf to reveal himself as an astute, enthusiastic salesman of Hammond Transport's services. Had that happened just before or just after he married Jill? Edward wanted to think it had happened earlier; it troubled him that his brother might feel he *must* make the firm bigger and more successful, just to pay off the debt they now owed Jill.

So now he was doing his spiel to Rogers, and Edward could see that despite himself Rogers was impressed.

'But mind you,' he said, 'you'd need a tidy fleet of vans to do the deliveries. What d'you do about vans? Sub-contract?'

'No, we have our own fleet,' Edward cut in, with the pride he always felt when he mentioned this recent venture. How the old man would have loved his own van fleet. 'We'll show them to you in a minute, Mr. Rogers. Could we just move on, if you've seen enough of the warehouse? I'd like you to look at our workshop. This way.'

The workshop had always been Edward's special pride and joy, ever since he joined his father on coming straight from school. Not for him the extended education that his younger brothers eventually received: he'd been down here in the servicing area with grease up to his elbows at an age when other youngsters were heading for university. But – except in moments of annoyance with David or Brian – he didn't really envy them their 'advantages'. *Here* was where you got your real education, here among the big rigs and their steady, throbbing engines – and among the men who drove them.

Edward was happily launched: 'Simulated testing bay . . . dummy run for M.O.T. . . . lubricant analysis . . . loading technique . . .' David listened with only half an ear. This wasn't really his department.

He was waiting for Rogers to give a signal. Had they hooked him or not? Grabbing new business was never easy, and the way things were at present, clients were looking for a transport service that pared every expense down to the bone.

Ah, here it came. Rogers was murmuring that he had other appointments. 'Some of your . . . ah . . . competitors are very keen to secure our business, Mr. Hammond. We're a cost-conscious firm. All this . . .' he waved at the workshop area . . . 'puts the pennies on, eh?'

'We provide a service, Mr. Rogers,' Edward said. 'That can't be done on the cheap.'

'My brother's got a good point there,' David said, catching the ball Edward had thrown to him. 'Hammond Transport make sure its lorries are well-maintained and of course, that costs money. But so do breakdowns. Collections and deliveries aren't made on time by vehicles that break down.'

'But all the same, Mr. Hammond,' Rogers protested, 'my firm would have to pay a price that's going to help you pay for this set-up. The rates alone . . .!' He swept a glance over the premises, which certainly were extensive now they'd added the van area.

'I think if you'll go through the figures I sent you you'll see that we are quoting a very competitive price. Other transport firms sub-contract the van work. We used to do so ourselves. But we tied ourselves in with another firm – you may recall the name? Carter Express?' Rogers nodded, and David went on: 'A year's experimenting showed us that the best solution was to run our own vans, set up our own maintenance, and retain complete control. It makes for reliability, Mr. Rogers. Believe me, this firm has a whole generation's experience behind us – we know what we're doing.'

An inner voice said to him: 'What we're doing is trying to justify the fact that we took all that the tax man left to Jill of her father's quarter-million, and sank it in this bloody business,' but he was learning to ignore these qualms. Money was money, nothing more: Jill's money or anyone else's, it bought goods and financed activities – it was the brain and the will behind the money that mattered.

He was annoyed when the Tannoy system interrupted his conversation with Rogers, so that he had to leave him to his brother. He charged up the iron staircase to the office, nearly falling over Brian as he got to the top.

'It's Chambers,' Brian said. 'He wants to move the wine out as soon as poss. And something about onward to Lyons – do you know what this is?'

'Oh?' David's mobile mouth tilted up at the corners. 'So he's nibbling, is he?'

'Didn't know Chambers exported?'

'Never you mind, Chequebook,' he said blithely, hurrying on. 'Go back to your little profit-and-loss account.'

Brian closed the staircase door and followed his brother more slowly back into the offices. Somewhere down below, he knew, Edward was squiring a client around the premises and in about half an hour they'd all gather in the boardroom to give him a pre-lunch drink. With a stifled sigh he glanced in at the boardroom as he made his way back to his own office.

One of the things he'd have to do soon was squeeze out a few pounds for boardroom improvements. Now that David was beginning to bring business contacts to the depot quite regularly, the ugly buildings were more or less on display. God alone knew what other people thought of the stark utilitarian décor of the boardroom . . .

When he looked back on the comfort of his old firm, it seemed like another world. But then, accountancy *was* a world away from the rough and tumble of the transport industry. There was very little here that was urbane or predictable, almost nothing that could be arranged in neat columns and added and subtracted to come out in a neat answer at the bottom of the page.

Yet he enjoyed it. No matter what Ann might say, there was a compulsive spell about the set-up. It wasn't as lucrative as being partner in an accountancy firm, and certainly not as gentlemanly – God, no! Not with Edward charging around and losing his temper when things went wrong!

But it was more fun. Now *there* was a strange idea. He couldn't ever imagine himself telling his wife that he enjoyed being a director of his dead father's firm because it was more fun. She probably thought him incapable of such a notion.

That very morning they'd had an odd conversation. It had come back into Brian's mind once or twice in the four hours since he left home for the office. How had it started?

It was when he said he might not make it to the school in Hampshire to see Nigel play Ben Gunn in 'Treasure Island'. Ann had pouted prettily.

'We ought to go, darling. We missed the soccer championship – although from what he tells me it's just as well. Eight-nil, poor love. He'll never be goalkeeper for England.'

Brain glanced through the other envelopes the postman had brought. Bills, mostly. There were always plenty of those.

'What day's the school play?'

'Friday.'

He shook his head. 'I'll check, but I'm pretty sure there's a cocktail party we're all attending. Some firm has contacted us . . . Ted's not keen but I think we ought to go so I'm raising it at today's board meeting.'

Ann was easing back a strand of long soft hair that had caught on the collar of her housecoat. 'Brian . . .'

'Yes?'

'Why is Edward chairman and managing-director of Hammond's?'

He was quite startled. It was very rare indeed for Ann to take the slightest interest in the business, except to ask why it didn't provide them with a better income.

'Well, Edward's . . . He just took it on when Dad died. We all agreed that he should.'

'Yes, but as a stopgap measure, surely?' She gave a little shrug that moved the fine patterned silk over her shoulders. 'I mean, chairman perhaps . . . okay, he's the oldest. But is he the one best qualified to be chief executive?'

Brian was mystified. 'Who else is there?'

'Why not you?'

The idea struck him as laughable. Yet, funnily enough, he'd been touched that she should say such a thing. 'Ann,' he replied, amusement in his voice, 'I've no ambition to be managing-director!'

She leaned a little towards him, flicking at the shoulders of his dark suit to remove a speck of dust that ought not to have been there, for he'd used the clothesbrush energetically before he came downstairs.

'I'm not talking about ambition, darling,' she murmured. 'I'm talking about the good of the firm. You were telling me the other day you're aiming to become a really big company – didn't you say you'd probably be quoted on the Stock Exchange—?'

'But that was for the future, dear—'

'Ted's nice,' she swept on, 'but is he really up to that? You're the one with the financial brain, and that's what they'll need.'

'And just now I'm needed,' he rejoined, 'at work.' He gave her his usual goodbye kiss on the cheek and hurried out, but as he edged his car out of the garage he was wishing he'd paused to give her a real kiss, a kiss of gratitude because she'd said such nice things and had clearly been thinking about him and his prospects.

Managing-director . . . Could he do it, supposing the chance was ever put his way? He had the financial know-how, that was certain. It was thanks to him that the firm had weathered the storm into which they'd stupidly sailed when they got themselves mixed up with Carter Express. Both his brothers knew how much they owed him, and as for the fourth member of the board, Jennifer Kingsley – well, if the truth were known, she had a better head for figures than either Ted or David. If ever it came to the point of changing the managing director, he was almost sure he could rely on Jennifer's vote.

Brian sat down at his desk, suddenly colouring and glad there was no one there to see. What was he thinking about? Replacing Ted as managing director! Utter nonsense – and disloyal, too.

He hadn't quite got over this feeling when the board assembled late that afternoon for its regular meeting. He shuffled through the papers from his brief case, his thin face vaguely harassed as he prepared in his mind the various points he wanted to make. Proposal to redecorate the boardroom before too long; heating costs; watchman's equipment to be renewed; that long letter about tax – better summarise that . . .

He awoke to the fact that Edward had said something provocative, to which he seemed to expect an answer.

'I didn't quite catch . . .?' he said, raising his head.

'I said, they only want to sell us something.' Ted indicated the large, gilt-edged invitation cards he had just thrown on the board table. 'They want to drum up business, that's all.'

'They're a very large and reputable agency—' Brian began, aware he'd been forced on the defensive from the outset.

'We've always looked after our own advertising,' Edward interrupted. 'Why do we need an advertising agency all of a sudden?'

'Because until now we've never taken advertising seriously—'

'And it shows.' The new voice was Jennifer Kingsley's. She was sitting at the far end of the table, the picture of efficiency as usual, her pad and pencil at the ready for note-taking and her brow creased into the two little frown lines between her brows that meant she was concentrating.

Edward gave her a surprised glance. She nodded with emphasis. 'What we do is amateur stuff – placards in buses, ads. in the local paper—'

'After all,' said Brian, pulling one of the invitations towards him, 'what can we lose? It's a cocktail party for potential clients. A chance to meet, talk informally, see if they can be of any use to us or not. There's no commitment. But good advertising would certainly help David land the new business he's after.'

If he was expecting support from his younger brother, he was disappointed.

'Ted's right,' said David bluntly. 'They're not offering us free drinks for nothing! They expect to make something out of it.'

'Not necessarily. They don't clinch every contact they invite to a party, surely.' This was Jennifer again.

'And what about that new contract you were after with What's-his-name this morning?' Brian demanded. 'You said yourself that Mr. Rogers commented on our lack of advertising.'

This was only too true. As he and Edward hauled Rogers into his Rolls-Royce after lunch that afternoon, David recalled, he'd paused to purse his lips and look regretful. 'You don't do much advertising, do you?' His wary eye had rested on Edward. 'I knew very little about Hammond Transport until David got in touch with me.'

His tone carried a double implication: that they weren't very go ahead, that they couldn't afford to advertise. In a way it had been a feather in David's cap to have the man say that he was there only because David had put himself out to bring him – but David hadn't been entirely pleased.

Nor was he now. 'New commitments are out,' he said. His voice, which always sounded young compared with the others, was laced with annoyance. 'We can't afford any new expense.'

'I'm the best judge of what we can afford,' thought Brian. Aloud he said, 'Dave, things are going well, you know that. We've learned our lesson, we've reorganized, we're out of trouble . . . '

David could see that Brian was making a big effort not to be irritated over the way his judgement on new expense had been questioned. But that didn't prevent him from putting his point.

'Jill guaranteed us to the tune of nearly a hundred thousand pounds. What death duties didn't take, we did. Are you saying we're now in a position to release the guarantee?'

'If only we were!' he added to himself. 'God, to be free of this debt of gratitude . . .'

Brian shuffled his papers. 'Not at this moment, no. That would be premature. We must have backing for a while to retain the operating credit we need.'

Edward sat watching the lightning flicker between his two younger brothers. Not a bit like them . . . If there was a row in the boardroom it was usually yours truly who was to blame. But it seemed to him that today there'd been a touch of the old iron about Brian, and for a while now David had had a tendency to get edgy if they looked like throwing Jill's money around.

'All right,' David said with some truculence, 'so her money is still locked up and no matter how you phrase it, we're still in her debt. The day we're not, we can start talking about luxuries like advertising agencies.'

Brian decided he would scratch 'redecorate boardroom' from his list of proposals for today. He said in a tone of reason: 'Advertising's only a luxury if it doesn't work. If it generates extra business which we can handle profitably—'

'If!' grunted Edward. 'Will it?'

'Damn it, why can't he ever let me finish what I'm saying?' thought Brian. He said, losing his reasonable note: 'What harm does it do to find out? To go to the party?'

Jennifer had the courage to say what the men could not. She caught David's glance and held it. 'We all feel the same way about Jill's money, David.' She gave a little smile to take away the sting of this admission – that his wife had had to salvage them from their own angry incompetence last year. 'But these advertising bods have got to convince us, and if they don't – well, we can say no.'

Edward looked round the table. No one wanted to argue it further. As so often, Jenny had struck just the right chord. 'All right. We've got other matters to deal with. I suppose there's no harm in listening to what they've got to say. Agreed?'

'It's only the timing I object to,' muttered David. But once more Jennifer caught his eye. 'Oh, well, all right. Let's move on to the next item.'

As they filed out of the boardroom an hour later they had reason to be pleased with themselves. On the whole, business was good.

Edward fell into step with Jennifer as they crossed the blustery parking lot. The wind caught her light brown hair, lifting it into a swirl of bright movement in the evening sun. He felt, as he often did, an indefinable ache as he looked at her.

'I'll drive you to that cocktail party, shall I?' he ventured.

She shrugged. 'I don't think I'll bother going.'

'Brian and David are taking their wives. I'll have to be there.' He paused as she put her key in the car door. 'You could keep me company,' he said.

She gave him a little sidelong glance. Poor old Ted . . . Oldest of the brothers, yet the only one unmarried. That old web-weaving spider of a mother of his! She was never going to let Ted out of her clutches – not, that is, unless he chose to be fond of someone other than Jennifer Kingsley.

'I expect you'll find someone else to keep you company,' she said. She didn't say it spitefully, even though he had temporarily found someone else last year, just after his mother trampled all over the relationship that had been growing between Jennifer and Edward. She knew, and Edward knew, that their situation was almost hopeless.

In a way she was a lot luckier than Edward. When Robert Hammond died, all Edward was left with was a part-share in the company he'd expected to inherit entire, and his widowed mother.

But she, Jennifer Kingsley, had more – lots more. Robert had left her an equal share with his three sons in Hammond Transport. That in itself was substantial. But more than that, she had his daughter, Barbara – his daughter and hers. Barbara was the living proof that she had had Robert Hammond's love.

And for this Mary Hammond, Robert's widow, was never going to forgive her.

Naturally it had been a shock to Mrs. Hammond. Everyone had been shocked and astounded when the will was read – not least Jennifer herself. To have it admitted publicly that Barbara was Robert's natural daughter, that Jennifer had been his mistress for years . . . Well, it had been a bad time. For a while she'd been close to hating Robert for the pain he had caused her.

But as time went by everyone began to accept the situation. She and Edward had been drawn to one another first of all by a sense that the will had done them an injustice – he, in being given only a quarter of what he felt his years of work had earned him, and she, in being exposed to public gossip.

After a while the friendship between them had deepened. She was almost sure that on an evening twelve months or so ago, Edward had had an engagement ring in his pocket to offer to her.

And what happened? His mother arrived back from Bermuda unexpectedly. That evening of all evenings, she'd called all her sons to a welcome-home party. How could they refuse? If they did, she might have another of the heart attacks that had caused her doctor to pack her off to Bermuda in the first place.

The truth was that Mary Hammond must have sensed something in Edward's letters to warn her of how he felt about Jennifer. And if it was the last thing Mrs. Hammond did, she would prevent her son from marrying her husband's ex-mistress. She was never going to come to terms with the fact that her dead husband had been deceiving her for seventeen years or more; she could only make it bearable by believing that Jennifer was to blame, an evil, scheming adventuress. Jennifer must be punished. Certainly she was never to have the happiness of being loved by Edward, of marrying him to become Mrs. Hammond. Mary was Mrs. Hammond – Jennifer could never be allowed to assume that title.

This had become the background to Jennifer's relationship with Edward, and it was in her mind now as she debated whether to accept his offer.

'I don't want to rake over the old ashes, Jenny,' he said, in a way that from such a big pugnacious man was curiously humble. 'But you know there are bound to be social occasions when I need someone with me.'

'All right,' she agreed. 'You can drive me.' She got into her car as he held the door. 'But I'll be wearing the same old dress you've seen before.'

'Good,' he said cheerfully. 'It suits you.'

He banged her door shut and stood back to wave as she drove out.

David had hurried home with a case full of paper work. He was after a haulage contract for a cosmetics firm which had expanded its sales beyond delivery capabilities. So far as he knew, no one else had cottoned on to the opportunity so if he got his offer in quick, he might get all the pickings.

As he put his key in the door of his flat he could hear Jill's high, clear voice, soaring up in excitement.

'When? When – oh! Well, I *could*, I think. I mean it's possible about the date. Hold on.'

He put his head round the livingroom door. She was skirmishing on the bureau with one hand, in search of her diary. He crossed, found it for her, and tried to give her a kiss as her head bobbed about while she turned pages.

A voice was clacking in the receiver urgently. 'Yes,' said Jill, 'but it *is* short notice . . . Yes, I know it's a marvellous opportunity . . .'

David raised his eyebrows at her. 'What is?' he mimed.

She wrinkled her nose and shook her head. 'Well, could I think it over and ring you back? All right . . . yes . . . yes, Andy, I will. 'Bye.'

As she put down the phone he swooped on her and kissed her with enjoyment. The curves of her body in his arms always gave him a deep pleasure, partly sexual, partly proprietorial. In a way it was still something of a marvel to him that she was his wife. He'd never owned anything so valuable before. Cars, yes. Even a powerboat. And other women too, of course – but he hadn't owned them. More a sort of lend-lease relationship, he thought, with a faint grin.

But Jill belonged to him. What was more, she'd given herself to him. All of her. 'With this ring I thee wed, with my body I thee worship . . .' All that. And 'With all my worldly goods I thee endow.'

She'd held nothing back. It was frightening, really. He knew damn well he didn't deserve it. Of course you could almost say that about any man – no one was good enough for Jill. But he less than most, he often thought. If she knew the half of what he'd done – things he was ashamed of now, things that would have hurt her deeply even in the days when they were lovers without the Wedding March bit. He had owed her loyalty because the affair had been serious and a bloke who's deep in a serious affair shouldn't be jumping into the sack with the first eager sexpot who comes along. And what had he done? He'd two-timed. Three- or four-timed, in fact.

And – get this, he thought – with her best friend.

Oh well. That was in the past. The present was here in his arms – perhaps the most beautiful creature he would ever lay his eyes on, gentle, desirable and deeply in love with good old David Hammond. He would make it all up to her – the past betrayals, the contemporary guilt that was always waiting to drag at him. He'd make her a good and faithful husband, and he'd get her money back from the firm with interest. One day, please God, he'd stop feeling guilty.

'What's a marvellous opportunity?' he inquired, depositing a kiss for luck on the nape of her neck.

'The chance to leave you.'

'Really? So soon?'

'A Festival of International Fashion,' she explained, 'promoted by a magazine.' She borrowed the pen from inside his breast pocket to scribble in her diary. 'It's to have television coverage, all that stuff . . . There are only three British girls going,' she ended with pride, 'and I'm to be one of them.'

David was impressed. He always tended to think of Jill's modelling as something of a hobby. 'Well, now, that does sound . . .' He broke off. 'Going where?'

'It's a German magazine,' she said, avoiding his eye.

'Published in—?'

'Hamburg. That's where the show is.'

'Oh, I see,' he said. Absurdly enough, he was put out. Hamburg sounded a long way.

Jill said, 'I thought perhaps you might be able to come with me.'

'*That's* a good idea.' A few days in sexy old Hamburg! 'When would you be going?'

'Tomorrow.'

'Tomorrow?'

'The truth is,' she said apologetically, 'I wasn't first choice. But the other girl's been taken ill, so they rang me sort of last-minute.'

'Tomorrow,' he said, holding a parade before his mind's eye of all the things he had to do before Friday. It was impossible to be away. 'I think you'll have to fly solo on this one, love.'

She wound her arms round his neck, and muttered against his jacket. 'I don't want to be away from you, Davie.'

'But you'd like to do it,' he prompted.

'If it was in London, I'd love to.' She shook her head, her face still hidden. 'Still, it isn't, so—'

David took her by the shoulders and held her off. He looked severe, which was only half acting: the truth was, he felt this was yet another thing he was going to feel guilty about, the giving up of the Hamburg trip.

'I'm away myself pretty often,' he remarked. 'It's goose and gander sauce, isn't it? No, darling, tell them you'll accept. Why not?'

They argued it back and forth while she prepared the meal. She'd embarked on a complicated French dish before he got home but now her attention wasn't on it. The sauce curdled; he was called on to stir while she added white wine, the whole thing being in the end more or less a veal cutlet in gravy. The funny thing was that he'd quite enjoyed all the pottering about beforehand.

As he'd done more than once recently, he tried to analyse how he really felt, sitting at home like an old married man eating a home-cooked meal and with an evening of office paper work ahead of him. Was this what life was going to be from now on?

He felt Jill's eyes upon him. If she said, 'What are you thinking?' what would he reply?

But instead she went to the sideboard for the fruit dish. Propped against it she found the invitation to the advertising cocktail party.

'Did you bring this in?' she asked.

'Yes. Just a business thing.' He realized that in her modelling career she might have run across the agency. 'Do you know them?'

'Quite well. They're very good. A Mr. and Mrs. set-up, with a lot of involvement.'

David shrugged. 'Well, I'll have to go on my own. I'll tell you about it when you get back.'

She made a little movement of rejection, as if to say, 'Who says I'm going?'

'Have you phoned yet?' he demanded.

'No.'

He glanced at his watch. 'Time's getting on. You'd better ring now.'

'Oh, David, I'm not really sure about it . . .'

'Why not?'

'Well, I'd have to postpone a fitting at the dressmaker, and I was supposed to lunch with a fashion editor tomorrow, and anyway I hate last minute packing.'

He couldn't help a trace of impatience. 'You could make a clean sweep of it and give up modelling altogether, if it's such a problem.'

'Oh, I . . .' She paused so as to choose her words carefully. 'I know you don't understand, David. It doesn't seem much of a job, standing about like a clothes-horse being photographed. But I like it and I'm good at it. Besides, what would I do, alone in this flat all day?' She looked at him keenly. 'I thought we'd agreed all that.'

'We had, so be logical about it! If it happens to take you abroad, well, that's the work you've chosen to do.'

'But you don't like the idea. I can tell you don't.'

No, he didn't. But why didn't he? Could it be because he was a selfish bastard and didn't like the idea of being alone?

'I shall be lonely,' he said, 'I shall miss you, and I shall be extremely bored. None of which is a fatal disease.'

She broke out into a little laugh, catching his hand in hers. Then she said, 'You *are* sure, darling? Because if you—'

He got up, and because she had hold of his hand she got up too.

'Jill, either pack it all in for good, or get on that phone and say you're going.' The abruptness of his manner brought a shadow to her face. He relented, adding softly: 'On one condition – that you call me from Hamburg every night.'

'I shall do that anyway,' she said as he handed her the phone. She smiled over it as she dialled, and he realized that for whatever obscure reasons of his own, he had done the right thing.

Brian was having a far less agreeable evening. He arrived home to the smell of something superb in the oven, and when he glanced in the diningroom there was his wife folding napkins into little cocked hats to grace an already handsome table.

His heart sank. He'd been looking forward to a nice quiet meal. 'Why all the trimmings?' he inquired. 'Is someone coming?'

'Your mother. We were talking on the phone and I found myself inviting her.'

Somehow this did nothing to raise his sunken heart. He knew his wife well enough to be sure she didn't get talked into inviting his mother. So what was it in aid of?

'You don't mind, do you?'

'No, of course not,' he said with a start. 'I'd better rush up and change.'

'You haven't got time, darling, and anyhow you look fine as you are.' This was a little bit of a reproach for being late home, as he often was. She didn't wait for any apology, but went on: 'Your mother seems to phone me quite often these days.'

In a way he could understand it. They had a lot in common. Both were women who, under a completely feminine exterior, hid a somewhat masculine desire to govern. Even their methods were not dissimilar: Ann used her looks, Mother used her ill-health – both of them weapons which the male members of the family found it hard to deflect.

Ann said suddenly: 'Did she ever meet Pamela Graham?'

Brian flushed. That was damn well below the belt.

'No,' he said in a flat voice.

His wife smiled artlessly. 'I'm only thinking about topics best avoided, darling.'

'I think it's best not only avoided but forgotten.' He could hardly bring himself to frame the words. Why was she doing this?

'Do you ever see her? Pamela?'

'No.' No, never since Ann came back to him. It had never even occurred to him.

There had been a time when he had been on the verge of love for Pamela Graham. She'd come into his life at a time of great loneliness and bewilderment. Ann had left him – not for another man, not to devote herself to some great cause – simply out of boredom.

At some time during that period Brian had asked himself if he was a very boring man and, if so, whether it meant no one would ever be in love with him. He'd been very frightened. The answer seemed to be yes. Then his little girl, Carol, had roused the anxiety of her schoolteacher, who'd asked to speak to her parents. Since Ann was away, staying with relatives in the country, Brian met the teacher – Pamela Graham.

Pamela had brought warmth and vitality back to his life. They had developed a deep relationship which could have become an enduring love – but at the point where Ann took a hand there had been nothing sexual in it. She had sensed that Brian was no longer missing her, had walked in one dreadful evening when he and Pamela were innocently watching television at his house, and by simple force of personality and superior tactics, had made them both feel guilty and underhanded.

Brian had wanted to hold on to Pamela. But Pamela's belief in both herself and Brian had been shaken. She couldn't be sure any longer that she had the right to break up his marriage – as if it hadn't already been broken by Ann. Nor could she be sure that Brian wanted his marriage broken. The whole tragi-comic debate ended not with a bang but a whimper; Pamela faded out, Ann occupied the citadel, and Brian found himself with an unexpectedly loving and devoted wife after several months of desertion.

'Perhaps you should see her, Brian,' Ann mused. 'Perhaps we ought to invite her for drinks one day. We got on quite well, in the end. Did you know that?'

The idea of the two women meeting for a cup of tea and a chat about him made Brian feel as shrivelled as a winter leaf. He tried to treat it as a joke.

'Really, a *ménage à trois* would be more than I could stand.'

'Do you miss her?'

He couldn't bear it. He had reached the point that his wife had been aiming for all the time, the moment he would admit he was hurt.

'Ann, you ask that as if . . . After you left me, when we were apart . . . I was lonely. I formed a friendship which went no further . . .'

She turned on him a brilliant smile; she saw the thin face strained with distress, the quiet mouth trembling – good, she'd made *something* happen. Maybe there was something more to be wrung from the joke.

'But darling, even if I believe it was all perfectly innocent, didn't you want it to go further? Weren't you even a little bit in love with her?'

The doorbell rang.

Almost in a sweat with relief, Brian hurried to the door. His mother, very elegant in a mink jacket and grey georgette, was a little surprised at the warmth of his welcome.

Throughout dinner he had a chance to retire into his usual cocoon of reticence. Ann talked about the children like an adoring mother and gave Mary the latest letter from Nigel. Mary made cooing Granny noises.

'He's obviously enjoying it enormously, Ann.'

'Yes, boarding school's worked out for Nigel, there's no doubt about that.'

'And what about Carol? How does she like her school?'

Ann caught Brian's eye. He said uncomfortably: 'Well, that may be another story . . .'

'It's taking her a while to settle in, Mother, that's all,' Ann explained.

'But she *is* very young to be away from home, dear.'

'The girls in her class are all the same age,' said Ann with some tartness.

'Yes, I know.' It was almost as if Brian's mother wanted to score a point over Ann. 'But as long as you're conscious that there could be a problem in sending her away—'

'Oh, we are, Mother. But we don't want to *invent* a problem which may not really exist.'

Mary Hammond perhaps realized that she wasn't going to win this round. She shifted her ground. 'And how about you? Any problems there?'

'Oh, we're both very fit,' said Brian in complete innocence.

'That's not quite what I mean, dear.' There was meaning in her glance.

'More coffee?' said Ann – which for her was a second-rate ploy.

'Thank you,' said her mother-in-law, and watched her pour it. 'I don't mean to be tactless,' she resumed placidly. 'but you did both confide in me. I *would* like to know if everything is all right now.'

'I don't know,' Brian said, with a desperate glance at Ann. 'Is it?'

'*I* don't know, darling. What do you think?'

Brian wished that the parquet floor would open and swallow him. But after that the evening improved a little – because it could hardly get worse.

Next day it was a relief to get back to the office. There might be troubles there, but they were out in the open. One of them began to loom at the Joint Consultative Committee meeting in the late afternoon.

This grandiosely-named committee consisted of three representatives from the work force – Bill Riley, Foreman Driver, and two drivers; and three from the management – Edward, David and Jennifer.

Brian was not one of the delegates, but he spent the half-hour before the meeting with Jennifer, going over the costs of a new scheme which they all hoped would be well received by the union delegates: this was a training school for drivers, to be financed by Hammond Transport and run on the premises. To be candid, this was a way of sweetening a particularly bitter pill – the recruiting of non-union drivers.

'We can't have that,' Bill Riley protested.

'We need the men, Bill,' Edward explained. 'We're far under strength—'

'You know what happened before, Mr. Hammond,' said one of the drivers. 'We all walked out.'

'If I were you, Mr. Hammond,' Bill said, 'I'd keep that particular can of beans closed.'

'Then don't blame me if I have to take on men I'd rather not have, and you'd rather not either. A union card only means that a man's paid his subs, nothing else!'

Said Riley: 'That's a risk we'll have to take, Mr. Hammond.'

Which stored up a heap of trouble for Riley.

David went home a bit perturbed about the meeting. His bid for the cosmetics firm's deliveries depended on a complete efficiency of the van service. Where would he be if he couldn't get the drivers?

He began to cheer up when he spoke to Jill on the 'phone from Hamburg. She sounded on top of the world, pouring out anecdotes about the day's fashion show and the magazine coverage.

'Now that's enough about me. Have you had a good day? What did you do about dinner?'

'Oh, I did all right. I had a frozen meal for one.' Jill would have been shocked to see the tinfoil container sitting in the midst of his papers and books on the bureau.

'And what are you doing now? Watching television?'

'No, no, slaving away . . . I brought a lot of work home—' He broke off as the doorbell rang. 'Hang on, love, there's someone at the door—'

'Who is it, darling?'

'Don't know, if you'll hang on I'll—'

'No, Davie, don't bother. I've said everything, and if you're busy—'

'You sure?'

'Yes, yes. Talk to you tomorrow. Night-night, darling.'

'Goodnight, love. Sleep well.'

He put down the phone and hurried to the door, where the caller seemed to be leaning on the bell. He swung open the door.

Julie Lane was there.

Julie was the girl with whom he'd cheated on Jill last year. She'd been Jill's flatmate, and it had seemed that every time Jill was away on a modelling assignment, she somehow got David to herself, either at her place or his.

To see her here in the same circumstances – Jill away, David on his own – was a shock. His safety lay in one fact: Julie didn't know he was on his own.

'Hullo, David,' she said calmly. 'Can I come in?'

What could he say but: 'Of course.'

She moved with her languorous stride through the hall to the livingroom. He saw her eye the empty tinfoil tray, the clutter of papers. She made no remark on those. Instead she said, 'I thought I'd come and have a gossip with Jill. Is she in?'

'No. You should have 'phoned.'

'Will she be long?' she asked, sinking into an armchair as if she intended to stay for hours.

'Well, yes . . .'

'What's she doing? Eating out?' She nodded towards the evidence of his meal. 'Left you to fend for yourself?'

'I had a lot of work to do.'

'Well, you carry on. I'll just sit quietly and wait with a drink, if that's all right.'

'It's a business dinner,' David lied desperately. 'She may be quite a while. So there's not really much point in waiting . . .'

Julie smiled. 'Can't I have a drink before I go?'

'Oh yes. Of course.' He leapt to the sideboard to fix her a

whisky and water. Meanwhile she got out her cigarettes and lighter. He groaned inwardly. He couldn't with decency get rid of her in less than half an hour. He handed her the chunky glass without a word.

She sat forward to sip the drink, her dark hair falling forward.

'Super weather we're having, isn't it?'

'Delightful.'

'Aren't you drinking?'

'I've still some work to do.'

'So you're not expecting Jill in the next hour or two?'

'No.' He fidgeted. 'How's everything with you?'

'Oh, fine.'

'Still in demand?'

She gave him a long, quizzical look over her glass.

'As a photographer,' he amended.

'I'm doing a lot of new things.'

'That's good. Er . . . Found a new flat-mate?'

'I thought,' said Julie, 'that I'd stay on my own for a while. It might be more convenient. Should I want to invite a friend back. That sort of thing.'

'Yes,' David said uncomfortably.

'You know I like my own way of life. It's a way of life you used to like, too.'

'That was a while ago, Julie.' He shrugged, sat down, and picked up a list of figures.

She stubbed out her cigarette half-smoked. David got up at once, ready to show her out.

'All right,' she murmured with irony. 'There's no need to jump about in a state of nervous apprehension. I'm going.' She tossed off the whisky and put down the glass. 'Thanks for the drink. Tell Jill I'm sorry I missed her.'

'Yes, I will,' he answered, walking her to the door.

'When does she get back from Hamburg?'

'On—' He broke off. He was realizing he'd been led right round the garden.

'Andy's a friend of mine,' Julie explained negligently. 'When Linda dropped out, he asked who I could recommend and I mentioned Jill.'

'Why did you come here then,' he demanded, his voice hard, 'when you knew she wouldn't be here?'

'You'll have to think about that.'

'I'm not very interested, Julie.'

She gave her slow smile. 'No. That's why you've been behaving like an uneasy adolescent. Goodnight, David.' And out she went, without haste.

While he was asking Jenny next day to get his figures typed out, he felt a sudden rush of almost brotherly affection for her. Jenny Kingsley was a nice woman – simple, uncomplicated, rather like Jill in character.

'You're looking nice today,' he said.

'Am I?' She was genuinely surprised. 'Well, thanks. I hope somebody says that to me at the party tonight when I've got my glad rags on.'

'Mm . . . yes . . .' He didn't want to talk about the agency party. He was still worried for fear they got themselves involved in expensive advertising campaigns. To change the subject he inquired. 'How's Barbara?'

'Oh, fine, I think. I tried to ring her last night but she must have been out gadding.'

'Still away?' he asked.

'Yes, in Manchester.'

Which was odd. Because at that moment Jennifer Kingsley's daughter Barbara was in her mother's flat in South London with a young man called Johnny Trent.

CHAPTER TWO

The party given by Pageant Advertising was a glittering affair. The directors of Hammond Transport were by no means the only guests, or even the main ones. As Edward arrived with Jennifer he felt decidedly un-swinging compared with the assembly in the beautiful penthouse room.

Jennifer was a credit to him. The dress was certainly one he'd seen before, but she looked calm and relaxed, her skin gleaming and her eyes shining. She made him feel rather special to be escorting her.

A handsome, thirtyfive-ish man hurried forward. 'Hullo. You're Edward Hammond. I'm Tony Bromley, your host for the occasion.'

They shook hands. Edward introduced Jennifer, and in a moment they had been provided with drinks from a tray a waitress brought. Jennifer held up the firm's brochure, which she'd picked up from a display on the way in. It was a handsome product, with a sky-blue glossy cover patterned with stars, addressed to 'Dear Client . . .'

'I was just glancing at this,' Jennifer said.

'Oh, don't bother with it now, Miss Kingsley. It's just designed to tell you a little about us but it would be better to take a few and glance over them at leisure.' He glanced round as another man approached. 'Oh, Nick – this is Miss Kingsley from Hammond Transport. Miss Kingsley, Nicholas Fox.'

Jennifer raised her eyebrows. 'Fox?' she repeated as Edward was led away by Bromley.

'That's right. I believe your daughter Barbara was one of my students.'

'I remember.'

'A nice girl, Barbara.'

'I think so,' Jennifer agreed.

So this was the man her daughter had had a schoolgirl crush on when she started art school. Jennifer had heard a lot about him – how talented he was, how sensitive, how understanding. Now, it appeared this talented, sensitive, understanding chap was an employee of an advertising firm, which caused the question to rise in Jennifer's mind: What's a nice art teacher like you doing in a place like this?

'I don't know if Barbara told you I'd gone into advertising?' Nicholas said.

'She mentioned it,' Jennifer said in ironic understatement. 'I didn't really pay attention.'

'Oh?' thought Nick. 'Cool.' She perhaps bore him a bit of a grudge for not living up to the kid's impossible ideals. 'Barbara thought I'd sold out to the god Mammon, didn't she?'

'Something like that,' she agreed.

'I'm afraid she was suffering from a touch of hero worship. It wasn't serious, we both knew that.' He smiled at her gently, not allowing her to sense any of the anxiety he was feeling. If she took agin him over some imagined slight to Barbara, that would put paid to the Hammond account and Tony would *not* be pleased.

Jennifer decided to let the matter drop. Barbara had got over whatever she felt for Nicholas Fox and no harm done. She sipped her martini and allowed her glance to rove across the room and then beyond to the sparkling night scene outside – London in its party dress of floodlighting and skyscraper windows.

Her attention was recalled by Nick. 'I've met Brian Hammond,' he remarked, indicating him with a nod. 'But who's the lady with him?'

'Ann, his wife.'

Ann was looking wonderful tonight, in a dress of pale green with dangly jewels from the Dior boutique. She was pleased with herself, and even rather pleased with Brian, who always made a good showing in the severe black of a dinner jacket.

She, like Jennifer, had been surveying the room, but more from interest in its occupants than in the view. The tall man with Jennifer looked interesting: at the moment she formed the thought he turned his head and met her gaze.

She experienced a strange feeling, almost as if she'd received a spoken message. A touch of colour came into her cheeks. She turned away on pretext of asking Brian for a light, yet all the time she knew that the tall man was watching her.

Nicholas had quietly manoeuvred Jennifer round so that he could look at Ann without turning. 'How's Barbara getting on at art school?' he inquired.

'She left at the end of the year.'

'Really? Why?'

'I think there were several reasons. She just seemed to feel she'd made a false start,' said Jennifer with a sigh.

Nicholas nodded. 'She may be right. She had considerable ability, quite enough to make a living – but I think she was looking for more than that.'

'How good was she really, Mr. Fox?'

'She had a talent, and by no means a negligible one. But whether it was for painting . . .' He paused and shrugged. 'The world of art's a jungle, like advertising. Perhaps that's why I like them both. What has she decided to do?'

'No plans as yet. She took a long holiday abroad, met some friends she was at school with. She hasn't been home for . . . oh, months.'

'Give her my best wishes when you see her,' he said. And, satisfied that she was kindly disposed towards him, led her off to meet some of the other account executives.

It amused Jennifer to see how, one by one, the Hammond Transport board were taken aside and made much of. She was not taken in, and she very much doubted if any of the others were. David, particularly, seemed a bit disgruntled about the whole thing. She guessed he was complaining about the way advertising people threw money about on such things as cocktail parties.

Bromley had an answer for that. 'Come on, don't you ever entertain a prospective client to lunch? Cost-wise, this is a more economic version – look around and see how many people we're talking to at once.'

It was said with good humour and ought to have raised at least a polite smile, but David was no longer listening. Because Julie Lane had just sauntered up.

'Hullo, Tony,' she said, offering her cheek to be kissed.

'Hullo, darling,' said Tony, kissing her. 'Glad you could make it. Let me introduce . . . David Hammond – Julie Lane.'

There was the flash of an impish grin. 'We know each other,' she said.

'Really? Fine,' Tony said absently. 'In that case, if you don't mind . . . See you later, David.'

David considered Julie for a second. 'How do you fit into this scene?'

'I do photographic work for them from time to time. They

like my ideas, I like theirs. Do you? Like their ideas?'

'I'm neutral. It's all talk so far.'

'What do you want?' she asked, taking a glass from a passing tray. 'A sample of the action? I imagine that can be arranged.'

David decided to ignore that remark. He talked doggedly about cars for the next ten minutes.

Meanwhile Tony Bromley and Nick Fox were planning tactics to get Brian off by himself for a little chat.

'Tell you what, you keep Mrs. Hammond talking and I'll come and join you,' Tony said.

'Okay.' Nothing could have pleased Nick more. He approached the couple with a polite inquiry about their drinks.

'Thank you, we're being looked after splendidly,' said Brian. 'Darling, this is Nicholas Fox. My wife, Ann.'

They murmured hullo to each other. Bromley arrived on cue and plunged at once into a conversation with Brian that soon led them off to a quiet corner. Nick said to Ann: 'I hope you're not finding all this too boring, Mrs. Hammond.'

'Shall we say a little tiring?'

'Then let's sit down.' He ushered her to a nearby settee which, because of its angle to the rest of the room, gave an illusion of privacy. 'Someone told me you have two children?' he queried. As she nodded he went on: 'Who's looking after them while you're here?'

'They're both away at boarding school.'

'Ah. I see.'

If he had said, 'Good, that makes the coast clear for us,' he couldn't have made his meaning plainer. Ann was amused, and not averse to playing this well-known game of 'Let's see if it's going to be serious.' Yet she was uneasy; she had a terrible feeling that this time it might get out of hand. The man beside her on the settee attracted her almost irresistibly, and she sensed that he felt the same way about her. There was no logic in it. It was a simple matter of chemistry.

'Is your wife here?' she asked.

'I'm not married – at least, not now. Have you been here before?'

'No.'

'It's almost always used for this kind of function. The view from the roof terrace is stunning – would you like to see it?'

'I'd love to. I expect Brian would too.'

Neatly done, thought Nicholas. This wasn't the first time

she'd played this game. All the better – it added a touch of uncertainty to the preliminaries. But only to the preliminaries. One thing he was sure of – this woman was his kind of woman.

Jennifer and Edward were the first to say their goodbyes and slip away. After them went David, from whom Julie cadged a lift. Short of actually saying no, he had no alternative. He put her in his car and drove briskly away from the tall building.

'In a hurry?' Julie inquired.

'I am, rather. I want to get home.'

'Expecting a 'phone call?'

'Later, yes,' he admitted, colouring. Somehow she made it seem juvenile.

'What happens,' she said, as she lit a cigarette, 'if you're not there?'

'I shall be there.'

'Mm . . .' she said dubiously. 'Always?'

David was cross. He hadn't wanted to go to the damnfool party in the first place and now look where it had landed him! He zipped up his lip and gave his attention to his driving. He'd never seen a better view than the façade of the Bayswater house which contained Julie's flat.

'Here we are,' he said.

'Care to come in for coffee?' she invited.

'Better not. I told you, I'm—'

'Expecting a 'phone call. Quite.' She said no more, and stepped out briskly when he drew up.

But she'd carefully left her gold cigarette-lighter tucked in the fold of the passenger seat.

Brian had some difficulty getting away from Tony Bromley. It had all been very interesting; everything that Bromley said was valid and, what made it more intriguing, he was saying it to *him*. Not to Edward the managing director, not to David the young go-getter; it seemed to trouble Bromley not at all that those two had gone.

But enough is enough. Brian wanted to get away so as to have a chance to mull over what had been said. He sought out his wife, who was fortunately quite happy in conversation with Nicholas Fox. Fox was as persuasive as Bromley: it ended with their having dinner as a threesome.

It struck Brian that Ann was unusually quiet throughout the meal but that might have been because the two men talked amiably about business, their former careers, the football season which was drawing to a close, and cars. Now and again when he glanced at her, to see if she'd like a change of subject, he thought she seemed in some way tense.

When they reached home at last it was quite late, at least for a couple who'd been promising themselves an early night. They'd only been in a few minutes when the 'phone rang: Nicholas Fox inquiring if they'd got back without trouble and thanking them for their company.

'Very attentive,' Brian observed as he hung up.

'Darling, he's only trying to get what he wants!'

'But at least it's agreeably done . . .'

It seemed to him Ann looked pale. 'Are you all right?' he asked.

'A slight headache. It's nothing.'

'Are you sure? Can I get you anything?' He touched her gently on the shoulder, where the gauzy folds of chiffon fell away to display the creamy skin.

Rather to his surprise, she hunched her shoulder up and turned her head so that her cheek touched his knuckles. 'Brian . . .'

'Yes?'

She moved nearer. 'We didn't have a holiday last year. Could we have some sun? Go away somewhere quiet?'

'Well, not just at the moment . . . It would have to be August anyway, because of the children.'

'They're at school. You and I could go together – we could have a family holiday later.'

'Ye . . es . . .'

'Wouldn't you like to?'

'You know I would.' He got the sudden extraordinary idea that she was practically flirting with him. Her face was turned up to him as if expecting a kiss. The logical thing seemed to be to kiss her.

She responded at once, then drew away. 'Why don't you kiss me more often, Brian?' she asked.

'I . . . I'm never quite sure whether you want me to or not.'

For answer she clasped her hands behind his head and, pulling him down towards her, kissed him fiercely. He slid his arms round her, beginning at once to want her. The rich sweet perfume she used was like a cloud of intoxication engulfing him.

Ann had got what she wanted. But whether it was from the right man, even she was not sure.

Edward and Jennifer meanwhile had been chatting prosaically in Jennifer's flat for an hour or more over the coffee cups. 'I still think we need a proper advertising policy,' Jennifer maintained, 'but whether we need an agency, and if we do, whether *that's* the agency, I'm not sure.'

'Because of Nicholas Fox?' Edward asked with unexpected shrewdness.

He sighed. He was fond of Barbara in a tolerant, paternal way. He still felt he would have made a good father-substitute for her. 'Where is she? Still with those friends in Manchester?'

'I suppose so. It's been a week or more without a proper letter. I don't like to 'phone. It seems . . . interfering.'

'Little monkey,' thought Edward, 'worrying Jenny like this.' He gave her hand a comforting squeeze. 'Maybe now she's tried her wings for a while, she'll be ready to settle at home.'

Jennifer sighed and nodded and began to clear up the cups. He took the hint and said goodnight. When he'd gone, she couldn't sleep and after about an hour she got up and went in search of a book. She was halfway through an Agatha Christie which, if she remembered rightly, was on the arm of her favourite chair in the livingroom. She went in, not bothering to put on the light.

As she picked it up, she froze. Someone was opening a door – the front door!

A million little fears shot through her. She remembered a sense of uneasiness she'd had earlier in the the evening, when she got home from work – a sense that everything wasn't as she'd left it. The coffee mugs on the kitchen shelf were out of line. The wiping-up cloth hadn't been folded when it was replaced on the towel rail. There were dents in the sofa cushions.

She'd had the feeling then that someone had been in her flat while she was out. But she'd dismissed it as nonsense. Now, as the sounds from the hall became more definite, she realized she'd been right.

She edged towards the telephone, holding her breath. With infinite care she lifted the receiver from its cradle. Her finger was in the first 9 of 999 when the livingroom light went on.

And there, standing in the doorway with her hand on the light switch, was her daughter.

Jennifer gasped, unable to speak.

'Hullo, Mum,' said Barbara.

Jennifer recovered her wits. 'You frightened me to death, Barbara! I thought you were a burglar.' She replaced the telephone, feeling foolish.

'Sorry,' said Barbara. 'I couldn't hear anything and you weren't in your bed so I supposed you were out.'

'Why didn't you say you were coming home?'

'I was going to. Then I thought I'd surprise you.'

'You did that all right,' her mother confessed. She gave her a big hug. 'It's lovely to see you again! How are you, darling?'

'Great. Wonderful.'

The way she spoke the words was odd – tense and apprehensive. Yet she did in fact look wonderful, with all the young and pretty vitality of her eighteen years. Jennifer eyed her with concern. What did that high colour mean?

'Are you upset about something?'

'No.'

'I expect you're just tired. Did you have a bad journey?'

'No, it was fine.'

'I wish you'd let me know!' her mother lamented. 'Your bed isn't even made up. Are you hungry? I've got some—'

'Mum, don't start doing all that, please – not yet. Let's talk first.'

Once again that odd tone. Jennifer glanced at her aslant. 'All right, darling. I'm dying to hear all your news. I didn't even know where you were half the time. Give me your coat and sit down.'

Barbara slipped out of her blue poplin raincoat. Jennifer took it out to the hall to hang it up. A thought struck her. She surveyed the hall. No luggage. She came back to the livingroom to find her daughter wandering about uneasily.

'Where's your case? Did you leave it downstairs?'

'No, it's not here.'

'You must have brought something, surely? Your night things?'

'I shan't be sleeping here tonight.'

Jennifer drew back in surprise. 'Why not?'

'There's something I have to tell you,' Barbara said.

'What?' The two women stared at each other. 'Tell me what?' insisted Jennifer.

The girl's eyes met hers and then looked down.

'I'm married,' she said.

'You're what?'

'Married.' She held out her left hand. On the third finger there were a plain gold band and a garnet ring.

Jennifer put out an arm to lean against the door-jamb, for fear she'd fall. A moment's giddiness had seized her. She looked at her daughter with eyes slightly unfocused.

'I was married a week ago,' Barbara said.

She was watching her mother with anxiety, knowing she was doing this all wrong but not knowing how else to do it. She really couldn't explain why she'd kept her marriage a secret; at the time it had seemed right. But how was she to explain it to anyone else?

With a slow movement her mother came into the centre of the room, close to her but turned away a little.

'Where did you meet him?' she asked.

'Italy. When I joined my friends in Turin.'

'But you weren't in Italy long—?'

'They suggested I go back with them to Manchester. Johnny was staying there too.'

'Where were you married?'

'In a register office, by special licence.'

Anger moved in Jennifer. She pointed with a shaking finger. 'There's a telephone which rings when you dial this number, and the postman delivers letters right to the door.'

Barbara understood. '*No one* was there, Mum. Not Johnny's parents, no one – just the witnesses.'

'You could still have let me know,' Jennifer said with a bitterness she could not repress.

'It was between the two of us . . . just Johnny and me . . .' This was the difficult bit, the thing that had seemed right at the time yet now seemed so difficult to account for. 'We didn't want to have to explain, or answer questions, or defend ourselves.'

'Was there something you had to defend?'

'No,' said Barbara, hurt.

Jennifer turned towards the door, her head still averted. 'Excuse me,' she said in a voice that trembled.

'Mum, don't cry!' Her daughter stretched out a hand.

'Please don't cry!' But Jennifer eluded her grasp and went out.

Left alone, Barbara sank down on the nearest chair. 'Well, award yourself nothing out of ten for that, B. Kingsley,' she thought. How could she have been so inept? She'd meant to convey to her mother something of the happiness and warmth she was feeling deep inside – and all she'd done was make her cry. Damn, damn, damn . . . But if she could just get her thoughts organized . . . put together a few words in advance . . .

Trouble was, she'd never been much good with words. How much easier life would be if all you had to do was tune in to someone else's thought processes and emotions! If her mother could only do that, she'd understand that Barbara hadn't meant any slight or neglect in being married in secret.

Lost in thought, she sat quietly in the livingroom. She was quite startled when Jennifer came in with a tray.

'I thought you might like a hot drink,' she said.

Good old Mum. Always the good provider. 'I'll pour,' Barbara said, leaping up.

She was mingling hot milk and coffee in the second cup when Jennifer suddenly said: 'Are you pregnant?'

Barbara checked. For a moment she stood motionless, bent over the tray. Then she resumed pouring.

'We fell in love, Mum. That's all. No other reason.'

'How old is he?'

'Twentyfour.'

'He's got a name?'

'John Trent. Johnny.'

'Do his parents know?'

'They live in Carlisle. We went to see them.'

'How did they take it?'

'They weren't too surprised.'

'Why? Does he make a habit of marrying girls without telling them?'

Once again, it was Barbara who remained calm. She handed Jennifer a cup of coffee, her hand quite steady.

'They know he's impulsive and whatever he does he's enthusiastic about.' She tried to convey something of Johnny's character. 'He's easy to know, Mum. He doesn't hide anything. Would you like to meet him?'

Jennifer's jaw went tense. 'At the risk of being thought conventional,' she said with heavy irony. 'I would quite like to be introduced to my son-in-law some time, yes.'

'I'll fetch him, said Barbara, putting down her coffee. 'I left him sitting outside in the car.'

'No! No, not now, Barbara. Not tonight.' Her mother sighed deeply. 'I might say something I'd regret later.'

'All right. Let's leave it for a few days.'

Jennifer sighed again. 'I may already have said a few things I'll be sorry for!'

'Nothing you didn't have a right to say,' Barbara burst out. 'Nothing that matters.'

'I just want you to be happy . . .' Jennifer's voice was deeply wistful. She'd wanted for Barbara what she herself had so totally missed: a happy, open courtship, a wedding with friends and a two-tier cake, a nice, steady, honest husband. Jennifer's love affair had been nothing like that: no one had been allowed to know of her relationship with Robert Hammond although it had lasted seventeen years. She had known happiness, yes – but only in short, stolen interludes. For Barbara she'd wanted a more steadily-glowing flame . . .

'Oh, Mum . . .' Barbara murmured, 'I *am* happy. I wouldn't want to change any of it. I've got everything in the world I want.'

Her mother got up and patted her hand. 'Where are you staying?'

'We've got a place of our own. It's not far.'

'Already?' Jennifer was surprised. 'Well, you go home now, darling. We'll talk again another time.'

'All right.' Perhaps that was best. 'Goodnight, Mum.'

'Goodnight.' They exchanged kisses. Barbara was moving away but Jennifer detained her. 'Does he know about your father? That he was Robert Hammond?'

Barbara nodded.

'You told him?'

'Yes.'

'You were right. Goodnight, dear,'

'Goodnight.'

For a long time after the door had closed behind her, Jennifer sat staring at the tray of cups and saucers. Her mind seemed incapable of functioning. She tried to picture her new son-in-law, but no image would form.

At length, since it was no use thinking of sleep, she took the coffee things into the kitchen and began the washing-up.

If she'd had any sense she'd have gone in late next day,

for she wasn't in a fit state for work. But a sense of duty, and a stubborn refusal to give in, drove her to arrive at her usual time.

She found Edward already hard at work, as usual. He was keeping tabs on the day's loading, the fourth of which was a container being gingerly lowered on to a trailer under the supervision of Bill Riley. But, surprisingly, Edward and Bill weren't the only people standing by. The proceedings were being watched by Nicholas Fox and a tall dark girl whom Jennifer had seen at the party last night talking to David.

Jennifer wasn't best pleased to have these two underfoot. It appeared Brian had given permission for their presence during a dinner with Nicholas Fox after the party, without consulting anyone else. She couldn't understand why Edward didn't object as strongly as she did.

'I just don't see why they have to take over the depot without warning,' she complained.

Edward was a bit taken aback. He wasn't used to that note of irritation from Jennifer. 'They're not taking over,' he said. 'They're looking round and getting the feel of the place. And it wasn't without warning. They 'phoned me this morning at seven-thirty to okay it.'

'*I* wasn't told,' she objected.

'You've been told now. I haven't had the chance to clue you in until now.'

'Perhaps another time you'd try to keep me informed,' she said stiffly.

'Yes, well . . . I will,' Edward said. 'I'm sorry.'

What the hell was the matter with her? It wasn't like Jenny to stand on her dignity. And great black smudges of sleeplessness under her eyes, too. She was as jumpy as a cat in a thunderstorm, and as far as he could tell nothing had happened at the depot to account for it.

'All right,' she said in acceptance of his apology. She was so preoccupied that it didn't even strike her as extraordinary that he should apologise. She was marching out of his office when he called her back.

'Jenny—'

'Well?'

'What's up with you today? It's not like you.'

'What isn't?'

'All this fuss over nothing.'

'I wouldn't describe it that way. You know there's not

enough space for our own cars in the parking area and now we get all these advertising people—'

'Jenny,' he protested, 'it's an argument about nothing. Come on. What is really bothering you?'

'The efficient running of this depot, that's all!' And with this splendid exit line, she left.

Damned peculiar, Edward told himself.

The advertising contingent split up around then: Julie went off to the docks on one of the lorries to see if there was anything worth photographing there, while Nicholas Fox explained the purpose behind the visit to Brian. Brian was the one who interested him: David seemed antagonistic, Edward was unconvinced, and the quiet-looking Jennifer Kingsley had surprised him by growling at him all morning. But Brian Hammond, as he took him for a working lunch in the boardroom, was willing to listen to tentative ideas.

'One or two schemes have been drifting around in my head,' Nicholas said. 'We might get out a weekly broadsheet—'

'Broadsheet?' David repeated, looking up from his plate of cold beef. 'Who for?'

'Your prospective clients. To let them know how go-ahead you are. What new developments you are planning, any interesting loads you've carried – ten tons of plastic gnomes for front gardens in Zurich – that sort of thing.'

David snorted and reached across the table for the Burgundy. Brian said: 'I'd have thought that was P.R. rather than advertising?'

'P'raps you're right. It was just a thought.' For the rest of lunch he brought his considerable powers of persuasion to bear on Brian: he was not only listening, but discriminating.

As they were finishing Julie drifted in again, lifting her cameras from around her neck. She stopped beside David, who was offering brandies. 'Yes please,' she murmured.

He looked up in surprise. 'I thought you'd gone to the docks?'

' "There and back again, sir." '

'I didn't hear Riley's rig come back?'

'He's still there. I took a taxi back, having seen all I wanted to see.' She sipped her drink. 'I hope you didn't mind me ringing you about my lighter?'

'Not at all. It arrived safely, did it?'

'You needn't have bothered to send it by registered post.'

'It looked quite valuable,' he said.

'Then perhaps you should have made sure of handing it to me personally.'

'I didn't expect to see you.'

'You have no faith in serendipity, David,' she said with a smile.

'What?'

'The faculty of making happy and unexpected discoveries by accident,' she explained.

Nicholas, seeing she was on some ploy of her own, left her to it. He shook hands with Brian, assuring him he could find his own way out to the car park, then who should he see walking towards him across it but little Barbara Kingsley.

He wasn't quite sure how she'd react. She'd been in a bit of a state about him for a while during her studies at art college, and though he was pretty sure she'd grown out of it he didn't want any unpleasantness marring the set-up here.

But when she spoke she was completely affable. '*Hu*llo, what are you doing here?'

'The Hammonds are considering using our agency.' He studied her. She'd changed. 'I thought you were away?'

'I came back last night.'

'Did you? Fine. Well . . . we must have a drink together some time.'

'Lovely. I'll ask my husband if it's all right.'

'Your what?' Nicholas said, already halfway past her en route to his car.

She held out her left hand for his inspection. She was laughing.

'Well! That was quick. Congratulations.'

'Thanks,' she said, and with a nod walked on, leaving him shaking his head in astonishment.

She went into the office building by the iron staircase, but when she looked into her mother's room there was no sign of her. She went to Edward's office, waiting on the threshold until he ended a conversation with a Mr. Rogers who was clearly important. As he put down the phone he caught sight of her.

'Hullo, Barbara! When did you get home?'

'Yesterday. Where's Mum?'

'Business Efficiency Exhibition.' He waved her to a chair.

'Will she be back this afternoon?' Barbara asked, shaking her head at his invitation.

'No, shouldn't think so.'

'Oh . . . Well, I suppose I could 'phone her . . .'

'But you'll see her when she gets home—'

'I'm not living at home now,' she said quickly.

He frowned. Was this what had been troubling Jenny? A family row? 'Why not?' he demanded.

'Because . . .' She held out her left hand.

Edward drew in a long breath. '*Married*?'

'Well,' she replied, a little too brightly, 'I'm not just wearing it for the sake of appearances.'

She'd expected more warmth from Edward. But in fact he wasn't thinking about her at all.

'Why the devil didn't your mother tell me?' he muttered.

This was a question he pursued as soon as he could. He went straight from the depot to Jennifer's flat, where he found her putting together what, to his masculine eye, looked a damned skimpy meal.

'She says she's been married a week. I think you might have told me, Jenny.'

'I didn't know. I didn't even know he existed until last night!'

'So that's why you've been like a bear with a sore head,' he exclaimed, light dawning.

'I have not!'

'Complaining about not being kept informed—!'

'Oh well,' said Jennifer, looking a little ashamed.

Edward was hurt. 'I do think you might have confided in me.'

Jennifer understood only too well what he was feeling. It was a lesser version of the hurt she'd experienced last night when she heard Barbara's news.

'I was trying to get used to the idea,' she said. 'I didn't want to talk about it.'

He laid a surprisingly comforting hand on her arm. 'Jenny . . . don't you know that if you ever need me, I'm there? You only had to say—'

'There's nothing you can do,' she said with a sigh.

'I can be here when she brings him on Sunday, for a start!'

Jennifer began to see something faintly comic in his knight-errant attitude. 'Edward, it's nothing to do with you,' she protested.

'Oh yes it is! It's the Hammond money he's after.'
'Money? What money? What are you talking about?'
'Was it before or after he proposed that she told him she was Robert Hammond's daughter?'
'I've no idea. What difference does it make?' she demanded, baffled.
'Remember the will, Jennifer—'
'I do. I should do.' Her tone was bitter.
'Right. What did it say about Barbara?'
'"A thousand pounds to my daughter Barbara Kingsley—"'
'The residue of the estate,' Edward reminded her. 'It's held in trust during my mother's lifetime. When she dies, half goes to Barbara.'
'I'd completely forgotten,' Jennifer said in a troubled way.
Edward's pugnacious chin was thrust out. 'She'll be well off. Did her new husband know about that?'

CHAPTER THREE

David wasn't pleased when Julie Lane turned up on his doorstep the next evening with roughs of the photos from her day at the depot. But as he studied them his personal feelings gave way to a rising admiration: the shots were good, she'd managed to make it all look quite exciting.

When he said so, she smiled. 'Excitement's something I'm good at.' He was just getting worried about that when she swept on: 'Most of these I wouldn't use. They've no sense of direction. But—' she picked up one and laid it alongside another, each showing a lorry in transit – 'if we put those two in juxtaposition, they begin to tell a story. Do you see what I mean?'

'Yes, my word! Blown up they'd look terrific!'

'What I haven't got yet is an angle, a hook for the ordinary person glancing at—'

She was interrupted by the telephone. David got up quite unwillingly, but then when he discovered it was Jill from Hamburg he was pleased – it would be a demonstration to Julie of their 'togetherness.'

It turned out to be a short demonstration. Jill was in a tearing hurry, a bunch of German journalists were waiting to take the girls out to dinner, was he all right, she was fine, she would ring again tomorrow, 'bye darling, 'bye – and that was that.

Julie was watching with some amusement as he turned back. 'Some millionaire publisher is giving them dinner,' he explained.

'Have you eaten?'

'Not yet.'

'Nor have I.'

David refused to take the hint. He looked at his watch, then the proofs. 'How long will this take? I don't want to hold you up.'

'We could always talk over a meal.'

'I haven't enough for two,' he said unwelcomingly.

'In a restaurant,' Julie said, not the least perturbed. 'You could tell Jill we ran into each other by accident.'

'There's no reason why I shouldn't tell Jill the truth!'

'Fine. We'll take my car, shall we?'

'Why?' he demanded, immediately suspicious.

She raised her eyebrows at him. 'Don't be so defensive! If we go in your car you'll feel obliged to take me home, and I'll feel obliged to ask you in, and you'll either feel obliged to say no and risk offending me, or say yes and sit on a hard chair in case you get set upon. I'm only trying to save you embarrassment.'

She'd succeeded in amusing him. It was a thing he liked about this leggy, sexy girl – she was fun in more ways than one.

'Okay,' he said, and made for the door. Over his shoulder he added: 'Don't leave your proofs the way you did your cigarette lighter!'

'Oh, I never use the same ploy twice,' she said as she passed him, putting the photos in her portfolio. And then she said, very lightly: 'The next move is more subtle. You won't even know it was my move. You'll imagine it was yours.'

Fun, but unnerving.

His brother was having a less exciting evening. After dinner coffee and a Western on television – what better relaxation could a man want, thought Brian. His wife was cuddled in the corner of the settee, watching sleepily and looking very beautiful in lounging pyjamas of shimmery satin.

'We've seen this film before,' he remarked, memories of it stirring in his mind. One evening of a family holiday . . . when the hotel staff were baby-sitting for them . . . 'Paignton, wasn't it?'

'That's right. The one in black gets shot in the end.'

'The one in black always gets shot in the end,' Brian said, grinning. 'Can I have some more coffee?'

Ann uncurled herself to pour it. He turned his attention to the soft movement, but then the ambush was sprung in the dusty canyon and a fusillade of gun shots grabbed him. 'There he goes, biting the dust . . . By the way, Nick rang up. While you were in the bath.'

'Who?'

'Nicholas Fox.'

'Oh.' She put sugar crystals in his coffee. 'What are they doing, anyway? Spending all that time at the depot?'

'Umm . . .' He was half-watching the check-shirted hero

running and ducking into cover. Amazing how they were never hit – half the gun-owners in the Old West must have needed glasses. 'They're . . . umm . . . doing what they call a "presentation".'

'And what might that be?'

'Oh, the image of Hammond Transport that they might put over . . . There!' He pointed in delight at the television. 'I'm sure that's the same bit of canyon they use for "Lancer"!'

'The image of Hammond Transport?' Ann repeated. 'You're getting quite trendy. Since when did lorry firms have an image?'

'Well, it might be good for business . . .'

'What did he want?'

'Who?' His wife thrust his coffee cup into his hands, insisting he look away from the screen to take it. 'Oh, Nick? He wants to discuss the way it's shaping. I said we'd join him for lunch on Sunday.'

He didn't sense the uneasiness that seized Ann at his words. He took a sip of the sweet strong coffee. 'It's a hotel in the Thames valley . . . got a good reputation for its food . . .'

'Not Sunday,' Ann said. 'We can't, darling.'

'Why not?'

Invention always came easily to her. 'We're taking your mother on a picnic.'

Even half a day of her mother-in-law's company seemed preferable to her than a lunch *à trois* with Nicholas Fox. She was only too well aware of the current of physical attraction that had run between them at the agency party. Ann didn't mind a mild flirtation, or even something a little more exciting; but she didn't want to endanger her marriage, not now when Brian's firm was beginning to make money and amount to something and life in general was rosy.

She didn't even want to cheat Brian. Conventional though he was . . . dull, happy to spend an evening watching second-rate Westerns on TV . . . he was a *good* man, kind and honourable. And one day he might be important. If Hammond Transport went on as well as it had done in the past half-year, from the springboard of Jill's money, Brian might one day be a member of a board of directors whose activities counted for something in the City. She pictured herself momentarily at glittering functions . . . the Lord Mayor's Banquet, perhaps . . .

Brian was still trying to get over the surprise of the proposed picnic. 'Does Mother like picnics?' he asked, bewildered. 'In any case . . . why?'

'She's getting old, Brian – she must be lonely a good deal of the time. I thought it would be nice for her, that's all.'

He looked at her with genuine admiration. 'It's good of you to make the effort. I know you don't really like her.'

'Oh, nonsense, darling—'

'You've said those very words to me.'

'Perhaps I'm mellowing. Anyhow, I can't lunch with Mr. Fox. I couldn't back out now.' She knew he would accept that. 'You go, though. You don't really need me there.'

'I think he enjoys your company,' Brian replied innocently. 'I'll ring him.'

'Dear heaven,' Ann said to herself, 'I think I shall scream.'

Mary Hammond was surprised but pleased at the picnic invitation. It wasn't really her kind of thing – she'd have preferred lunch in the comfort of her own diningroom – but it was kind of Ann to think of her. However, it meant rearranging the usual Sunday routine.

'What are you doing on Sunday?' she asked her eldest son just as he was setting out for work next morning.

'Sunday? Why?'

'I was wondering about meals. Brian and Ann have asked me out for the day.'

Edward thought that a bit unusual but he was behind time. 'I'll be out,' he said, 'at Jennifer's. I'm meeting Barbara's husband.'

'Meeting—? *Barbara Kingsley*'s husband?' Mary gasped. 'She can't be married, surely?'

'She is, Mother.' He picked up his raincoat from the back of a chair and made for the door.

'But when, Edward?'

'See you tonight. I must dash.'

He was gone. Amazed, Mary pushed aside the morning paper she'd been looking at, and tried to take it in. Barbara? Married? But she was only eighteen. Married, and no one had said a word to her. Of course she wasn't exactly related to the girl – unless the daughter by another woman is some relation of the legal wife. All the same she should have been informed. Barbara was part of the Hammond clan if only on the wrong side of the blanket . . . She shuddered as her mind formed the phrase. So sordid and . . . and *unnecessary*.

She went to the telephone, not quite sure what she was going to say but impelled by the need to have a share in what was going on. Jennifer Kingsley answered rather briefly, as if she'd just been on her way out when the call detained her.

'May I speak to Barbara, Miss Kingsley?' she requested.

'I'm sorry, she isn't here, Mrs. Hammond.'

'Edward's just told me that she's married now. I was quite taken aback.'

'Yes . . . well . . . It was quite a surprise for me too.' Mary could hear the unwillingness in Jennifer's voice. Was it just that she didn't want to talk to her, or . . . had the marriage really been a very big surprise?

'Tell me about the young man,' she said.

'I don't know him very well yet,' Jennifer confessed.

So she was hurt. She was suffering. Good. 'Well, I'm sure he must be very nice if Barbara is fond of him,' said Mary. 'Will you please give her my good wishes for her happiness, Miss Kingsley, and say I hope she'll bring him to see me.'

'Yes, I will.'

'You won't forget?'

'No, I'll tell her the next time I see her.'

'Next time I see her.' She'd lost Barbara: that was an admission. Mary felt a growing satisfaction at every word she heard. The love-child had fallen in love and walked away from her mother, which in a way was only right since Jennifer should never have had her in the first place.

Mary kept the conversation going a little longer. She knew that every second of it was adding to Jennifer's unhappiness and embarrassment. As she hung up at last she felt that her day had had an auspicious beginning.

She tried to garner more information about the marriage from Ann on Sunday, but Ann, usually so well-informed, knew as little as she did.

'Well, I think we should all try and help Barbara,' Mary remarked.

'How?' Ann asked, suppressing a smile.

'I shall certainly ask Barbara and her husband to come and see me, and I'll suggest to David and Jill that they do the same. If you were to invite them as well . . .'

'Oh, I see. Make them feel wanted.' Ann shrugged. 'But after all, it's a somewhat distant relationship from my point of view—'

'She's Brian's half-sister.' Mary had learned to face that fact and could say it without wincing. 'What I want to do is make her feel part of the Hammond family, give her roots . . .'

Brian said, 'Mother, she's *got* roots. She's Jennifer's daughter.'

'But if her husband has his way to make . . .? The Hammonds could be very useful to a bright young man. Ann understands – don't you, dear?'

'Yes, I think I do,' Ann said with something of a sigh, 'very clearly indeed.'

Brian caught her eye over his mother's bent head, and they exchanged a wry smile. Neither thought that Jennifer Kingsley was going to enjoy the next few days.

The bright young man that Mary Hammond envisaged was being introduced to her son Edward at that very moment. Edward had lunched with Jennifer; the young couple were to arrive about two. But two-fifteen came, then two-thirty. He hated unpunctuality. Jennifer had made excuses: 'It's Sunday . . . they may have been held up . . . they'll be here.' And at last they walked in. Barbara, he noted, was surprised to see him.

'Edward said he'd like to join us,' Jennifer explained. 'I hope you don't mind.'

'No, no,' said Barbara. But she didn't look too pleased. It didn't occur to Edward that this was simply because she didn't like the idea of an inspection.

She went to the door, returning hand in hand with a tall lad – well, a young man, Edward supposed – with an open, friendly face and an eager smile. Anything less like the fortune-hunter he'd expected would have been hard to imagine. His clothes had an element of fantasy which, Edward was to learn, reflected something in the boy's character.

'This is Johnny,' said Barbara. She led him across the livingroom. 'My mother.'

'Hullo, Johnny.'

Johnny offered his hand. His handshake was warm and firm, if a trifle over-enthusiastic.

'And this is Edward Hammond.'

'How do you do,' Edward said.

'How do you do,' said Johnny, turning to shake with him. 'I've heard about you.'

'Oh?'

'That you're Barbara's half-brother. *Fantastic*,' Johnny said with approval, as if every home should have one.

'I see,' said Edward. He was quite at a loss, and remained so during almost the entire conversation. He gathered that the two kids had had a bit of a whirlwind romance, beginning in Italy. It became clear later that Johnny had been in Italy looking for fashion clothes for his men's shop – no, sorry, 'boutique' – which was about to open in a turning off the Penge High Road. A shadowy character called Vince – 'my partner' – had found and refurbished the shop – no, sorry, 'boutique'.

'We're going to call it "Roman Style, South",' Johnny explained. 'Italian, you see? Then as we open new branches, perhaps Kilburn will be "Roman Style, North" and Shepherd's Bush "Roman Style, West", and so on.'

'What happens when you get to Penzance or Wigan?' Edward inquired coldly.

'I don't know,' Johnny confessed with a sunny smile. 'What do you think?'

'Yes,' said Barbara, with a good deal of malicious amusement, 'what would you suggest, Edward?'

Edward felt a fool. They were all looking at him. Moreover he felt a patronizing fool. 'All right,' he said, 'perhaps it was a silly question.'

He was quite glad when, after tea, he could claim work at the depot as an excuse to leave.

'You don't work on Sundays, do you?' Johnny said in surprise.

'Pretty often, yes.'

It didn't seem to fit in with Johnny's view of him. 'I'd have thought you'd just tell others what to do . . .'

'The buck stops at the top,' Edward said. 'You'll find that out soon at "Roman Style East or West".'

' 'Bye,' Barbara said on a laugh. She knew he felt discomfited.

In the afternoon a few days later, David went to the airport to welcome his wife back from Hamburg. He was genuinely delighted to see her. The flat had been empty without her. To see her back in the bedroom as the light began to fail, slipping her blue dressing gown on and hunting for her bath oil, was like having a kind of a non-birthday present.

'How about a dinner somewhere special, to celebrate?' he suggested.

He had to repeat the question; it was drowned by the sound of the bath water the first time. She came out of the bathroom stretching and relaxing her back muscles. 'Let's go tomorrow,' she said. 'I just want to lie in the bath, and snooze, and not bother.'

'All right.' He began to rub the spot between her shoulder blades. She sighed in enjoyment.

'It's good to be home,' she said.

'Instead of touring round all those boring night-clubs on the Reeperbahn.'

'Well, they *were* boring.'

'A likely story!'

'Did you miss me?' she asked, turning towards him.

'You know I did.'

'I bet you had a ball,' she said, tapping his cheek with one finger.

'Oh!' It was a protest. 'From a girl who's just got back from one long rave-up!'

'I was working. Well . . . most of the time.' She giggled, then yawned. 'I'd better have that bath before I fall asleep on my feet.'

He pottered about getting a meal for them both, feeling protective and domesticated and rather enjoying the sensation. When they reached the coffee and brandy stage, Jill settled for hot milk. 'I don't want to spoil this big sleep that's coming on,' she explained.

'Umm . . . How long will it last, Princess Aurora?'

She smiled and buried her nose in the mug of milk. With her hair carelessly tied back and in her blue wrap, she looked about twelve years old.

'By the way, Julie said to give you her love.'

She looked up. 'Have you seen her?'

'She was at the depot. That agency – the advertising bods – they've hired her to do pix.'

'Oh, I see.'

'And then we had dinner to discuss them.'

'Really? When?'

'That evening when you could only make a quick phone call.'

'Oh.'

'We went out afterwards,' David ploughed on, determined there should be no secrets.

Jill glanced about. 'She was here?' She set down her mug and got up.

'She brought some proofs . . . wanted an opinion . . . afterwards we discussed it over a meal. That's all.'

Why couldn't he just have said, 'She was at the depot' and left it at that? The more he said, the phonier it sounded. Yet it was the literal truth, and between husband and wife there was supposed to be honesty.

'You didn't mention it on the 'phone?' Jill said.

'I was going to, but if you remember you were in a hurry that night—'

'But I rang again the next night. You didn't say anything then.'

'I forgot about it, I suppose.' Damn. That sounded as convincing as a political broadcast. 'You don't mind, do you?'

'Why should I?' said Jill. 'I don't quite understand how you could forget to tell me, that's all.'

'It wasn't important. Anyway,' he said valiantly, 'she sent you her love.'

'Well, you'll probably see her before I do, so perhaps you'll give her mine.'

'Jill,' he said, with real concern, 'come on . . .' He put his arms about her but she didn't respond.

'I'm so tired I can scarcely keep my eyes open,' she murmured moving away. 'I think I'll go to bed.'

'I'll clear away. I shan't be long,' he said.

'I expect I'll be asleep. Goodnight.'

'Goodnight, Jill.' He was left staring at the littered dinner table.

Brian's wife was still very much up and about. She'd been watching television earlier in the evening while she waited for Brian to come home, and perhaps feeling that there'd been a bit too much television-watching in her life recently – when the doorbell rang, and there was Nicholas Fox.

She was startled, but recovered. 'Brian isn't back yet,' she remarked.

'I know.' He invested the statement with an extra meaning. 'At a meeting of the Association Finance Committee. Correct?'

'Quite right.' So he had come here knowing he'd find her alone. All sorts of warnings tugged at her nerve ends, but when he looked inquiringly at her she heard herself say: 'Come in.'

He said a few nice things about the livingroom décor while she crossed to switch off the set. 'Television's good company when you're alone,' he added.

'I was watching earlier,' she said. 'I just forgot to switch off.'

He put down the folder of papers he was carrying. 'I was sorry you couldn't make it for lunch on Sunday.'

'We had a prior engagement.'

'Brian told me. Never mind, there'll be another time. I'd like you to see the place, The Flying Fox – do you know it?' She shook her head. 'You'll like it.'

'How do you know?' she asked curiously.

'Because I know quite a lot about you.'

Ann preferred to go back to the last topic. 'It's Brian who's the important one to take to lunch. I don't really have to be there.'

'No, but I'd prefer it, myself.'

'Why?'

'I like you both. You know how it is when you take to people. What could be merely necessary becomes a pleasure.'

It was gracefully said. Ann couldn't help feeling pleased.

'Besides,' he went on, 'you remember that conversation we were having over dinner? I'd like to continue that.'

'*I* didn't contribute very much,' she protested.

'You're an extremely intelligent woman. That's why the conversation was so interesting.'

And that was practically irresistible. Ann was accustomed to being complimented on her looks, which she didn't underrate, but she'd often had the urge to say to some ponderous rich businessman: 'I'm not just a pretty face!' To have Nicholas speak approvingly of her intellect made him special. That is, more special.

To cover her pleasure, she said: 'Well, around here one doesn't often discuss the relation of beauty to truth over dinner . . .'

'You must have been young when you married,' Nicholas said, somehow implying that she'd married beneath her class intellectually.

'Eighteen.'

'Was Brian your first boy-friend?'

'He wasn't a boy,' she answered, remembering, 'he was a man. He knew far more of life and what it was about than I did.'

'Perhaps you've overtaken him since?' Nicholas suggested lightly.

She felt impelled to defend her husband. 'Brian is kind and considerate . . . and there are depths that . . . well, he's always dependable, and that's a great deal – as much as anyone can expect.'

'Yes,' Nicholas said.

She'd expected him to argue. She looked up, and their glances met and held.

'I've done some silly and self-indulgent things in my life,' he said, 'for no better reason that that I wanted to. You know?'

'Yes.'

'Yet I'm aware that there's something better somewhere. The thing is not to be afraid to reach out to it. We all let ourselves be held back, you know, Ann . . .'

'I know . . .' But that was altogether too dangerous. Any minute now she'd be admitting she'd often felt stifled in her marriage, describing the frustration that had prompted her to pack up and go about a year ago.

So she decided she'd take his last remark as being about his work, and the talk turned to that, and to his painting. Beginning as a safety measure, it ended by being genuinely interesting.

'I'd like to see the kind of thing you were attempting to do,' she said. 'You must tell me where I can look at your pictures.'

'Well, as a matter of fact, one gallery still has two paintings of mine I'm not ashamed of. I'll meet you one lunch time and take you there.'

She saw a warning light. 'I don't think that would be a good idea,' she said.

'Going to look at my paintings?' he queried, though she was sure he knew what she meant.

'Arranging a lunch.'

'Why not?'

'The same reason you shouldn't have come here tonight when you knew—' She glanced at her watch, and was startled. Time had flown by as they talked. 'You'd better go. Brian will be home in a minute.'

But he resisted her gesture towards the door. 'Since I'm here,' he said, 'I'll wait and see him.'

'Why?'

He tapped the folder on the occasional table by his chair. 'We have things to talk about.'

Oh, very cool. Armed with a reason, an excuse, if anyone should walk in on them. All the same, Brian would be surprised. Even Brian . . . Because Nicholas *knew* Brian was at the Association meeting and could only have got the information from Brian himself. So why come here when Brian was elsewhere? Even Brian would wonder.

She heard his car draw up outside. 'There he is now,' she said, with an anxious glance at Nicholas.

He sat placidly where he was. 'I shan't have to wait long.'

Ann didn't know what to say. He was determined not to leave and anyhow it was too late now. In some apprehension, she heard her husband's key in the lock, the slam of the outside door. He came in, hefting his briefcase into an armchair.

'Hullo, darling.' He kissed her cheek. 'Hullo, Nick, you're here already?'

Already? Already? She went hot and cold with anger. The bastard! He was here at her husband's invitation. He had played her like a difficult fish, laid out his bait, and she'd fallen for it hook, line, sinker and fishing-rod.

She avoided looking at him but she knew instinctively that he wouldn't have shown any triumph. He wasn't that kind. She knew he'd been proving something to her – oh yes, a perfect proof, perfectly arrived at, like the last line of an elegant algebraic equation.

He had been showing her who was master.

Despite herself, she felt a surge of pure admiration. No one else in her life had ever bested her – at least, not since she got out of pigtails. No one in her environment could manipulate others as well as she could, with the possible exception of Mary Hammond. But Mary was clumsy: part of her success was due to her lack of finesse.

Ann had finesse – in great quantities. But that hadn't prevented this hateful, handsome, clever man from giving her a hiding to nothing.

She mustn't, simply mustn't, get involved with him. She felt fear. He was the only man who had ever made her afraid. But that in itself was exciting – a new sensation: and who knew what others he could teach her?

He and Brian were having a friendly, nonchalant chat about the Association committee, while Nicholas picked up his folder and began to sift through his papers.

'Sorry, darling,' Brian said as she moved uneasily, 'we have to talk business.' He headed for the stairs. 'I'll just clean up. Shan't be long, Nick.'

'Of course.'

'Perhaps you'd give Nick a drink, dear? And I'd like some coffee if there's any going.'

'I'll get it,' Ann said.

Nick tilted his head towards Brian. 'I've just invited your wife to come and see a couple of my paintings, one lunch time.'

'Good idea,' Brian said, making his way upstairs. 'You'd like that, wouldn't you, Ann?'

'No,' thought Ann. 'Yes. I don't know. Do I want to find out?'

CHAPTER FOUR

Jennifer and Brian were due at a board meeting. In fact they would already have been there if Brian hadn't glimpsed from the corridor window one of the big continental lorries moving out of the yard below. He detained Jennifer with a hand on her elbow.

'That's where the future lies, Jenny,' he murmured. 'Look at it. London–Milan.'

She smiled at the almost dreamy note in his voice. 'Well, we're making a start.'

'Yes, but we're late arrivals. We've a lot of leeway to make up.'

'Come on,' she said briskily. The board of directors ought not to be hanging about in corridors when it was needed at a meeting.

Everything went smoothly until towards the end, when they reached Item 8. 'New business,' Edward announced. 'It's just a report on the Rogers contract, isn't it, David?'

David nodded. 'Position's much the same. He's wavering, but he's still talking about that firm with a depot in Leeds.'

'Who's that?'

'Trunk Haulage.'

'Oh, *them* . . .'

'We did, as I recall,' said Brian, 'have an approach from a small firm in Leeds. Six lorries, wanted to sell out . . . I could look up the name.'

'Well, perhaps we could keep that warm,' David took it up, 'but I've pointed out to Rogers that with our regular collections, a local depot's hardly needed. I've promised him priority for any emergency collection, although I don't see why there should be an emergency with biscuits!'

'Fine, fine, and I agree that if we're talking about depots, Leeds may not be top priority.'

Edward looked at Brian to see if he had finished, then back at David. 'Is that all?'

'For the moment, yes. I think I'll have to go and see Rogers again in Leeds, but let's leave it for the present.'

'All right, let's move on—'

'Just a minute. Arising from that . . .' Brian began.

'Arising from what?'

Brian took a deep breath. This was the moment he'd been waiting for. 'I've been giving this whole question a lot of thought, and there's no doubt in my mind we should be treating it with a lot more—'

'Treating what?' Edward said. 'Which item is this?'

'The same item, new business, Mr. Chairman. Like it or not, we're members of the European Community.' He could hear Edward stifling a groan. He plunged on. 'Traffic is bound to increase, and we ought to be fighting harder for our share. Which means we should be examining the case for a depot in one of the Channel ports, Dover for preference.'

His elder brother glowered. 'I'm going to cut you off there, Brian. I see that Dover's important, but you're moving right away from the item under discussion.'

'I'm sorry, Mr. Chairman, but I dispute that ruling.' He glanced at the others, wondering if they would support this palace revolt. 'I think it arises directly under new business. New business has to be serviced as well as obtained. If we landed a big European contract, we'd be hard pressed to deal with it.'

'I agree,' said Jennifer surprisingly. Though she always made her own decisions, she didn't often jump right in at the start, preferring to hear all the pros and cons first.

Edward had no intention of giving way. 'We've got a heavy agenda to get through without trying to deal with an additional matter like that. You should have put it on the list beforehand, Brian, so we could have a think—'

'Surely we could spare a few minutes now? Or if you wish, I could propose we convene an extra meeting—'

'All right, all right,' Edward growled. 'But keep it short!'

Brian had his thoughts arranged. He'd rehearsed this opening once or twice inside his head. His long, narrow face was alight with an unusual enthusiasm as he continued.

'We've already got a handful of roll-on, roll-off contracts—'

'Which are easily serviced from London,' said David.

'David, that isn't always so! I've been looking into the figures, and some of those contracts involve us in a lot of empty mileage, and time lost in detours.'

'Besides which,' Jennifer chimed in, 'what about return traffic? With a base at Dover, we could service the South and the South-east, without hauling the loads to London first.'

Brian nodded at her. 'Precisely. And with the eventual motorway pattern, the same might apply to the West and part of the Midlands.'

'Brian,' David said, 'you're talking as though we had all the money in the world at our disposal. Let me repeat: we haven't. We're still backed by Jill's guarantee.'

'That's no reason to stop looking ahead.'

'You're talking about buying land . . . building a depot . . .'

'Not necessarily. It may be we could share facilities with a firm already established in Dover.'

Edward had listened to this altercation with growing alarm. The meeting had got away from its chairman, and he knew it. 'Calm down, this is a board meeting, not a saloon bar argument,' he said, but no one paid any attention.

'A firm already established could ask the earth—'

'It does no harm to think about it.'

'We could use our time more effectively—'

'All I'm saying, David, is that I should be empowered to look into the possibilities and report back.'

'Brian,' Edward said loudly, making a break in their duologue. 'You're the *finance* director on this board. Don't you think you're exceeding your brief a little bit?'

'Mr. Chairman, the bigger this company becomes, the less it will become possible to manage it by knowing what it's like to drive a lorry.' This was a nasty dig at his elder brother, who gloried in the fact that he'd done just that, and not just a couple of times but as a regular truck-jockey when their father was alive.

Edward flushed, and Brian felt a pang of remorse. But he believed in what he was doing. He cleared his throat and continued: 'My figures enable me to interpret the needs and trends of this firm at least as accurately as anyone else on this board, no matter what their experience. It's not too soon to be thinking about Europe. If anything, it's rather late.'

There was a moment of heavy silence. They all knew that Edward had been hurt, and felt guilty. Yet, there was truth in what Brian was saying: the cost account was at least as good a barometer of the haulage business as Edward's know-how.

David said after a moment: 'I'm not saying that Brian

shouldn't investigate Dover. That wouldn't do any harm so long as we're not committed.'

Brian gave him a sharp stare. 'Any commitment is a matter for this board, not me,' he pointed out.

Jennifer, who had been doodling on her shorthand-book, suddenly spoke up. 'I move that Brian should go to Dover, see what the situation is, and make recommendations.'

It sounded commonsense. There was an atmosphere of relative calm now. David said. 'I don't think we need a formal motion. We're all agreed, aren't we?'

That was how they left it. But though David had put up no objection in the end, he wasn't quite easy about it. And it didn't do anything for his peace of mind when he walked into the flat to find Jill and Julie nattering over the tea-things.

When he'd kissed Jill, Julie began explaining how she'd felt she just must hear all about the Hamburg trip. David trusted her about as much as he would a riverful of piranha fish, and his mistrust was justified a minute later.

'I owe your husband a meal, Jill. Did he tell you?'

'Wouldn't you be delighted if I hadn't,' he thought.

'I heard all about it,' said Jill.

'I'll take you to lunch one day soon, David.' As an afterthought Julie added: 'We must try and arrange so you can come too, Jill.'

'Thank you,' Jill said.

Luckily Julie relented a little after that, and began to ask about Hamburg. The talk flowed on between the girls about people they both knew, Jill as model, Julie as photographer. David took no part. He poured himself a drink and thought about Rogers and his blasted biscuits. It was no problem, really: Hammond's could handle the business and Rogers knew it. The shilly-shallying was to get another penny or two off the Hammond rates.

'Who else was there?' he heard Julie inquire. 'How about Frank?'

'He came to take a look. And all of a sudden he's offering me work. Trouble is, it's in Liverpool.'

'Liverpool! My God!'

'Oh, good backgrounds for travel coats and such. But it's a long way, and I'm only just back from Germany . . .'

'It's all go,' said Julie.

'Isn't it just.' Jill stifled a yawn, which made Julie look at her watch.

'Good lord, I'd no idea it was that late. I was only supposed to be dropping in for half an hour!' She jumped up. 'Can I 'phone for a taxi?'

'Haven't you got your car?' David asked.

'I cadged a lift here. I suppose . . .' She smiled artlessly. 'I couldn't cadge a lift home?' She looked at Jill. 'You wouldn't mind?'

What else could Jill say but: 'Of course not.'

'Then I can give him that hat of yours to bring home.'

'Hat? Oh – the one with the poppies round the brim. Did it photograph well?'

'Splendidly. I've been meaning to give it back for months.' She tugged at David's sleeve. 'Come on!' She turned back to drop a meaningless kiss in the region of Jill's ear. 'Lovely to see you.'

'Nice to see you,' Jill murmured.

'Shan't be long, darling,' David said as he followed Julie.

'I shall go to bed,' his wife replied. 'I'm exhausted.'

David wondered if this was a usual ploy between married couples when the wife was annoyed. A damn' dangerous one, in his opinion.

He might have expected what happened once they reached Julie's flat. She couldn't find the hat. He was supposed to pour drinks while she looked, and this he did, but he wasn't the least surprised when she appeared looking helpless in the bedroom doorway.

'It's no use. You'll have to help me. It's in a box on top of the wardrobe.'

'Where?' he asked bravely, though it could only be the bedroom.

'Let me have my drink first.' She took the gin and tonic he had mixed and gulped down a large mouthful. She looked at him expectantly. Your move, she was saying.

'Have you finished at the depot?' he inquired, aware that he sounded prim. 'Have you got all the material you need?'

She shrugged. 'Nick wants to go back, I don't know why.'

'Isn't he Art Director?' She nodded. 'That's not the Art Director's job, surely, working on a potential client?'

'He has his reasons, I expect.' She gave it some thought. 'He may want to get some account work experience. I think he fancies himself as a top executive. Don't worry, Tony Bromley's got his finger on the pulse. You'll get a good job – if you decide to take them on. Shall you?'

'We can't afford it.'

'I think they'd say you can't afford not to.'

'Yes, I've heard that line. But the money's simply not available, not at the moment.'

'So everyone's wasting their time?' She stroked her straight nose. 'Except me.'

He made a sound of protest.

'I mean that I get my fee as a photographer,' she said. As he relaxed, she added, 'And it's been nice to see you every day.'

He sighed and decided the only way was direct action. 'Julie, I'm married now.'

'That makes a difference?'

'Too true it does.'

'Don't you want to see me?'

'It's not that.'

'So what is it?'

'I wish I knew what rules you play by,' he groaned.

'Play?' she said. 'Who's playing?' Then she laughed. 'That hat is still on top of the wardrobe.'

David reached home with it in a plastic carrier labelled Harrods, where it might very well have come from. To his surprise the lights were still on and Jill was in the kitchen.

'Hullo,' he said, putting his head round the door. 'I thought you were going to bed?'

'I felt like some coffee. Want some?'

'No thanks. Here's the *chapeau*. Where shall I put it?'

'Oh, anywhere.' She seemed totally uninterested.

'Sorry to have been so long,' he called over his shoulder as he stowed the carrier in the hall cupboard. 'Julie eventually unearthed it on top of the wardrobe.'

Jill went into the livingroom carrying her coffee. He went in with her. 'I didn't really want it back anyway,' she remarked. She drank from her cup then put it down with rather a bang on its saucer. 'David.'

'What?'

'I think I'd like a car of my own.'

He stopped ferreting about in his briefcase for the Rogers file. 'You can't drive,' he pointed out.

'I had lessons. I'm sure I could soon get my licence. I could get to my assignments more easily and . . . and if a friend of mine needed taking home, I could take her.'

He decided that he'd better ignore the last bit. 'Perhaps later on,' he murmured.

Jill seemed taken with the idea and determined to talk about it. 'I think it should be a new one, don't you?' she ventured. 'I saw one the other day I'd quite like. Lots of room on the back for luggage. I think it was about fifteen hundred pounds.'

'You could get a good second-hand one for half the price,' he objected.

'I expect I could.' Her voice was tart. 'But I'd rather not, thank you.'

David realized that, for reasons having nothing to do with the car, she was annoyed. He tried sweet reason. 'Listen, Jill, we can't afford fifteen hundred pounds at the moment, not for a second car.'

She misunderstood. 'David, I'm sorry I even have to ask you. Normally I wouldn't, as you know, but I don't have the free use of my own money for the time being. I don't expect you to *give* it to me. I'll pay you back.'

He knew his face was as bleak as his words. 'I should have known you wouldn't be able to resist using that, one day.'

'That's a horrible thing to say!'

'All right. I'm sorry. I'll put it another way. Money's not important. *You* said that once, not me. But just the same we're in your debt, and I know it better than anyone.'

She couldn't bear the sombre gaze he had fixed on her. His face was a stranger's face.

'David . . . please . . . don't look at me like that . . .'

'You have every right to anything you want, in the way of money, and it's up to me to find it somehow—'

'David, forget the car, damn the car, I wish I'd never mentioned it!' Her voice broke.

He was unmoved. 'I'll go to the bank in the morning and—'

'No! Please – I don't know how all this started, but let's stop now,' she pleaded.

All her little-girl charm had gone, despite the scrubbed-clean face and the blue dressing-gown. She looked haggard and much older.

David surveyed the flat. Not much of a place for an heiress, really. 'This is where you realize how being married is different,' he observed in a matter of fact tone. 'We can't go to our own places and cool off. There's nowhere to go. If anyone leaves, they leave.'

Jill was too frightened to say a word. 'If anyone leaves, they leave . . .' It wasn't a threat: he wasn't the kind to make threats. No, when he'd had enough he would just go. She must be very, very careful from now on.

Ann Hammond had sent Brian off to Dover with lots of encouragement for his ideas. She wanted them to come to fruition: it would be a step up for him vis-à-vis the other directors, and the expansion of business must surely result in more money.

She knew that the others were lukewarm about the depot in Dover. Edward would be against it because it meant change: he was the sort who liked things to run on predestined lines, like a tram. As for David, his touchiness concerning Jill's money was, in her opinion, childish – he'd get over it if Brian could make him see the wonderful prospects from handling freight from a Channel port.

She had listened with real attention to all Brian told her, surprising him somewhat; he'd always felt she found it dull.

'But at that time there was nothing in it for you, darling,' she pointed out. 'You gave up excellent prospects in accountancy, and for what? For a salary you could have got anywhere, with fewer problems. But now . . . well . . . the things you tell me are wonderful!'

'I don't know whether I'll be able to pull it off,' he warned.

'You'll do it! You've got more ability and more authority than you've ever given yourself credit for. It won't be so long,' she prophesied, 'before Hammond Transport becomes really big business, and when that day comes I want you to take your rightful place, the position you deserve.'

She wondered afterwards if she'd overdone it a bit, but Brian had looked so starry-eyed that on the whole she thought she'd done a good job. While he was away, she decided, she would put up the summer curtains and change the loose covers. She was vacuuming down the creases in the armchair when the phone rang.

It was Edward. 'I've got someone in the office who wants to speak to you,' he told her.

Next moment Nicholas was saying hullo.

Unconsciously she patted at the kerchief in which she'd tied back her hair. She knew she looked a mess.

'How's Brian?' he asked.

'He's in Dover.'

'I wondered if you'd heard from him?'

'Not so far.'

'Oh . . . Well, you remember when I called to ask Brian for his comments?'

Would she ever forget? 'I remember,' she said.

'I left a file with him. . . Is it anywhere around? A plastic folder, with Hammond Account on it. I rather need it, you see. It had some sketches and notes . . .'

'Just a minute.' She put down the phone. A moment's search at Brian's desk revealed the file. She went back. 'It's here. Where are you? The depot? Suppose I bring it in to you?'

'No, no, I don't want to put you out like that.' She could imagine him now, in Edward's office, glancing at Edward for agreement. 'Look, Ann, when I've finished this meeting here, I'll come and collect the file.'

'But I could come—'

'It's my fault so I should do the leg-work. I'll drop by later on – say around two, two-thirty?'

It seemed impossible to refuse. As soon as she put the phone down she hurried through the rest of the housework then bolted upstairs to change. However she might tell herself that she wasn't going to get involved, she certainly wasn't going to let him see her with her head tied up in a dust-cap.

When the doorbell rang she came downstairs without haste. It was a beautiful day in May so she had chosen to wear a soft silk dress with full sleeves and a pleated skirt – a dreamy, romantic dress.

She took her time about opening the door. She didn't want to look flustered. 'Come in,' she said in her coolest tone. Leading him into the livingroom, she gave him the file. 'I hope this is it?'

'Yes. May I?' He was asking permission to sit down at Brian's desk so as to check the contents.

'Do,' she replied.

He disregarded her completely while he made sure the things he wanted were in the file. She was just deciding to walk away when he looked up with his sudden brilliant smile.

'Sorry to impose. I hope you weren't in the middle of anything?'

'Not at all.' But she glanced at her watch to let him know he wasn't the big event of her day. 'Though I have some shopping to do now.'

'My car's outside. May I drive you?'

'It's not worth it, really. I prefer to walk – it's just the local shops.'

'I could carry your shopping bag.'

She gave him a faint smile. 'I'm sure you're very busy.'

'Yes, I am,' he surprisingly agreed.

'In that case—'

'But as I didn't take my lunch break, I'm entitled to have it now. So let's go.'

Since it would have been schoolgirlish to keep on refusing, she gave in. She punished him by buying a great many heavy items which he then had to carry back.

'You bought half the shop,' he complained.

'It's for a dinner party tomorrow. Thank you,' she said as they reached her door again.

'I'll bring it in,' he offered. 'The file's still indoors anyway.'

He didn't wait for her to say yes or no, but as she went in walked past her and by instinct found the kitchen. 'Anywhere special?' he called.

'No, just put it down. I'll see to it later.' She was fetching the file from Brian's desk as she replied. Just as she picked it up she noticed a sheet of notes in her husband's writing. She offered both file and paper to him. 'Brian must have read it all. He's made some comments.'

'May I see?'

'I suppose so. It's got cross references to the file.'

Nicholas gave a glance to the paper and tucked it in the file.

'Very helpful,' he remarked.

Ann gave him a very wry survey. 'Are you cultivating Brian?'

'In what way?'

She nodded at the file. 'He seems to be on your side.'

'That's not surprising.' Seeing her raise her eyebrows he went on: 'He's got more foresight than the others.' He stopped rather abruptly. 'Was that tactless?'

'Somewhat. Also I wonder if it's true.'

'Brian understands that advertising has clearly defined powers, clearly defined objectives.'

'Which *your* agency can achieve?'

'Why not?'

She hesitated. 'Brian likes you.'

'I like him. But if you think I'm using him—'

'I do, rather,' she cut in.

Nicholas laughed. 'He's using me, too.'

'How?'

He glanced about. 'May I sit down?'

'Yes of course. Sorry.' He'd succeeded in making her feel remiss.

He settled himself on the sofa, while Ann chose an armchair some distane away. The afternoon sunshine made a pattern on the pale carpet.

Nicholas said: 'Brian can see a very different future for Hammond Transport, many times the size, a public company, operating all over Europe. He's talked to me about it.'

'So I gather,' she commented with a certain dryness. She'd take a bet none of the directors of Hammond's knew as much as Nicholas did of Brian's schemes.

'One thing he'll need is a good advertising agency. Brian needs a case the others on the board can't turn down. It's as simple as that – we need each other.'

'I see.' She stifled a sigh. In a way it was rather sad that Brian should need an ally against his own brothers. 'I suppose I should offer you some tea,' she said.

'After all the weight-lifting, it would be very welcome.'

When she went to the kitchen he followed.

'Lemon, or milk and sugar?'

'Lemon.'

'Or you can have a drink if you'd rather?'

'No thanks. You can give me that tomorrow.'

'Brian's back tomorrow,' she said.

'I know.' He nodded at her shopping bag. 'Your dinner party. Tony Bromley and I are coming here.'

Ann threw up her hands in a gesture of defeat. What was the use? He always seemed to be about two moves ahead of her. She began to understand how Spassky felt while facing Fischer.

Brian returned from Dover next day but went straight to the depot from the station. He paid off the taxi quickly and ran up the iron stairs to the office. He went into Edward's room still carrying his week-end case.

'I'd like a meeting arranged at once.'

'At once? Wouldn't tomorrow do?' Edward queried, indicating the paper work on his desk.

'Ted, this is urgent.'

'But you can't expect a board meeting at a minute's notice!'

'It doesn't have to be a formal meeting, just a get-together.'

His brother glanced at his watch. 'We can't do it now. Jenny's got a couple of people with her.'

'Are the others lunching in?' Brian asked.

'I've no idea—'

'Well, could they? That's not asking too much, is it? To talk over lunch?'

In the face of so much enthusiasm Edward had no option but to ring round the others and tell his secretary to ring the canteen for the usual cold meal. They sat down soon after one o'clock. Brian chatted generally in reply to polite questions until they'd disposed of the cold meat and salad.

'Well, I think it's been very useful,' said Edward at length, 'even if you didn't find us anything.'

'I didn't quite say that.' He reached for his briefcase, opened it, and took out a small sheaf of papers which he distributed, one to each. He was looking pleased with himself, an unusually confident smile on his quiet features. 'All the relevant information is there . . . the dimensions of the building at the top, the access directions . . . Sorry about the typing. I was up at six this morning, tapping away on the hotel typewriter.'

He looked at the others as they studied the paper. Jennifer, he gathered, was receptive. Edward appeared dubious – well, he'd expected that. David was the only one who was scowling in antagonism at his inoffensive sheet of flimsy.

'I found it through a local estate agent. Formerly a warehousing firm's, very reputable but for internal reasons they want to let off one warehouse.'

Edward read from his notes. 'A seven year lease?'

'And just what we need . . . the right size building. There are even petrol pumps on the site. Plenty of parking space and no planning problems—'

'You're sure of that?' Jennifer put in.

'I've checked. We could pretty well move straight in, do modifications later.'

'It's the price of the lease that bothers me,' David said, speaking for the first time.

Jennifer checked the figure. 'I don't know, David. It seems reasonable enough.'
'It's certainly worth considering,' said Edward in a warmer tone than he'd used since they first sat down together.
'We have to make a decision pretty well at once. They're negotiating with someone else, a discount store, but if we make an improved offer, it's ours.'
'Improved by how much?' David asked.
'An additional ten thousand pounds for the lease.'
'Ten thousand!' David was aghast.
Brian hurried on. 'That's not per annum, that's just extra on the purchase of the lease—'
'Ten thousand on top of all this?' David demanded, waving his sheet of notes. 'We can't. We haven't got it.'
'Hold on a minute, David,' said Jennifer. 'We shouldn't write it off like that, not premises as good as these.'
'How do we know they're so good? Can we rely on Brian to survey buildings?'
'Oh, come on—' Edward began.
'No, fair enough,' Brian said. 'I suggest we all go down to Dover tomorrow. If I'm wrong, you can tell me so. If I'm right, we can sign up and make an initial payment.'
'Using what for money?' David inquired.
'I'll set things in motion this afternoon—'
'I don't know why I have to keep on saying this,' David burst out. 'We're operating with loans and overdrafts all over the place. Those are debts.'
'Working arrangements,' Brian corrected.
'*Debts!* Partly secured by Jill's guarantee, to the tune of about a hundred thousand pounds.'
'That's not precisely a debt, it's—'
'Morally it's a debt,' David stormed on, his face dark with resentment. 'Until that's paid off or the guarantee released, if that's the technical term, we're not entitled to buy leases, employ advertising agencies, or indulge in any of the fancy schemes that have started floating around here.'
Brian saw that he would have to try another tack. 'David, in principle I agree with what you say—'
'Right. The subject's closed.'
'No, it isn't,' Brian persisted. 'This is a special case.'
'Why? Because this depot in Dover is your baby?'
Brian's temper, slow to rouse, was beginning to come to the boil. But he held it down. 'It's not that. Of course I—'

'It's not a personal issue, David,' Edward put in.

Brian spoke over Edward's plea. 'This is a golden opportunity—'

'To spend money we haven't got!'

'We can find it,' Brian persisted.

'At Jill's expense.'

'Not at her expense. We'd be acquiring an asset—'

'While *her* money remains tied up.'

'Would she mind?'

'That's not the point,' David said, faltering a little.

'Can we talk to her? Explain what we intend?'

'It's nothing to do with—' David stopped himself. He'd been about to say it had nothing to do with Jill. In a strange way, that was true. It was to do with him, with his pride and his freedom. 'What do you want?' he demanded. 'Another personal favour from her?'

'If you want to put it that way,' Brian said, his voice going up. 'It's for the benefit of the firm—'

'Look, for God's sake,' said Edward, 'there's no point in having a shouting match—'

'I didn't want to use Jill's money in the first place. I only agreed because I saw it as a short term measure, to save this company from collapse—'

'And that's what it is, a short-term—'

'But it's grown into a damn great albatross around our necks! Until we're rid of that we're not free to do anything!'

Brian didn't care now. 'You mean it's an albatross round *your* neck, and *you're* not free.'

'If we're getting personal,' David snarled, 'you seem very keen to finance your own empire-building with someone else's money—'

'My empire building, as you call it, has only one object, the good of this company and—'

Jenny leapt to her feet. 'Stop it, stop it!' she cried. 'You're both being ridiculous!'

David shoved back his chair and stood up. 'There'll be no Dover depot on these terms so forget it,' he said, and screwing up the notes he flung them on the table.

'That's not for you to say—'

'Oh yes it is, Brian!'

'Let's take a vote. Let's find out what the majority feel.'

David leaned towards his brother, his face contorted. 'Don't try that one, Brian. Jill can withdraw her guarantee

any time I advise her to, and then where would you be?'
Straightening, he stalked out of the room.
There was a long pause during which everybody took several deep breaths and listened to the echoes of David's words.
Then Brian said, 'He's cutting off his nose to spite his face.'
'We must have his agreement, Brian,' Edward persisted.
'He's one director among four. He has no power of veto.'
'No. But he has a moral right in this case,' Edward said gravely.
Brian collected his papers together and made ready to leave. 'Are you ready to endorse that by voting on his side?'
'I'd rather not be put in that position.'
'But you might be. Would you vote his way?'
'As chairman of the board, yes, if I think it right.'
Brian gave him a long, fierce stare. 'For the first time, Ted,' he said, 'I wonder if you ought to be chairman.'

CHAPTER FIVE

David walked out of the boardroom, out of the office block, and out to his car. Looking neither to right nor left he climbed in and drove off. If he had seen Brian running out trying to attract his attention it would have made no difference; he had said all he wanted to say to Brian.

He knew instinctively that the hunt would be up after him. They'd go to his flat to try to make him see sense. So he wouldn't go home. He drove round for an hour or so, then dropped in at a pub for a beer and a sandwich. But he couldn't eat, couldn't drink. And it was lonesome. Other people sat together, talking and laughing. He had no one to talk to.

Certainly not Jill. The last person to whom he could talk about the board meeting was Jill. Yet he felt a simple longing for human contact.

When he left the pub he didn't know that he was going to Julie. But it was to her place that he drove. Her eyes widened as she opened her door to him.

'You see a political refugee,' he said, trying for lightness. 'Can you offer political asylum?'

'Of course. No questions asked in this asylum.' She stood aside to let him pass and as he did so looked at him keenly. She closed the door and followed him.

He looked very tired. 'I've been driving around, trying to think where to hide out . . .'

'Who's after you?' she asked, smiling.

'My brothers, I suspect. There's a difference of opinion so I felt it best to disappear.'

'Ah, I see. They could reach you at home if you went there.'

'Exactly. But all will be well around seven o'clock. Jill leaves for Liverpool then, so I can go home and refuse to answer the 'phone or the doorbell.'

'Fine. Or I could give you dinner if you like. I still owe you a meal.'

She was so undemanding. How calm and restful it seemed here, compared with the continual tension at home and the rows at the office. It had never occurred to him there could be anything restful about Julie Lane.

But in fact she was quiet and understanding all the time he was explaining what had happened. She listened attentively, occasionally putting in a question. He poured it all out; he was far beyond discretion or reticence. His marriage, his job, his plans, his disappointment, his sense of guilt . . .

'So it really wasn't about the depot in Dover,' Julie observed.

He shook his head. 'As a matter of fact, *that's* a good idea.' He sank back in the comfortable armchair, legs thrust out, head thrown back.

'It's about Jill's money,' Julie continued.

'Yes.'

Julie leaned forward, her chin on her fist. 'You think she bought you.'

He sat up. 'I know she didn't. It's not the sort of thing that would occur to her. She's not like that.' He reached morosely for his brandy glass. 'It was a generous thing for her to do,' he ended.

'But just the same,' Julie said, 'the result of her action is that you feel as if she bought you.'

'No . . .' He was too tired now to be sure what he had said. 'I shouldn't be telling you all this . . .'

'We're old friends,' she said.

'Are we?' If you judged by her tolerance of all his self-pity, they were friends. But some faint memory stirred . . . something she'd said once. What was it? Something about making a move. 'It'll be subtle. You won't even know it's my move. You'll think it's yours.'

He rubbed his forehead to try to clear his thoughts. 'I suppose if you'd known about Jill's guarantee, you could have predicted all this.'

'With unerring accuracy.'

'I wonder. Are you really so perceptive?'

She got up abruptly. When she spoke she was surprisingly hard. 'Never challenge me, David. I can't resist it.'

'It wasn't a challenge. I want to know if you can really see . . .'

'I'll tell you how you feel now. You feel under an obligation to Jill, you feel bound to her—'

'I want to be, mind you.'

She frowned. 'But of your own free will, surely? Free

will implies choice, and just at present there is no choice. Your freedom has vanished, you can't do or feel as you want, even your business judgement is impaired – because you're in her debt.'

'Right in every detail.' He hesitated. 'I've a feeling I behaved like an idiot today.'

'From the business point of view, perhaps.'

'Agreed. But I'm not a commercial automaton. I'm a person.'

'Well, speaking as a person myself, I think you should release Jill's money as soon as possible. Then you'll be free. Then you can decide how you really feel about . . . oh . . . everything.'

The advice was superfluous. It had always been his ambition to get Jill's money restored. Now it was more urgent than ever, that was all.

At last he looked at his watch. 'I should be going.'

'If you like,' Julie shrugged. 'But there's no one waiting for you, after all.'

However, it really was time to go. There was nothing more to say, and to move into the field of action would be a disaster. He might not know how he felt about Jill, but he knew perfectly well how he felt about Julie – and physical involvement he needed like a hole in the head.

He drove home through silent streets. The May blossom gleamed in the moonlight. The world was tranquil, almost like a child breathing in its sleep. David was feeling odd. It wasn't just the brandy – there had been a change in him in the last few hours. Perhaps it was a learning situation; he was learning that he couldn't go on for the whole of his life expecting to be on the crest of a wave. Today he'd had to face it – he wasn't a kid any more who could edge his way out of a difficult situation by throwing a tantrum.

He let himself into his flat with automatic quietness. First he went to the bedroom, but then he decided to get a drink of water. On his way through the livingroom he paused to switch on a table lamp. And nearly died of fright.

Jill was sitting huddled on the settee.

'Jill! I thought you were in Liverpool.'

She spoke in a flat voice. 'It was cancelled. They rang at five-thirty.'

'Good heavens . . .'

She held her wrist in the beam of the table lamp so that

the face of her watch could be seen. 'It's half-past three in the morning, David. Where have you been?'

A nightmare situation. His brain felt clogged and useless. The limited light of the lamp fell on Jill's slim wrist and arm, and on her face, filling it with hollows of shadow so that she seemed unreal, a Topolski drawing.

Desperately he sought for words. None came.

'I asked you a question,' she said.

He tried to summon up a phrase, not too defensive, not too apologetic, with which to begin his explanation.

Then, providentially, the phone rang.

Jill sat back. 'That won't be for *me*, not at half-past three in the morning.'

Like a sleepwalker he went to the telephone and picked it up.

'Hullo?' His voice was heavy, as if he'd been drugged – or slugged, he thought, with a flash of humour.

It was Julie. 'So you got home safely? Despite the car?'

'Yes. Yes I did.'

'How are you feeling now?'

'Fine. Quite okay, thanks.'

'Not lonely?'

'No, not a bit. Thanks for 'phoning—'

'Thanks for 'phoning?' Her voice sharpened. 'Are you sure you're all right?'

'Quite all right, thanks. Goodnight.' Thankfully he put down the receiver. But the relief was short-lived because when he turned back, Jill was still waiting, sitting on the settee, unmoving, not even looking at him.

No good trying to put it off. 'I went to see someone,' he said. 'When I left, the car wouldn't start. I had to send for the A.A. That's why I'm so late.'

'How long did all that take?' his wife inquired.

'I don't know. An hour or so, I suppose.'

'Otherwise you'd have been home at two, or thereabouts. I see.'

'I didn't know you'd be here!' David blurted out. 'Sitting here waiting to make a time-and-motion study!'

'I do apologize,' Jill said sharply. 'I see I've no right to wonder where my husband is at three-thirty in the morning.'

He flung away in rising irritation. 'I'm going to make some coffee. Do you want some?'

'No, thank you.'

He went to the kitchen and filled the kettle. Lost in the sound of the running water, he didn't hear Jill follow him.

She said, a straight question: 'Were you with Julie?'

They stood face to face, he with the kettle idiotically in his hand, she in her crumpled cotton dress of yesterday.

'Not in the way you mean,' he said.

He plugged in the kettle and switched it on. There was a little comfort in these everyday actions.

'What I don't understand,' she said, 'is why you should go rushing to her . . .'

'I had a rotten day. I didn't want anyone to find me. If I'd come home they'd have been pestering me. I knew they'd never think of Julie.'

Jill frowned. 'Who's "they"?'

'Edward and Brian. The terrible twins.' The attempt at lightness didn't come off. 'Julie gave me dinner and a couple of drinks. We sat talking. That's all.'

'Until this hour?'

He pointed towards the bureau and the telephone. 'Look, check up on me! Ring and ask her – she won't be asleep yet!'

'David—'

''Phone her!' he urged, his voice rising. 'Or would you like me to do it and report back?'

'I'd *like* you to stop shouting at me, please.'

He took a grip on himself. He'd made a vow not to escape into tantrums. Damn it, it wasn't Jill's fault . . .

He picked up the kettle as it boiled and poured hot water into a mug. Then he realized he hadn't spooned in the instant coffee. He got the jar down from the shelf to ladle in a big measure, then gulped down a mouthful or two, scalding hot. It did him good. Somehow burning the roof of his mouth took some of the sting out of the situation.

Jill had watched him with a complete lack of interest. As if she was seeking for something to say, she announced: 'Brian 'phoned.'

'When?'

'Several times. He sounded in a bit of a state. He left a message.' She fetched a piece of paper from the bureau to give to him.

He read it, crumpled it up, and tossed it away.

'He said it was urgent,' Jill said.

'That means it's urgent to him.'

'What's it all about? He really sounded upset.'

David grunted. 'He's got a pet scheme which I sat on. He wanted to keep talking, and I didn't. A continuing dialogue, it's called. Pointless . . .'

His wife hugged herself with her arms. It was now nearly four in the morning, the time when all life is at its lowest ebb. She spoke wearily.

'David, we're married. I thought the "forsaking all others" meant no other women . . .'

'Other women!' He was almost amused at the phrase – it sounded as if he kept a harem. But it was no laughing matter. 'I don't understand why you insist on thinking . . . She's supposed to be your best friend!'

Jill's mouth turned up at the corners in a smile of sad irony. 'Do you think I don't know about you and Julie?'

'There's nothing to know.'

'Before we were married.'

'When who I saw was none of your business.'

Although that wasn't strictly true, she made no objection. According to her code, he knew, a man who's engaged to one girl shouldn't be having an affair with another. But she said: 'It's my business now.'

'I've *explained* why I saw her tonight,' he said, as if he were talking to a dim child.

'Oh yes, and you explained why you saw her when I was in Hamburg. It seems very strange that whenever I'm not here there's always some pressing reason why you have to see Julie.'

'Is it my fault that she's working freelance for Brian's pet advertising agency?'

He put an end to the argument half an hour later by dragging himself off to bed. He left Jill leaning against the breakfast bar, fighting her tears.

He was wakened next morning by the sound of the telephone. At first he tried not to hear it, and then when he heard the ringing abruptly stop he realized Jill had picked up the receiver. He looked at the bedside clock: nine-thirty.

He stumbled out of bed, pulling on his dressing-gown. When he went into the livingroom he found Jill, dressed, made-up, and ready for work, answering the phone.

'No, it was cancelled. I'm just going in now to hear whether they've chosen a new location . . . Well, we had rather a late night . . . Is it important? . . . All right, I'll fetch him—'

'I'm here,' David said. 'Who is it?'

'Brian.'

He groaned as he took the phone. Covering the mouthpiece he said to her: 'You're going to the studio?'

'Yes.'

'Well, hang on a minute and I'll drive you.'

'I'll get a taxi,' she replied.

'Jill, I want to talk to you—'

'There's nothing to talk about,' she said over her shoulder as she went out.

The call from Brian was not, as he'd expected, about Dover. It was about the Rogers contract: Mr. Rogers had been on the phone from Leeds and no one could talk sense to him because David had the information.

He showered and dressed and was on his way in fifteen minutes. When he got to Hammond's, he found his two brothers and Jennifer waiting for him in Edward's office.

Edward said, 'Rogers wants you to call him back urgently. But sit down a minute first.'

He surveyed them. 'What is this – a board meeting?'

'A discussion.'

'The subject being—?'

'Dover.'

He turned to the door. 'I've nothing more to say.'

'All right,' Edward said on a note of command, 'just listen.'

David doubted the wisdom of it. He was shaved and dressed, but in no other way was he ready for the day's work. His mind felt as if it was full of dirty cotton wool. The few hours' sleep had done him no good at all.

But Jennifer fixed her appealing glance on him, and unwillingly he took up a stance that indicated he would hear what was to be said.

Edward spoke crisply. 'Brian found a depot he believes to be suitable in Dover. Jenny and I think we should go and look at it.'

'There's no point,' David said.

'We can leave now, and talk on the way—'

'About what?'

'David, this is a business matter,' Brian put in. 'We all

respect how you feel, but it's too good a proposition to let slip on a minor disagreement.'

'It wasn't minor, Brian.'

'All right, but there has to be a solution that you'd find acceptable—'

'Oh, so I'm the one who's being difficult and obstructive?'

'I didn't say that—'

David cut him short. 'What about you two?' he demanded, turning to Edward and Jennifer.

Jennifer had her opinion ready. She'd given the matter very deep thought since the fracas yesterday. She knew – better than anyone, perhaps – how strongly personal matters could influence practical decisions, but in the end good sense ought to win.

'Whether this depot is what we want, or whether we can afford it, I don't know yet. But we had a favourable report from Brian and I don't think we should ignore it, whatever your feelings, David.'

David waited for his eldest brother to speak.

'I'm not entirely sold on it either,' Edward said. 'But I agree we should take a look.'

'All we're asking is that you keep an open mind,' pleaded Brian.

David gave a sigh of exasperation. 'I wish you people would grasp the fact that I'm sometimes right! An open mind? How can you have an open mind about spending money we haven't got?'

'But we could get the money if you would stop looking at it as a personal problem—'

'Brian, it's a matter of principle—'

'Then in fact we're wasting our time talking to you?'

'Now just a minute, Brian,' Edward said. 'You shouldn't—'

'When I hear someone bleating about "principle" then I know that commonsense has flown out of the window! For "principle" read "prejudice"—'

'Thank you,' David said. 'That seems to end the discussion.'

Edward lost his temper. 'For God's sake, come to your senses, you two! David – all we're bloody asking is that you should come with us to Dover!'

'I've told you—'

'At best,' Edward said, speaking calmly with a great

effort, 'we sort out some sort of compromise. At worst, we waste a few hours of our time.'

David held up his briefcase. 'The Rogers file is in here. *This* is what keeps the wheels turning – not pie in the sky. I'll go and ring Leeds.'

'Are you refusing to come to Dover?'

Jennifer put a hand on Edward's arm, then took over the argument. 'David, three of us think we should go. Don't you think you ought to take that into account?'

'The majority isn't always right, Jenny.'

'So no matter how it's explained to you,' Brian challenged, 'you know better?'

'Yes, I do.'

'David,' Edward said, completely calm and very worried, 'do you realize what you're doing? You're claiming the right to a veto, no matter what we say.'

'While we're under an obligation of such a large amount to my wife – yes.'

'So when you get down to it, it amounts to this,' Brian said. 'It doesn't matter about the company's welfare. You don't like feeling in debt to Jill.'

David gave him a hard look. 'If she'd put up the money another way, Brian, I could have had effective control of this company.' And he walked out.

'Over my dead body,' Brian said. He hit the desk softly with his hand. 'When it comes to the point, Ted, he *can't* over-rule us.'

Edward rubbed his chin. 'This is a special case, Brian. It's no good trying to shut your eyes to it.'

'It's you that's shutting your eyes! As chairman and managing-director you've got to bring him to heel.'

'As chairman and managing-director, I'm telling you "no". We don't go ahead without David's consent.'

'That's not only shutting your eyes,' Brian said with contempt, 'that's allowing a difficult director to lead you round in blinkers!'

When he had gone, Edward shook his head. 'This is the way it begins, Jenny. When two men start acting like that, they can pull a company to pieces.'

She rose to her feet, seeming dazed. 'I can't understand what's happened to us. Brian seems so different.'

Brian had hesitated a moment out in the corridor, then hurried to his office. He dialled his home number. When his wife answered he said quickly: 'Ann, it's me. Look, I want you to do something. Ring Jill and ask her over this evening.'

'Jill and David?' Ann said, reaching for a pencil to make a note.

'Not David. Jill on her own. I need to talk to her. I don't know how you can suggest it – make some excuse. You want to talk about clothes, or you're after tickets for a fashion show – something like that, something innocent.'

'Innocent?' Ann echoed. 'And isn't it?'

'Ann, I'm busy. Fix this up, will you?'

It was with a frown of some wonderment that his wife put down the receiver, then dialled the number of Jill's model agency. She had some trouble tracking Jill down, but a lot less in persuading her to spend the evening. In fact, she seemed almost to jump at the chance.

At a local charity's bring-and-buy sale Ann had brought an Indian sari. When Jill arrived she took her up to her bedroom to show it to her, on pretext of wondering how best to use it.

They spent half an hour draping it round each other with pins. Gradually Ann introduced the topic of the transport business. From Jill's replies it was clear David had told her practically nothing.

'I gather our respective husbands are at daggers drawn,' Ann joked.

'Is it as bad as that? I know they'd had a disagreement . . .'

They went downstairs when they heard Brian come in. 'Nice to see you, Jill,' he said, as if surprised. Ann made pretended explanations, and they all sat down with a sherry.

'I was telling Jill a minute ago about your feud with David,' Ann said.

Brian caught the ball neatly. 'Hardly a feud. More a difference of opinion.' He smiled at Jill. 'It concerns you, in a way.'

'Me?' She was startled. David had said nothing of that.

He explained about the Dover project and David's opposition. Jill said loyally that it didn't sound like David to block a good business move.

'It's because it would mean we couldn't release your guarantee for a while,' he told her. 'He's discussed it with you, of course?'

'No, not in detail.'

He could see it was a cover-up. She hadn't a clue. He felt a dawning sense of triumph. His whizz-kid younger brother ought to cover all the angles if he was going to take on the entire board of Hammond Transport.

'It's a shame to lose this opportunity,' he said, 'but of course it *is* your money and it does restrict you to have it tied up with us.'

Jill gave a passing thought to the car she couldn't have. So that was why? But it was silly. If David needed the money for the firm, then of course he must have it.

'I've got enough,' she said to Brian. 'We're both working – we're all right without that money.'

'David's rather concerned about it.'

'David seems a lot more worried about it than I am, for some reason. Truly, Brian, I'm quite happy to extend the guarantee or whatever you call it, for as long as you like.'

'Well, thank you. We don't really need it extended, Jill. Our problem is that Ted feels David has an overriding moral standing in the matter, since he was representing your interest.'

Ann said, 'Obviously David didn't know how Jill felt about it.' It was just the right note.

'Brian,' said Jill, 'if it's for the good of the company . . .? Just tell me how I can help.'

'You're very kind. It'd set poor old Ted's mind at rest if he could hear this.'

'Why don't you ring him, darling,' Ann suggested.

'May I?' He looked at Jill for permission.

'Of course, why not?'

'You could have a word yourself, perhaps. It would be such a relief to him to hear it directly from you.'

'Go ahead.'

Edward wasn't at home nor at the depot. Brian began to feel the thing might go off the boil. Then he thought of Jenny, and it was there that he ran his elder brother to earth.

'Hullo, Brian?' he said in alarm. 'Trouble?'

'Quite the reverse,' Brian said. 'I've got Jill here. She wants to talk to you. Hold on.'

Edward raised his eyebrows at Jennifer. 'He's putting Jill on.'

'Jill?' Jennifer echoed. 'What's the—?'

'Ssh . . . Hullo, Jill?'

'Hullo, Edward. Listen, Edward . . . Brian's just been explaining what a muddle there is over my money.'

'The devil he has,' thought Edward. Into the phone he said, 'Well, it's not exactly a muddle. But David does seem to feel—'

'I know, and he's got it all wrong, really. I mean, I don't *need* it, and if the company can raise loans and things against it—'

'That's what we have been doing, Jill. We're grateful—'

'But now this thing in Dover . . .? It does seem silly not to. Don't you think?'

'I do indeed.'

'So don't feel you have to turn it down because of using my money, Edward. It would be unbusinesslike, wouldn't it?'

'That's true . . . Jill, would you let me speak to Brian again?'

As he waited he shook his head at Jenny, his forehead furrowed in a massive frown. She moved nearer, so that she was almost touching him.

'Brian? Does she understand what she's saying?'

'Of course she does. She isn't the least bit perturbed about the release of the guarantee.'

'But has she thought how David is going to feel about it?'

'She's going to talk to him.' Brian glanced at Jill, who nodded. 'So he'll know. Now look, what I suggest is this – you and Jenny, and David of course, go to Dover at the first opportunity. There's no point in my going again.'

'But won't the warehouse have gone to the original bid – the discount store?'

'I rang my contact in Dover. The discount store want alterations made and they're dickering. If we can make a decision within a few days . . .?'

'Okay,' Edward said. 'We'll talk in the morning.'

Jennifer had gathered the gist of the conversation. 'I suppose that's good,' she remarked.

'Unless David feels we've gone behind his back.'

'Do you think we have?'

'I'm inclined to think,' Edward said unwillingly, 'that Brian has.'

She sighed. 'A few months ago, I don't think he'd have got Jill on her own like that. Would he?'

'So you've noticed it too?'

Jennifer was the one most likely to notice. Quieter by nature than the brothers, her role as director i/c administration kept her within the office building to a greater extent. She had watched David struggling with some intractable problem inside his marriage. She had seen a growing anxiety in Edward. But strangest of all had been the change in Brian.

'It's as though he's grown impatient,' she murmured. 'As if he wants to . . . take the lead.'

'That's it exactly. And David too . . . You know, Jenny, I think I can drive a team but when they start pulling different ways . . .'

David had got home that evening to find a note: 'Supper in oven, J.' He spent a lonely evening, for which he got revenge by writing on the back of the note: 'Gone to bed, D.' But he was genuinely tired, and was sound asleep when Jill came in.

They met at breakfast next morning. Each was wary: it seemed safest to keep to neutral topics.

'By the way,' David said, 'I'm going to Leeds tomorrow.'

'For the day?'

'Away a couple of nights, I think.'

It was on the tip of her tongue to say: 'With Julie?' but she thought better of it.

'Ann asked me over for a drink last night,' she said instead.

'Oh?' He began to feel better about his lonely evening 'How is she?'

'Fine. I had a long talk with Brian.'

David felt his hackles rise. What about?'

'About Dover. I wish you'd talked to me about it, David.'

'Why?'

'Because there seems to be a complete misunderstanding somewhere.'

David threw down his napkin and rose from the breakfast table in anger. 'Jill, you put up all your money to guarantee our loans because we were up against it. All right, we needed it, and we're grateful, but the sooner we're not beholden to you in any way, the better!'

'Who for, David?' she demanded, throwing back her head. 'Not me, because I don't care.'

'You don't understand the implications!'

'The only implication is that I'm helping the firm! As far

as I'm concerned you can use the money for as long as you like. I told Brian I'd sign a guarantee for a fixed, long-term period, if that would help.'

'How long did you have in mind?' he exclaimed. 'A lifetime?'

'David, if it's for the good of the company—?'

He cut her off abruptly. 'Brian's taken you for a ride, don't you see that? Used you against me. How do you think I feel, when we're using *ex gratia* money from my wife all the time? Like a poor relation!'

Jill leapt up to face him, a momentary anger equal to his lighting up her eyes. 'Where did I get the idea that marriage was supposed to be a partnership!'

'I want to be my own man, Jill,' he said, in a desperate attempt to make her understand. 'I don't want to be kept by you.'

'Or is it because of Julie? Would you rather be with her, is that it?'

'Oh, for God's *sake*, don't drag that up as well—'

'Because if that's what you want, don't let that damned money stand in your way!' Her voice cracked. 'Go to Julie! I know she wants you, she always did, and she's welcome!'

'Jill—'

She shoved him aside and ran into the bedroom. The slam of the door sounded very final.

CHAPTER SIX

David obdurately refused to go to Dover: he said he had more important things to do before he went up to Leeds to see Rogers. Edward and Jennifer made the trip and were impressed with what they saw.

On the way back in the train, Edward said to her: 'Listen Jenny . . . Have you a free evening some time soon?'

'What for?'

'My mother . . . er . . . my mother would like you to come to dinner one night.'

Jennifer for a minute was sure she'd mis-heard him over the clack of the train wheels.

'She asked me to invite you . . . some evening convenient to everybody.'

She could hardly find the breath to speak. 'Your mother suggested this?'

'It came up in conversation.'

With the aid of a giant hoist, he thought wryly. He'd had a serious quarrel with his mother over it, this very morning. She'd said she was thinking of inviting David and Jill for next day.

'David's going to Leeds,' he told her.

'Oh. Then perhaps next week would be better.' She laid aside her engagement diary.

Edward put down the teacup which he'd been carrying around with him while he collected papers and documents; he always had a peripatetic breakfast, much to Mary's annoyance.

'While you're on the subject of invitations, there *is* someone I'd like you to have to dinner some time.'

'Of course, dear. Who?'

'Jennifer Kingsley.'

Colour came into his mother's cheeks. Her severe good looks became even sterner.

'Invite Miss Kingsley? Into my house? Certainly not.'

Edward sighed in exasperation. 'You invite Barbara,' he pointed out.

'That's different.'

'Make friends with the daughter, cold-shoulder the mother. It doesn't make sense.'

'It does to me!' his mother replied with vehemence. 'Barbara has done nothing wrong. I can feel affection for her because she is your father's child, your half-sister. Sometimes she has a look of Robert . . .' She checked herself. She wasn't going to let him know how much that affected her. 'But Miss Kingsley is not innocent as Barbara is. If I never see her again, that will suit me very well.'

Her son took a deep breath. 'I'm not really asking you, Mother. I'm telling you.'

She gave him a tolerant glance which, if she but knew it, infuriated him. 'You disappoint me, Edward. I thought you had got over that preposterous infatuation.'

'It was never that,' he rejoined. 'If you want to know what my feelings are where Jenny's concerned—' But he, too, had things he couldn't discuss. 'All I know is this. When I need to talk to someone when I need help – I turn to her.'

'That's natural. She's a business colleague.'

'Bill Riley's a business colleague. I feel no desire to spend an evening chatting to him.'

'Edward, you're being absurd.'

'Absurd, am I? All right – we all have our absurdities. Your need to get revenge on Jenny is even more silly.'

'Edward!'

'You see her as some sort of *femme fatale*.' He snorted at the idea. 'Why don't you grow up?'

Mary Hammond was genuinely hurt. She'd had the thick end of her son's tongue before – even as a boy he'd been high-tempered. But to have him use that tone of contempt—!

'I suppose *she* put you up to it?' she said through stiff lips.

'No, and I don't suppose she'll want to come any more than you want to ask her.'

'Then I suggest we drop the idea.'

'Mother, I am sick and tired of trying to deal with two people I'm fond of as though the other didn't exist. It's time we tried to be civilized.'

'What do you suggest we talk about at this dinner? Our mutual recollections of your father?'

'Talk about what the hell you like—'

'Please don't speak to me like that!'

'Then be courteous to my friend and fellow-director in what is, after all, my home as well as yours.' He gave her a very hard, unloving stare. 'I'm waiting for your agreement, Mother.'

And before he left the house she had given in. Now all he had to do was persuade Jenny to accept.

'I'm sorry,' she said, 'I don't have an evening free for weeks.'

'Jenny, don't just turn it down. I'm not inviting you just so you'll have a horrible evening. I'm not as thick-headed as you imagine, nor as malleable in my mother's hands—'

'Oh, Edward, I never—'

'I bet you did. You must have asked yourself why I never married. You've been with the firm a long time, Jenny. Remember Marguerite Barrett?'

Jenny's eyes darkened with recollection. Marguerite Barrett had been Edward's girl . . . oh, over ten years ago. Twelve, maybe. That was back in the days when Jennifer referred to him as 'Mr. Edward' and kept her distance. There had been a bit of a mystery about the breaking-off of his engagement. As she thought back, she realized it had taken Edward a long time to get over it. That was one of the periods when he'd gone out for weeks at a time as a lorry driver. Marguerite Barrett had gone away – Jennifer had heard she was married now.

Edward had buckled-to in the office and depot. His father's health gradually failed. And there was poor old Ted – trapped.

'Jenny,' he said, 'perhaps we rushed our fences, you and I. Tried to move too fast.'

'Forcing your mother to invite me to dinner won't solve anything.'

'I want you to accept, Jenny. We can't live in a kind of no-man's-land for ever.'

And she looked as if she might agree, however unwillingly.

Next day David was due to drive to Leeds. He tidied up some loose ends in the office during the morning, then went out to the pub down the road for a beer and a sandwich before setting out. Julie Lane was already there, drinking white wine and eating French bread and cheese. An overnight bag of bright red leather was at her feet.

'Hullo! Where are you off to?' He was surprised – she hadn't said anything about going away when he rang her.

'I've got a job on in Lewes. This won't take long, will it,

David? My train goes in forty minutes.'

He was a bit put out. In general Julie always had time for him. 'I'll drive you to the station,' he offered.

'Thank you. That would be a help.' She sipped her wine. 'So what's it about?'

'I need your help, Julie.'

'You should try the Citizens Advice Bureau.'

'Please. I'm serious. I'm in a real mess with Jill.'

'Then you should speak to Jill.'

'I can't. We don't talk, we quarrel. And it's no wonder. Her trip to Liverpool was cancelled the other night. When I got home she was sitting up, waiting.'

'Oh dear.'

'I tried to explain, but she's got it firmly fixed in her head that I meet you every chance I get.'

'What an odd notion.'

'I thought if you talked to her, explained that there was nothing in it—?'

Even as he said it he knew it was a naive proposal. Julie's reaction left him in no doubt.

'Why should I do anything? You came to me, remember. You stayed of your own free will. Don't expect me to bail you out.'

'Julie,' he said in despair, 'stop playing games.'

'I told you once before – I'm not playing, I never have been. Jill isn't very clever but she's more clear-sighted than you. You do have something to sort out with her, and one of these days you'll have to face up to it.'

'I'm trying to sort out my marriage, Julie.'

She glanced at her watch. 'I'll have to go.'

'Come on then.' He picked up her case and led the way, leaving his beer on the table. With a little grimace she followed.

He put her case in behind the front seat, then opened the other door for Julie to get in.

It was unfortunate that across the street his brother Edward was buying panatellas at a kiosk. Edward simply couldn't help seeing the two drive off together with luggage in the back of the car. He didn't know what to make of it.

David returned three days later with a fairly satisfactory report. Rogers was willing to give a limited trial period to Hammond Transport to see how it worked.

'Good,' Brian said.

'On condition,' David went on, as if Brian hadn't spoken, 'that we trim our quotation by five per cent.'

The others waited while Brian, muttering, did some calculations. 'It's tight,' he said, 'extremely tight.'

'I told him we'd have to consider it,' David said.

'On the other hand,' Brian suggested, 'if we satisfy them with this contract we *could* get the rest of their work in the end. They're very big in the food industry. It's a slight gamble but worth taking, I think.'

After a little more discussion it was agreed to try the Rogers contract at less-five-per-cent.

'Next item,' said Edward. 'The question of a depot in Dover.'

David stiffened, but said nothing while Edward reported that he and Jennifer had seen the building and approved of it. Brian reported that he had talked to the bank, who were entirely happy to provide the finance.

At this point, predictably, David intervened. 'But only if the finance is guaranteed by Jill's money.'

'Mr. Chairman,' Brian said, 'I'd like to put something on record, if I may. I have the personal assurance of Mrs. David Hammond that there is no question of the guarantee being withdrawn, and that she approves the scheme under discussion—'

'Let *me* put something on record, Mr. Chairman,' said David. 'I consider the approach made to Jill without my knowledge was underhand, to put it mildly!'

'Mr. Chairman, really!' Brian protested.

'Let him finish,' Edward warned.

'But I had a simple conversation, which I've reported—'

'I don't want any more interruptions. Is that clear? I want to know how David feels.'

But David was only able to say what he had said before – that though he thought the idea of a depot in Dover was good, he couldn't agree to going ahead with it until they were in a position to do it without help from Jill.

'But we do in fact have her backing,' Edward said. 'You accept that?'

'Jill's an interested party. It was right to consult her,' Brian insisted.

'Brian, the way it was done caused ill feelings and resentment.'

'That wasn't my intention, Mr. Chairman. My only consideration was the welfare of the company.'

'Do you wish to express regret, in that case?'

Brian looked resentful. 'Well, I suppose if it's caused any trouble . . .'

Edward turned to his younger brother. 'So you have Brian's apology. What I want you to do now, David, is consider the case strictly on its merits.' He glanced round the table. 'You've all read the proposal on the agenda.'

'Moved,' said Brian promptly.

'Seconded,' Jennifer said.

'Those in favour?'

Brian and Jennifer held up a hand. David didn't move.

Once again Edward turned to his youngest brother. 'David, I want us to agree on this.'

'I'm sure you do,' David broke in. 'But I'm going to vote against this and I beg you to vote against it also and then use your chairman's casting vote to defeat the proposal. I'm not going to go over my arguments again. This is a personal appeal to you, Ted.'

The chairman of the board looked down at the papers in front of him. He patted them so that they lay with their edges aligned.

'I want to explain the course I intend to take. I think this is a deplorable position. David is directly and personally involved and the arguments in favour of doing nothing without his agreement are very strong indeed.'

Brian sat back in his chair, his face grim.

Doggedly Edward continued. 'You asked me for my backing on a personal level, David – but in the end it's got to be what's right for the company. I have to say that, despite everything, I think we need Dover. I could abstain and so allow the motion to be carried by two votes against your one, but I must make my position clear.' He cleared his throat. 'With some reluctance, I support the proposal, which is therefore carried by three votes to one.'

Brian relaxed. No one spoke.

'Any other business?'

No response.

'The meeting's closed.'

Stony-faced, David got up and went out.

As if Brian wasn't there, Jennifer spoke gently to Edward. 'It had to be done, Ted.'

But being more or less ignored couldn't lessen Brian's sense of satisfaction. He went home with a load of papers, his forward survey of possible expansion at Dover. Ann was away for the day at her parents, so he settled down in the evening sunlight to study them.

He was disturbed by the sound of footsteps approaching the front door. He half rose, expecting the doorbell to ring. But instead a letter plopped through the letter-box. He went out to pick it off the doormat. It was unstamped, addressed to 'Mr. and Mrs. Brian Hammond.'

Puzzled, he opened the front door. Pamela Graham was walking down the front path.

'Pamela!'

She stopped and turned. 'Oh, hullo,' she said. 'I didn't think there would be anyone at home.'

'Well . . . come in.'

There was awkwardness for both of them in the encounter. Each was remembering how tamely, how lamely, they had let their friendship be extinguished. But she stepped into the house.

'I 'phoned during the morning,' she explained. 'No reply, so I thought . . .'

'Ann is visiting her mother today. Normally I wouldn't be here so early, of course, but I've brought some work home.'

'I really wanted to speak to Ann,' Pamela said.

Brian examined the envelope in his hands. 'I see this is addressed to both of us?'

'It's about Carol,' she said.

'Carol?' He was surprised. There could be no possible reason for Pamela writing a letter about their daughter. She had been Pamela's pupil at day school but now she was at boarding-school, there could be no contact.

'She 'phoned me last night.'

' 'Phoned you? Why?'

Pamela glanced about for a chair, realizing this would take longer than a mere moment or two. 'Some ridiculous question about French verbs. She said she was in a 'phone box.'

'Yes, there's one in the hall that thc girls can use.' He paused. 'French verbs?'

'I asked her why she didn't speak to her own teacher. She said her teacher was French so she couldn't understand what she said.'

Brian gave a chuckle.

'It's not funny, Brian,' Pamela said flatly.

'Well, no . . . I suppose it's a great compliment – to you, I mean.'

She looked almost impatient at his obtuseness. 'Brian, this was last night. I was at home. I've never given her my home number. Think what the child had to do – dial Directory Inquiries, get my number, dial again, put in the right money, her pocket money too – and why? To talk to me, using a transparent excuse.' She saw that Brian was beginning to take it more seriously. 'Yes, a lot of trouble just to do that, you'll agree.'

'What did she talk about?'

'Nothing much. The school sports, a film she'd been to, school lunch. And she asked about the girls who used to be in her class. "All my friends," she called them.'

Brian was feeling his way towards an assessment of the matter as Pamela saw it. 'I know you never thought boarding school was a good idea . . .'

'I felt you ought to know she had needed someone to talk to.'

'We go and see her as often as we can,' he defended himself. 'There were a few problems, but she seems happy enough.'

She made a little gesture of disappointment. 'A happy child would have forgotten her former teacher by now.'

'But she was very fond of you, Pamela.'

'Yes, but . . . If she felt lonely last night, or in need of reassurance, why did she 'phone *me*? Why not you or Ann? You'd think she'd turn first to you.'

He felt as if layer after layer of meaning was being unfolded in this simple action of his little girl. A strange uneasiness took hold of him: were there layers of meaning in everything? Which he was always unaware of?

'It is worrying,' he said. 'You're right. I'll talk to Ann. Maybe we should visit the school more often . . .'

'I think that would be a help.'

'If Ann should want to talk to you about it herself?'

'Oh, of course.'

'Perhaps one evening.'

'Well, leave it that she'll get in touch if she feels she wants to.'

When she had taken her leave he sat down again to his papers but didn't immediately begin work. Between the pages and his eyes a little girl's face appeared – Carol, in mute misery, as they had said goodbye on her first day at boarding school.

But after a while he picked up his pencil and began to add up figures.

His elder brother was also at work, planning the schedules for the Leeds collections. It was going to be no fun, keeping to this timetable. If only Riley and the works committee had been more co-operative about recruiting drivers! There had been two or three good applicants he'd had to turn down because they didn't hold union cards – and how he needed them now.

As if in answer to his prayer, Jennifer tapped on his door and came in.

'There's a Mr. Barker outside.'

'Who?'

'He says he's in answer to our ad.'

'Oh, yes – he rang. Send him in Jenny, will you, please?'

She opened the door to usher him in – a big, solid, friendly-looking man in his late thirties. Jennifer gave Edward an inquiring glance and a tentative thumbs-up as she went out again.

'Sit down, Mr. Barker.'

'Thank you, sir.' He obeyed, taking papers and cards from the breast pocket of a clean though worn windcheater. 'You'll want to see my licences.'

Edward studied them. 'How long have you been in heavy goods?'

'Pretty well since I left school, sir. Been on lorries for the last fifteen years – drove vans before that.'

Edward tried not to look too pleased. 'Who for?'

'Same firm all the time – Nolan's.'

'Nolan's. Don't know them.'

'Nolan Haulage, Hendon. A small outfit, ten lorries. I was sorry to leave.'

'Why did you?'

Mr. Barker began a complex explanation involving the ill-health of his wife's mother, moving home, and other problems, all of which Edward had heard before from men applying for jobs or giving notice.

'Brought your references with you?'

Barker scratched his head. 'Well, I would have done, but Mr. Nolan hasn't sent them on yet. Not much of a one for the paper work. But you could telephone him if you like, sir. He'll tell you anything you want to know.'

'Well, yes, perhaps that would . . .'

'Here's the number, sir.' He offered a much-folded scrap of paper.

'Right.' Edward dialled. The number rang.

It rang in a phone box on a street corner in Hendon. A man in a cotton-knit shirt was hanging about outside. As the phone began to ring he took a notice off the door; the notice said: 'Out of Order.' He picked up the receiver.

'Nolan Haulage,' he said.

'Could I speak to Mr. Nolan?' Edward inquired.

'Nolan speaking,' said the man, whose name was James Lowe.

'This is Edward Hammond of Hammond Transport. I'd like to ask you—'

'Oh yes, Mr. Hammond – I've heard of you. Excuse me being out of breath – I had to dash in from the yard to answer the 'phone. My girl's popped out to fetch the tea. Now what can I do for you?'

A few questions and answers established for Edward that Jim Barker had worked for Nolan Haulage for fifteen years and was honest, reliable, punctual, a hard worker. He thanked Mr. Nolan for his information and was saying good-bye when Jim Barker said: ''Scuse me, sir, could you let me have a word?'

'Of course,' Edward said, handing over the phone.

As he took it, Barker gave him a look of inquiry. 'What d'you think, sir? Can I say you . . .?'

'You'd better see our foreman driver but I'm sure that's a formality. Can you start Monday?'

'I can start tomorrow.'

'Monday'll do,' Edward said, amused.

Barker said into the phone: 'Hullo, Mr. Nolan, this is me, Jim Barker. Yes.' Some kindly chit-chat followed about his domestic problems. He ended with: 'Thank you, Mr. Nolan, for speaking for me. I think it's . . . well . . . touch wood, but I think so.'

He hung up. At the other end of the line, the man in the phone box did likewise. He grinned, patted the phone, and left the phone box.

Across the street a nondescript blue Ford was parked. He leaned forward to speak to the man at the wheel.

'He's in,' he said.

CHAPTER SEVEN

He was, of course, a union man with his subs paid up to date, otherwise Bill Riley would not have accepted him. He lived up to his verbal references: completed his runs on time, looked after his lorry. Everybody's blue-eyed boy, that was Jim Barker.

It came on Hammond Transport like a thunderbolt, therefore, when late one afternoon in June a call came through from a police station in Kent. Riley was reporting that the lorry he and Barker had been bringing back from Dover with a load of expensive German cameras had been hi-jacked.

Jennifer took the call, and came flying into the loading-bays in search of Edward. She blurted it, short of breath after taking the iron stairs and the car park at break-neck speed.

'Hi-jacked? How? When?' Edward was aghast.

'That's all I know. Riley came through, then Kent C.I.D. They said to fetch you.'

'Bloody hell!' groaned Edward. 'Is he hurt? Bill?'

'Not so far as I can make out. Come *on*, Ted.' She dragged at him, and he gave in to her pull then shook her off and ran past her to cross the distance between the loading bay and his office in record time.

Little was to be learned on the phone. Brian hurried in as he talked, alerted by Jennifer. It took no time at all for them to agree to drive down to Kent.

The story, when they heard it, was infuriating. It was almost beyond belief that Riley had fallen for this simple trap of the pretty girl in a stalled car, the helpful lorry-driver pulled up alongside, and the one-two-and-away of the snatch. Riley had run after his disappearing vehicle – even managed to grab the tailboard – but it was no use. He and Barker were left on a lonely stretch of road with a stolen car, an empty lorry, and a lot of egg all over their faces.

The Kent C.I.D. were saying very little but it was easy to see they weren't impressed by Riley's story. After some hanging about it became clear they weren't going to let either him or Barker go, at least not tonight.

Edward was in a jam. Tonight, of all nights, was the dinner party his mother was giving for Jennifer. After weeks of delicate negotiation he'd actually achieved the impossible: a date had been arranged when Mary could give the dinner, Jennifer could come, and actually *would*.

He and Brian sat about in the vestibule of the police station. His restlessness at last got through even to his imperceptive brother.

'Is something wrong, Ted? I mean, extra to . . .?'

Suddenly Edward decided to confide. 'It's Jenny. She's having dinner with us.'

'Us?' Brian's eyes went round. 'You and Mother?'

'I'll have to ring and cancel, and God *knows* when I'll get it together again.'

Brian was always rather good in an emergency of practicalities. 'Look . . . you go home. I'll hang on here. Yes, I insist.'

'No, no, Brian. It's my responsibility—'

'It'll be all right. I'll represent Hammond's.'

'But Riley will—' Riley will expect *me*, he'd been going to say.

'They're not going to let Riley see anyone for a bit,' Brian said grimly. 'No, you go, Ted.'

And after some discussion and a further abortive conversation with a cagey detective-sergeant, go he did.

In a way, Jennifer was almost disappointed. The one bright spot in a really dreadful day had been that the dinner-party must now be cancelled.

In the morning she'd had a quarrel with David. At least, David had quarrelled with her. It began in an 'ideas' meeting with Nicholas Fox, David, and herself, about possible advertising for Hammond Transport.

Predictably, David had been obstructive. The more Nicholas spread out graphs and art-work, the more David became bloody-minded. He raised every objection he could think of – expense, time-lag, printing strikes, phoney image – the lot. What made it bad was that Brian wasn't there to counteract his kibbitzing: Brian was with their banker, spreading out sugar. Jennifer felt obliged to take the line Brian would have taken, simply to balance out the discussion.

When Nicholas Fox took his leave, David turned on Jennifer. She took the wind out of his sails by saying, 'I'm not necessarily against what you were saying, David. But don't just dismiss this advertising plan out of hand. It has to happen some time, you know.'

That made him pause. 'But . . . that's in the future . . .'

'It was you who always used to talk about expansion. You pushed for the warehouse here, for buying the extra land, for taking over Carter Express.'

'In the past, yes . . .'

'So why not now?'

'I think it's getting out of control. Brian seems to have developed a strange sort of euphoria.'

Jennifer had had very similar thoughts, but she wasn't going to say so to David.

'You've switched roles, haven't you?' she observed. 'You and Brian. Once upon a time you were the hare and he was the tortoise.'

'Yes, but we could always rely on you and Edward to keep the balance.'

'And can't you any more?'

'You, perhaps,' he said with earnestness. 'I know you'll always come down on the side of commonsense.'

Jennifer couldn't prevent a smile. 'Are you by any chance lobbying my support against Brian?'

'No, no. I can deal with him.'

'Really?' She was surprised to hear it. At the moment she didn't quite see who could 'deal' with Brian, who seemed to be a prime example of local-boy-makes-good. 'Who are we talking about then? What's your problem?'

'I feel there's a sort of . . . power vacuum.'

'So we're talking about Ted.'

David glanced at his watch. She was relieved to think he was about to go. Behind-the-scenes manoeuvring always distressed her.

'Perhaps we could get a moment to chat about it this evening.'

'I have a dinner date this evening,' she said, repressing a shiver though it was a warm day.

'I know. So have I. Same one.'

'You're coming?'

'Jill and I. She had a dressmaking session with Mother last night, and came home saying she'd accepted for both of us.'

Jennifer wasn't sure whether David had agreed to go out of idle curiosity or because he wanted to keep an eye on what happened between his mother, Edward and Jennifer from a business point of view. Whichever, it was something of a relief not to have a *diner à trois.*

Brian came back with good news from the bank but was annoyed to have missed Nick's presentation. He was rather short with Jennifer when she reported on what had happened. She thought to herself: 'He gets more and more like a tycoon every day!'

She lunched with Barbara, which did nothing to cheer her. When she asked how her son-in-law's shop was going, she got scanty information.

'It's fine, Mum. Johnny's re-organizing.'

'Re-organizing? He's only been open five minutes!' She tried to make her daughter meet her eye. 'Everything *is* all right, Barbara?'

'Super, Mum, really. Johnny's interested to hear about your advertising plans. He thinks it's maybe just what the boutique needs. Could you let me have the name of your agency?'

Jennifer was staggered. 'Our agency? But that's a big-time firm. Now, Barbara!'

She lectured. She knew she did, but she couldn't stop herself. She had the feeling Barbara was glad to get away, afterwards.

Then, in the afternoon, the phone call came from Riley. After that, the day disintegrated. She had to contact the insurers, the customer expecting the load, the despatchers, and fend off the local reporters. When Edward rang through to say he was leaving Brian to cope at the police station and would see her at his mother's, her heart – already in her summer sandals – went through the soles and into the office floor.

She'd had a hair appointment, but that had had to be jettisoned. All the same, she managed quite a good job with some bobby-pins and setting lotion. The new dress spread on her bed gave her a little confidence: she'd paid more for it than she usually did, and the shop assistant had looked genuinely admiring when she tried it on.

But no such expression dawned in the eyes of Mary Hammond when she opened the door to her at eight o'clock that evening. If Edward hadn't appeared immediately, making welcoming noises, Jennifer might have bolted.

Jill and David were already there. It occurred to Jennifer

that they'd been asked to come early, and for one startled moment she wondered if Mary was as nervous as she was. But she dismissed the idea as absurd.

But if Mary had expected support from Jill and David, she was going to be disappointed. It was clear they'd been quarrelling before they arrived. Mary placed them all at table then escaped to the kitchen to bring the soup. David, invited to pour the wine, began to complain that it hadn't been chilled enough.

'Just pour it, David, will you?' Edward said on that sudden note of command that sometimes came to him. And David, quelled, did so.

A lovely start to a lovely evening, Jennifer thought.

Mary eased the situation, as a good hostess should, by asking about the stolen lorry.

'Nothing to tell, Mother,' Edward said. 'A good, clean, professional job.'

'No one was hurt?'

'No, no violence.'

'That's a blessing.'

Jennifer, who so far had said nothing but 'Good evening,' felt it was time she uttered. 'The police seem to take it for granted they won't find the load.'

'They probably know it's already been disposed of,' David said.

Conversation languished.

'How was your trip to Boulogne yesterday?' Jill inquired of Edward.

'Oh . . . fine.'

'Was it choppy in the Channel?'

'No. Flat.'

David couldn't resist. 'Rather like Norfolk, I imagine.'

'What?'

'Very flat – Norfolk.' But none of the others knew Noel Coward well enough.

'And poor Brian's still down at the police station?' Mary resumed.

'Well, one of us had to be there. It's our lorry.'

David looked as if he was about to say no one had asked *him* if Brian should represent them.

'Lovely soup, Mary,' said Jill valiantly.

'Thank you,' Mary said. It was a measure of her helplessness that she couldn't think of anything else.

By the time they reached the dessert, the good wines that had accompanied the two previous courses had brought about a slight thaw. Jill had more or less entertained them with an account of her Hamburg trip, though in deference to her mother-in-law she didn't describe the Reeperbahn night clubs.

'Tell Edward about your trip to Caen,' Mary encouraged.

'Oh, I've heard that,' Edward said. 'The time you went with that photographic girl – the one Pageant Advertising have been using.'

'Julie,' Jill said, losing her sparkle.

'How *is* Julie these days, Jill?' Mary inquired.

'I haven't seen her lately.'

'Wait a minute, didn't I see her the other day?' Edward said. 'The day you went to Leeds, wasn't it?'

David gave him a cold glance. 'Was it?'

'Coming out of the Dragon with a red suitcase – you gave her a lift. Remember?'

Jennifer, who had no reason to care one way or the other about Julie, became aware that Jill had become very tense.

'Oh yes,' David said casually – too casually. 'She was going down to Sussex. I gave her a lift to Victoria.'

'I remember,' Jill said. 'She mentioned it on the card she sent me.'

Edward was the only one who believed her, just as he was the only one unaware that he had put his foot in it.

The meal dragged to an end after that. They coasted through the coffee and brandy stage by listening to Edward's dogged chat about Continental motorways, which he'd recently been sampling on behalf of Hammond Transport. Jill's social conscience seemed to have deserted her: she didn't care if the dinner-party foundered, all she wanted was to get away.

As soon as she decently could, she stood up. 'We really must go now,' she said.

'Must we?' said David.

She wheeled on him with unexpected sharpness. 'You know I've got an early start in the morning.'

'Oh, what a shame,' Mary said, well aware that something was very wrong.

'I must get back too,' Jenny said. 'If I could just use your 'phone to call a taxi, Mrs. Hammond—?'

'Of course.'

'I'll drive you back,' Edward said in a huffy voice, 'if you *must* go.'

Jill seized her chance to make her escape. 'Good night, Mary, and thank you for a super dinner.' They exchanged affectionate kisses, and Mary went with her into the hall.

David was annoyed. He said to Jennifer, 'It seems we won't have time for that chat after all.'

'Never mind. Tomorrow, perhaps.'

'David, Jill's waiting,' his mother called.

With a suppressed exclamation he went out. Edward touched Jennifer's arm. 'Jenny, what's the hurry?'

'I'm tired. It's been a bad day.'

'Relax a little, then—'

'Relax? Here?' She stared at him. 'I don't want to stay any longer, Edward, and your mother's made it perfectly clear she doesn't want me to either . . .'

'Why? What did she say?' he demanded.

'It's what she *doesn't* say. Now let me ring for a taxi.' But just as she reached the phone, it rang.

Edward picked it up. 'Hullo – Brian? You're still . . .? Why, what's wrong?' He looked at Jennifer, frowning. 'What on earth for?'

'What's wrong, Edward?'

'He's what? *What*? But that's ridiculous!'

'What, Edward? What is it?' Jennifer begged, alarmed at the anxiety behind his angry exclamations.

'You get back home, Brian. I'll get down there and sort it all out.'

'You're surely not going out again tonight?' his mother protested, coming in from the hall.

When Edward spoke it was more to Jennifer than to Mary. 'They're keeping Riley overnight.'

'What on earth for?'

'God knows. They must be round the bend. Come on, I'll drop you off on the way.'

And so ended a pleasant social evening.

For David and Jill it ended just as badly. He knew she would ask for an explanation of the encounter with Julie, and that she wouldn't believe it when he gave it. He was proved right on both counts.

'You took her to Leeds with you, David! You couldn't even bother to be discreet about it!'

'I did *not* take her to Leeds!' he shouted.

'For God's sake stop lying to me. It's the one thing I can't stand!'

'I am *not* lying! But lies or truth, you don't listen—'

'You admit there have been lies, then?'

'God damn it, Jill, stop accusing me—'

'It's myself I'm accusing, really,' she said, her anger dying. 'Maybe it's all my fault. Maybe I should never have married you.'

And since he'd sometimes had the same thought, he didn't dare reply.

Brian overslept badly next morning after getting home from Kent well past midnight. It was after nine when he came downstairs struggling into his dressing-gown, to find Ann buttering wholemeal toast in the kitchen.

'You should have woken me, Ann.'

'You were sleeping like a log. What time did you get in?'

'About one o'clock, I think.'

'Must have been quite a session!'

'Oh, they had some absurd idea that Riley was involved.'

'That wouldn't surprise me.'

'You've got to be joking,' he said, staring at her as he picked up the percolator.

'Don't I often see in the papers that the drivers are accomplices in hi-jackings?' she inquired, crunching her toast.

'Oh, Ann! Riley?' He put down the percolator. 'I must ring Edward.'

'Have your coffee first.'

He poured it, gulped down half a cup. Then it occurred to him that he'd been very self-engrossed. 'Did you have a nice evening?'

'Not bad, thanks.'

Brian hadn't been able to see Nicholas Fox for the advertising presentation the previous day. He'd therefore arranged to meet him in town for dinner with Ann, but naturally had to withdraw when he rushed down to Kent. He'd insisted that Ann should go, however.

'Where did you go?'

'Consuelo's.'

'Was the food good?'

'So-so.'

'Has the post come?'

'Behind you.' Ann felt a need to make Brian aware that

she and Nick were becoming close. Perhaps if she alerted him, he'd somehow prevent it. 'Nick suggests I should take sculpture classes during the day.'

'Good idea,' Brian said, slitting open an envelope.

'Is that all right, then?'

'What?'

'Taking sculpture classes.'

'Oh yes, splendid.' He dragged himself away from his letter. 'You don't have to ask my permission.' Having reacted correctly, as he felt, he resumed reading.

Ann took a sip of coffee and watched her husband scanning the letter. 'What if I said, "I'm falling in love with Nick"?' she wondered. 'Would he say, "Oh, yes, splendid"?'

'Well, anyway,' she said loudly, 'we owe him a dinner.'

'Who?'

'Nicholas Fox.'

'Oh yes. Well, we'll fix it up.'

'When?'

'Ah . . . ' Brian gave it some thought. 'I think I'm likely to be home early next Thursday. Is that too soon?'

'No, that would do. We'd want someone to make up the four, though.' She paused, as if thinking it over. 'How about Pamela Graham?'

But her husband refused to justify her own feelings by showing guilt for his. 'If you think she would like it,' he agreed.

Mary Hammond, who dearly wanted to find out what was wrong between David and his wife, was provided with the perfect opportunity by finding one of Jill's rings on the kitchen draining board. She rang her at the studio.

'You must have left it when you rinsed the wine-glasses. Would you like to drop by and collect it?'

Jill couldn't help thinking it symbolic that it was her engagement ring. 'I'm going into Chelsea for lunch. I'll call in on my way. About eleven-thirty?'

'Lovely.'

Mary had coffee ready, but Jill refused it. 'I mustn't stay – it's a working lunch.'

'Just a cup.' Mary poured it anyway, as a cover for her next remark. 'I thought David looked a bit peaky last night?'

'Did you?'

'He's rather irritable too. I suppose he's working too

hard.' Then, as Jill made no response: 'I suspect you both are.'

'Meaning I was irritable too?' Jill said, astoundingly.

It was like being bitten by a thrush. Mary stared at her. Then she came straight out with it.

'Jill, is there anything I can do to help?'

'Help who?'

'Both of you.'

'I don't know what you mean.'

'Jill dear, we've always been able to talk frankly, ever since you first became engaged to David—'

'Has David been—?'

'He hasn't said a word. But I can see for myself that things aren't going well.'

'Is it that obvious?' Jill sighed.

'It has been, for weeks. Tell me what's wrong.'

Jill pushed her engagement ring up and down over her knuckle. 'A classic situation . . .'

'Another woman,' Mary murmured. And then: 'Your friend Julie.'

'You could hardly call her a friend,' Jill said bitterly.

Mary studied the gentle, almost dreamy features. Poor child. She simply wasn't equipped to deal with this situation. 'She's always been after him, hasn't she?' she remarked.

'You knew that?'

'Oh, yes, I sensed it. Ages ago, when you and David and Julie were here together.'

Although Jill was expected elsewhere, and although she had vowed never to discuss her troubles with anyone, she couldn't resist asking for advice from the only woman in her circle who could be said to be a mother-figure to her.

'What does one do in these circumstances, Mary? I'm afraid I'm not the type to go and scratch her eyes out! In any case, that would only make things worse.'

'Perhaps if I talked to David . . .?'

'No, Mary, please don't. If he . . .' her voice trembled . . . 'has to be "talked to", then I'd feel humiliated.'

'I understand. But I can't sit by,' Mary said, with the light of battle in her eye, 'and watch you two drift apart.'

Jill was too naive to take warning. She talked unhappily about her day-to-day existence, ending with: 'I think sometimes it would be better to make a clean break, rather than have this long-drawn-out agony.'

Her mother-in-law looked at her in genuine unhappiness. Could such a thing really happen? In her family?

'I've almost decided,' Jill said, about to utter the dreaded word. 'I shall ask him for a divorce.'

Mary was utterly against it. It was against her religious principles: 'Whom God hath joined together . . .' She tried to describe to Jill the ups and downs of her own married life, and then broke off – for her marriage was a poor example.

'Jill, you said you wouldn't go and see this woman.'

'I'm no match for her, Mary.'

'Then I won't try to persuade you. But I do intend to see her myself.'

Now that the danger was plain to Jill, it was too late. 'No, please, Mary . . . I'd really rather you didn't. This is really between David and I—'

'You must remember that my life was wrecked by another woman,' Mary cut in. 'I'm not going to sit by and watch it happen to you!'

When Jill left, she was very uneasy. Fond though she was of David's mother, she very much doubted whether she wanted her as her champion.

Edward, too, was to act as champion – for Bill Riley. During that day it became obvious that the Kent police had the framework of a case against Jim Barker and Riley. Barker's references were soon shown to be fake. But, incredibly: Riley was found to have a police record.

It dated from twenty-five years ago. He'd just come out of the Forces, got drunk, broke into a warehouse with two other men, and stolen cigarettes (then very scarce) valued at thirty-two pounds.

As far as Edward could make out, this seemed to convince the police that he was the kind of man to plan a big-scale theft from employers he had served faithfully for the intervening years. He was a little unjust to them in this estimate, because Jim Barker was so dim he didn't understand what he was saying: he'd admitted being shoe-horned into Hammond's by two men who paid him what seemed a lot of money at the time. And when asked if they had an arrangement with Riley to accept him, replied, 'I didn't even know he was in on it.'

Edward had an interview with Detective-Inspector Parsons. They both came very near losing their tempers.

'Damn it, I've known Bill Riley all my life!' Edward protested.

'Mr. Hammond, if we let him go and it turned out he was involved, you'd be the first to turn round and accuse us of not doing our job!'

'I should like to put up bail for him,' Edward said, taking a grip on himself.

'I'm sorry, I shall have to oppose that, sir.'

'You can make application to the magistrates tomorrow,' his sergeant said helpfully.

Edward gave him a glower. That was at three o'clock in the morning.

He went storming back to London to call an emergency meeting of the directors, after hiring a lawyer for Riley and filling him in on what he felt – *knew* – about Riley. He was angry with everybody – himself most of all.

'This is the latest position,' he said, his voice rasping with fatigue. 'There's no trace of the load. We must regard that as lost. A lorry load of cameras is easy to dispose of.'

'Damn,' muttered Brian.

Edward shot him a glance. 'You're thinking of our insurance. The premiums will shoot up after this, all right. Jennifer has informed the despatchers—'

She nodded. 'I've been on to them twice.'

'And I've spoken to the customer.'

'That must have been uncomfortable!'

'It was, Brian. As you can imagine, they don't intend to use us again.'

'I worked hard to get that client,' David said morosely.

'Then you'll have to find one to replace them.'

'If we get a reputation for losing loads . . .'

'Let's not have any recriminations,' Brian urged. 'What's happening about the drivers?'

'The man Barker has admitted he was a plant. We were taken for a ride, and for that I must take the blame.'

'Oh, come on, Ted,' Brian said in a tone of kindness, 'any one of us could have been fooled.'

Edward's glare more or less told him what he could do with his patronizing forgiveness. 'When it comes to assessing drivers, I'm not supposed to be a fool.'

'I suggest,' said David, giving a slight turn to the knife, 'that we don't take on any staff in future without written references.'

'What about Riley?' asked Brian.

'He was charged, along with Barker, at half past three this morning.'

David had not been in touch. He was staggered. 'Riley?'

'Conspiracy to rob Hammond Transport Services of goods to the value of forty-eight thousand three hundred pounds. He goes to court at midday today and the police will ask for a remand in custody for seven days.'

'Have they got proof?'

'Not in my opinion.'

'Then they won't get a remand.'

'The solicitor thinks otherwise.' Unwillingly, Edward reported what he had learnt about Riley's criminal record.

'But the magistrates won't be told of that.'

However, as they discussed it they began to see that even with legal representation Riley's chances might be poor. Jennifer even queried whether they should brief a barrister: 'After all, it's us who've lost a load.'

'But not through Riley!'

'Can we be absolutely sure of that, Edward?'

The three male members of the board stared at her in horror. She stuck out her chin and went on: 'After all, he does seem to have been incredibly careless. All drivers of high cost loads are instructed never to leave their cabs.'

'But I've been on the road, Jenny, and men do.'

'We ought to give the police some credit for knowing what they're about. They sorted out Barker as a crook, and now he's confessed. *We* didn't suspect him.'

'He held a union card,' Edward said bitterly.

'So does Riley. But you never knew he had a record, did you?'

'Never.'

'He's always been a close one,' Jenny said, shaking her head.

Afterwards Edward sought her out in her office. 'You weren't serious about Riley, surely?'

'I'm trying to keep an open mind.'

'If he wanted to steal from us, he's had hundreds of opportunities over the years.'

'And *we've* had pilferage,' she reminded him. 'The same as any other firm. Most of it never traced.'

'Jenny, are you saying Riley's dishonest?'

She couldn't bring herself to assent to that. 'As I said

before, none of us knows much about Riley,' Her thoughts went back into the past. 'Except perhaps your father. I wonder, Ted . . . if he knew about his police record.'

'He certainly never gave me any hint,' Edward declared.

'He wouldn't, would he? He was a close one, too – kept secrets for life.'

Edward gave her a rueful smile. '*That's* true.'

'He may even have given him the job to help him back on his feet.'

'That would be typical of Dad. I gather Riley got two years' probation – he'd have needed a job.'

'And later on,' Jennifer said, her voice and look softening, 'he kept your father's secret in exchange.'

'About you? *He* knew?'

'One weekend, when your father and I were in the cottage,' Jennifer said, lost in her recollections, 'Riley 'phoned. Something urgent had to be sorted out. I asked Robert if Riley knew about me since he'd been able to ring, but I didn't get a clear answer – it just passed off. Later, after Barbara was born, a big bunch of roses arrived at the hospital. No card, no message. Those deep red moss roses with the lovely scent . . .' Her voice almost tailed off for a moment. 'A couple of years afterwards I went to Riley's house with a message from the depot. His garden was full of those roses. I think he knew, Edward – the only person who ever knew.'

'And never said one word.'

'That's Riley, isn't it? Wild horses wouldn't make him talk.'

'So what chance have the Kent police?' Suddenly Edward looked a different man. 'Jenny, even if he is involved in this business, I'm standing by him. If only because of those roses . . .'

CHAPTER EIGHT

The news about the hi-jack had cooled off some of Hammond's customers. At an informal get-together at coffee time on how to handle this, Brian began handing out orders to David. At first David seemed too pre-occupied to notice, but when it came home to him he flared up.

'You're not in the chair yet, Brian!' he snarled, and marched out, almost colliding with Edward who was joining them a little late.

'What was that about?' Edward inquired of Brian.

'God knows.' Brian put down his cup. 'Excuse me. I must get on.'

'I'm off to hear the court case in a couple of minutes, Brian.'

'Shall I come with you?'

'No need,' Edward replied. To Jennifer, when his brother had gone, he said: 'What was that remark about the chair?'

'Oh, just a brotherly squabble.'

'They seem to do nothing else these days! And David's a bag of nerves. Last night – he was twitching like a marionette.'

'Oh, you noticed, did you? I didn't think it had registered.'

'It did after a bit. Jenny, did I put my foot in it about that girl Julie?'

'Yes. Both feet.'

Edward sighed. 'Bully for me. Well, must be off. Wish me luck, Jennifer.'

'I wish Riley luck,' she said. 'He's the one that needs it.'

But he didn't, as it happened. When Edward walked into the interview room, he found Riley with Detective-Inspector Parsons, who said calmly: 'You can take him back to your depot, Mr. Hammond.'

'On bail?' Edward asked, startled.

'No. I'm withdrawing the charges.' He didn't mention the embarrassing results that his inquiries on Riley had revealed: deputy chairman of the bowling club, past president of his local British Legion branch, on the parents' committee of the local school which Riley's children had attended with the children of the sergeant of the local nick – who knew him well and liked him. It had got sillier and sillier by the minute. *And* they had no evidence against him, not a shred – only guilt by association.

'You can largely thank your boss for this,' he said to Riley. 'It's hard to make a case when the man who's lost the goods speaks up for the suspect.'

'Aye,' Riley said grudgingly. 'Well, it'd take him a while to train another foreman, wouldn't it.'

Riley being restored to them, Edward felt free to go down and get things rolling in Dover. In his absence, David took the chair at the board meeting. The two younger Hammond brothers seemed incapable of discussing anything without crossing swords, Jennifer felt. The depot at Dover now being a *fait accompli*, David did most of his sabre work over the proposed advertising campaign. But he lost on that one too; Jennifer and Brian were in favour and Edward had left a proxy vote also in favour so he was outcounted three to one again.

He was coldly angry, and would have been angrier yet if he could have heard the conversation going on between his wife and his mother. Mary Hammond had turned up on the doorstep at mid-morning and should have counted herself lucky to find her daughter-in-law at home.

'Is it a bad moment?' she queried, with a gesture to the aerosol of furniture polish.

'No, I'm just feeling house-proud. One of my rare days without appointments.'

'And now I've interrupted you.'

'I was just going to stop for a coffee anyway.' She led Mary in, put away her polish and duster, and rinsed her hands.

Mary plunged straight in. 'I saw Miss Lane yesterday.'

'Julie?' Jill paused with the towel in her hand. 'Oh . . .'

'I'm afraid it wasn't a very fruitful meeting.'

'I didn't think it would be.' She filled the kettle noisily and plugged it in. She was telling herself she didn't want to hear this. But of course she did. 'You went to see her?'

'No, I invited her to tea.'

'And she came?' Jill said, utterly astounded.

'She did. But I'm afraid it was in a spirit of defiance. She was quite bare-faced about it all. Aggressive from the moment she arrived.'

Jill could understand that Julie would use attack as the

best method of defence – not that Julie felt she had anything to defend, she was certain. 'She can be very direct,' she murmured.

Mary bridled. 'She placed the whole blame on David, made the wildest accusations against him . . .'

'Oh? What?'

'I've no intention of repeating them to you, Jill.' She could still hear the echo of Julie's frank statements: dates, places . . . The dates were so hurtful, even to Mary: the day before his wedding, Julie claimed. And the day after he came back from his honeymoon. If Jill knew, it would destroy her.

Most frightening of all had been Julie's parting shot. Mary, foolishly angry, had cried: 'What's the matter? Can't you get a man of your own?'

'I happen to want David,' Julie replied.

Mary had once been taken to see a rather scandalous musical in which a lady of doubtful repute had sung: 'Whatever Lola wants – Lola gets!' She was frightened, because she felt the same might be true of Julie.

'I suppose it's possible David was infatuated with her for a while,' she said to Jill.

'Yes.'

'She clearly has some sort of animal attraction for him. But nothing more than that.'

'Perhaps that's all that counts,' Jill said sadly. 'I'm afraid it's something I lack.'

'Jill, David fell in love with you for what you are . . .'

'I doubt that. I was the right choice for a particular section of his life – to be introduced to his business friends and make the right kind of noises—'

'My dear—!'

'And be accepted by you – because that's important.'

'Jill, this is complete nonsense.'

'No, it isn't. He brought me home to you as the nice girl he was going to marry.'

'And is there something wrong with being a nice girl?'

'No, providing you're nasty underneath, or vice versa. Being like Julie has advantages.'

'She's a liar, Jill,' Mary protested.

'No. If she said that David has deceived me, it's true. But what she may not have told you is that he hates himself for it.'

Her mother-in-law was indignant. 'I cannot think why you defend the woman!'

Jill made instant coffee and brought it out to the living-room. They sat down side by side on the settee.

'Julie and I used to be good friends,' Jill said in a musing tone. 'I still find it hard to dislike her, despite all this.' She talked on for a while, recalling the life she'd shared with Julie when they had lived in the same flat. They had had fun. Perhaps it wasn't Julie's fault that she had begun to want David just as David had decided he ought to marry Jill.

Mary put down her cup and caught Jill's hand in both of hers. 'You're putting a very brave face on it.'

'I'm not. I just feel differently from the other day. Now it's out in the open I feel . . . perhaps I can cope with it.'

'Then you're not thinking of divorce any more,' Mary said thankfully.

Jill gave an optimistic smile. 'Well, we'll see how it goes.'

It was difficult for it to 'go' in any fashion except more complicated. Once the Pageant Agency was hired, Julie was legitimately employed around the depot. David couldn't avoid her. But he did try. He wanted a reconciliation with his wife.

On the following Sunday he and Jill lounged in bed with a tea tray and the Sunday papers. It was somehow symptomatic of the new, more relaxed atmosphere that had recently developed.

The Sunday Times slipped away from him. He was too lazy to retrieve it. He switched the supplement out of Jill's hand and said, 'Tell me what you've been doing at the studio this week.'

She was pleased. 'Oh, two piece suits . . . rainwear . . . complete with fake apple blossom.'

'Apple blossom? In July?'

'These shots are for next spring.'

'Ye Gods!'

'What have *you* been doing?'

'Running around. Having a board meeting.'

'But I thought Edward was away?'

'He is. In Dover.'

'So who took the chair?'

'I did.' He made an 'important' face.

'Did you enjoy that, Mr. Chairman?'

'Yes, I did, rather.'

'Getting a taste for power, David?'

'Who, me? I only took the chair because Ted asked me.'

'Then that was very flattering.'

'I suspect the idea came from Jenny. A great peace-maker, Jenny.'

'Blessed are the peace-makers.' She laughed. 'It's ages since you talked to me about work, David! Why does peace have to be made?'

'Are you sitting comfortably?' he inquired. 'Then I'll begin. It all arises from a sort of battle I'm having with Brian . . .'

The recital took them more or less up to lunchtime. Jill really seemed to be paying attention.

'It's strange,' she remarked as she laid the table. 'Brian always seemed to me to be rather reserved and not terribly ambitious.'

'He's changed quite a bit in the last few months.' David drew the cork on a bottle of Bordeaux.

'What's brought on the change?'

'Ann, mainly, I suspect.'

'I thought she wasn't very interested in the firm—?'

'Not when it was the scruffy old lorry depot that Dad left. But now she can see big improvements, she may like to see him in charge.'

'And he goes along with this?'

'Unconsciously, perhaps. She left him once, don't forget. He may feel it's a way of holding her.'

'And is Edward likely to give up the chair?'

David shook his head.

'And what's your rôle in all this?'

'I support Ted.'

They had finished lunch when the phone rang. David had retrieved the Sunday Times, so Jill answered.

'It's Bill Riley, David – from the depot.'

Groaning, David levered himself off the settee. 'Hullo, Bill, what's the problem?'

'It's these advertising people, Mr. David. They want to get into the warehouse for taking pictures.'

'Oh, for heaven's sake!' David said. 'Nobody mentioned on Friday that they wanted to get in there for Sunday. I could have left the keys with you.'

'What's the trouble?' Jill asked.

'Damn publicity people,' he muttered. To Riley he said:

'They'll just have to do without. I'm not coming out for that on a wet Sunday afternoon.'

A new voice spoke in his ear.

'Sorry to drag you away from your Sunday paper, David,' Julie said. 'But this is for your firm's benefit, not mine. I've discovered that we've got no coverage of your warehousing capacity and the press date is Tuesday.'

'Then Monday will do.'

'It won't. Do you want me to come round and collect the keys from you? Would you prefer that?'

He drew a sharp breath. God forbid. 'No. I'll bring them. Fifteen minutes.' He slammed the phone down. 'I've got to nip over to the depot. Shan't be long.'

'Oh, David, what a shame! Couldn't they come and fetch them?'

'I want to be sure I get them back.'

He grabbed up his raincoat and prepared to go.

'Who were you just speaking to?' Jill asked.

He hesitated, but in the improved atmosphere felt he could risk the truth. 'It's Julie and her assistant.'

'Oh, I see,' his wife said.

'She's working on the advertising account now.'

'Really? You forgot to mention that.'

'I was going to—'

'Don't keep her waiting,' Jill said, bending and making a great to-do of getting the Sunday papers together.

'I'll be right back,' said David.

At this point in the afternoon, the other brothers were widely dispersed. Edward was in Dover, enjoying himself hugely. Without fuss, he had invited Jennifer to spend Sunday with him, and he had welcomed her at the station about mid-morning.

They had gone sailing with a new acquaintance, rapidly becoming a friend, who owned a yacht. They had spent a hilarious two hours leaping about at Dyter's command, learning now to handle sail. He had then taken them to lunch at the Yacht Club, and afterwards they'd gone on a tour of Dover Castle. Edward had never expected to enjoy looking round ancient monuments, but it all depended on the company you were with.

Brian was down in Hampshire visiting his son Nigel at his boarding-school. The original idea had been that he and Ann should go together; Pamela Graham's conversation about emotional needs of children had prompted the visit.

But at the last minute Ann had cried off: she had a headache, she said. She'd persuaded Brian to go so that Nigel wouldn't be disappointed.

She went straight to the telephone when he'd gone – not to ring Nicholas, though she would have done so if she could. Nicholas was in Brussels on business.

No, Ann rang Pamela Graham. Her motives were mixed; partly it was a desperate need to confide in someone, and since she had no women friends, Pamela was the next best thing. And partly it was due to something Nicholas said when she told him at dinner the other evening that Brian had once been attracted to Pamela.

'You mean he *could* find comfort?' he asked.

She wanted to know whether the possibility existed. Supposing – just supposing – she allowed her feelings for Nicholas to get the better of her, would Brian have someone to turn to?

So far, nothing had happened between herself and Nicholas, nothing more than holding hands as they walked, a kiss or two, and one embrace. She was trying to find herself a justification to allow it to go further.

Pamela was surprised to be invited to lunch but not perhaps to be reduced to a listening role. Ann chatted brightly about Hammond Transport Services, about the brothers and their personal affairs: David might not have been pleased to hear the confidences she bestowed.

At last she got on to the real topic. 'God knows how I got myself into it,' she murmured in a much more subdued tone. 'I fought it and fought it . . . really tried to keep him at arm's length . . .'

Pamela said: 'The chap . . . who was here with me for dinner that Thursday?'

'Was it that obvious?' Ann said, blushing prettily.

'Noticeable.'

'Do you think that Brian . . .?'

'You should know that better than I,' Pamela said, refusing to be involved.

'I keep getting the idea that he's actually encouraging it. He seems positively to throw us together.'

'How far has it gone, then?' asked Pamela despite herself, stirring her coffee.

'In one sense, nowhere at all. But in one sense I'm already defeated. I can't get him out of my mind . . . I don't sleep, I don't want to eat . . . that's it, isn't it? The dreaded incubation period.' She prowled the livingroom restlessly.

'And what does *he* feel about it?'

'Hard to tell. But he's made all the moves.'

'Culminating in clearing off to Brussels the moment you started falling for him.'

'But that trip was arranged some time back.'

'But he made no effort to cancel it.'

'Not that I know of. Oh, I've no illusions. Women don't come first in his life.'

'And that's what attracts you.'

'It's always the ones you can't hold, isn't it?'

Pamela frowned. 'What you mean is, there's no future in it.'

'I doubt it.'

'Then what can I say, except drop it?'

'Then you think,' Ann said with slow clarity, 'that there's no point in getting involved with a man if you can't imagine it getting anywhere.'

'It depends what you're doing it for.'

'But I'm not *doing* anything. It's happening to me.'

'I don't believe in natural victims, Ann,' Pamela objected. 'Things happen to us because we choose not to resist them.'

Ann stood looking down at her. 'Was that the case with you and Brian?'

Pamela looked taken aback. 'I don't think that's terribly relevant. We stopped before it reached that point . . .'

'The point of no return? And what was that point, Pamela?'

'When it threatened his family.'

'But you agree it's all right up until then.'

'I didn't say that.'

'You agree that an occasional affair stimulates a marriage, though?'

'Not a bit. It's an excuse, that's all.'

'Though we proved it to be valid.'

'We?' repeated Pamela, displeased at being dragged in in this way.

'You and I. When I started to think you and Brian were serious, I came back.'

'Ann, you can rationalize your way out of anything,' Pamela said in despair, and getting up to go.

'But you really have been the most tremendous help, Pamela.'

'I find it difficult to believe.'

'You have, Pamela. Just to be able to talk about it to someone.'

'You wouldn't consider talking it over with Brian?'

'How could I possibly?' Ann asked, astounded.

'It's his marriage that's in danger as well as yours.'

'But what could he say? It would only worry him sick.'

Pamela had had enough – more than enough. Desperate to get away she said, 'If you really care about that, Ann, stop it right now. If Nicholas Fox rings, put down the phone. If he writes, return the letter unopened. Close him out, Ann.'

'Stop living, you mean?'

'Goodbye, Ann,' Pamela said, opening the front door.

'Goodbye, Pamela. I'd have felt awful on my own here if you hadn't come.'

When she was gone, Ann began on the washing up, and went over their talk. She felt she had got the best of the discussion. Which must mean, mustn't it, that she was right?

About this moment David was driving into the Hammond's depot and parking near the warehouse. Julie, in jeans and T-shirt and hung about with cameras, was waiting under the loading-port. Her assistant, Arnold, was carrying the tripod.

'Has Bill Riley gone?' David asked.

'He had to get home.'

David unlocked the big warehouse doors. 'How long are you likely to be?'

'Not long.' She waved Arnold ahead.

'I'll be in my office. Will you lock up and bring the key to me there?'

She waved negligently, intent on studying her surroundings. He left her to it.

He spent half an hour quite productively on draft letters. Julie tapped on his door and tossed him his keys.

'Give my apologies to Jill for dragging you out,' she said.

'She didn't mind.'

'And just in case your mother has briefed a little man in a raincoat, tell her this was strictly business.'

'My mother?' David paused with the keys in his hands.

'What's it got to do with her?'
'You may well ask,' she replied, about to go.
'Julie! I *am* asking.'
'You didn't know she'd been giving me a lecture?'
He was totally at a loss. 'What about?'
'Seducing her youngest son. What else?'
'When was this?' he asked flatly.
'Oh, the other night.'
'I don't believe it.'
She shrugged. 'I was summoned to the presence. Actually it was rather disappointing. She completely ran out of steam.' She went out of the door, pausing beyond it to call back: 'There won't be time to show you proofs of the warehouse pix so you'll have to trust my judgement. See you Wednesday.'
David scarcely remembered making the drive to his mother's house. He rang an impatient fanfare on the bell. His mother might possibly have been having a nap; she looked pink and sleepy.
'How dare you say idiotic things to Julie Lane, Mother!' he exclaimed, pushing past her.
'What are you talking about?'
'You asked her here and talked nonsense.'
'She told you this?'
'Of course she did.'
'I should have expected that. She was bound to.' Mary felt a certain contempt. So she'd gone running to teacher, had she? Couldn't fight her own battles? But Mary had not yet understood her son's anger.
'I was completely humiliated,' he said. 'How could you—'
'I think it is Jill who's been humiliated,' she replied in a dignified, judicial fashion.
'Who asked you? Who asked for your opnion? You do not have the right to interfere in my marriage, Mother.'
'I was trying to save it—'
'Save it? You don't know what you're doing!'
'But I know what *you* are doing, David, and I would have spoken to you about it instead of to Julie Lane, if Jill hadn't begged me not to—'
'So Jill's been running to you to complain? I didn't think she'd—'
'She didn't. I raised the—'
'That, I believe,' he said through gritted teeth.

'But there is no reason in the world why she should *not* discuss her problems with her mother-in-law!' Mary began to feel an anger to match her son's. 'I am extremely fond of Jill, David. You have caused her a great deal of suffering and you should be thoroughly ashamed of—'

'Now don't start lecturing me,' he warned.

'It's high time someone did. In my view Jill has been far too tolerant over the whole sordid business—'

'Who says it's sordid?'

'Oh, for heaven's sake! With a woman like that?'

'You know nothing about her.'

'She's a slut,' she said unwisely.

'Is that your objection? It would have been all right to go to bed with someone you approved of?'

She drew herself up. 'It would be quite reprehensible under any circumstances, David!' Then she heard the shrillness of her own tones and tried to get a grip on the situation. 'Don't let's descend to shouting at each other. That isn't going to help.'

'I just want your assurance,' he said, coming close and staring down at her, 'that in future you are going to keep out of my private life.'

'I'm not prepared to give it,' she answered, facing him without a tremor.

'Then you're going to make things worse.'

'Can things get worse? Jill is already talking about a divorce.'

He hesitated. 'When was this?'

'Just before I saw this woman. That is why I taxed her.'

'Mother,' he almost groaned, 'what did you hope to achieve?'

'Well, had she been a reasonable person—'

'You mean willing to obey. Did you imagine Julie was like that?'

'Well, I . . .' She faltered. She felt on unsafe ground.

'You just wanted to tell her how much you disapproved – correct?'

'I certainly don't see why she should get away without some comment.'

Her son cast his eyes to the ceiling. 'Then it was for *your* benefit. Not mine, not Jill's. Simply to give you the satisfaction of giving a lecture on morals.'

'I never mentioned the word, David.' She heard herself beginning to sound defensive and ended with spirit: 'And if I had, I doubt if she would have heard of it!'

'What words have you stopped hearing, Mother?' David demanded. 'Forbearance? Goodwill? You're very quick to condemn others. You're a churchgoer – have you never heard the passage "Judge not, that ye be not judged"?'

'David,' she gasped. It had literally never occurred to her that she could be wrong.

'I think there are a few words in the Bible about the self-righteous, too. You would know them better than I do. It strikes me as ironic,' David said, 'that you can go to church every Sunday morning and never once take any of the comments as applying to yourself, only to others!'

'That's not . . . that's not so, David. I *do* examine my conscience—'

'But the examination results in a "pass" mark for Mary Hammond. Never mind about anybody else, though.'

She sat down slowly, feeling for a handkerchief. 'I only mean to do the best—'

His snort of derision cut her short. 'Good intentions! Who gives you the right to intend good or bad when other people ought to be consulted first?'

She could think of nothing to say: her mind was whirling. Made to face her own actions, she had to admit that her own good sense should have told her Julie was beyond any words of hers.

'You're right, David,' she confessed brokenly. 'Right in everything you've said. I do interfere . . .' She felt tears welling up. 'I've done it with all my sons. I can't help it, though I know it's wrong.'

Her son relented a little. 'We've got to work out our own lives . . .'

'I know. But it's so hard when you see them going wrong . . .'

'But we're not children, Mother!'

'Perhaps I'm too old to change.'

'Perhaps.' He even smiled a little, then added comfortingly: 'It's not at bad as you think with Jill and me. Over the past few days, we've . . . I don't know, we suddenly seem to be getting on better.'

Perhaps David would not have said so if he could have seen Jill at that moment. She was ringing his office at Hammond Transport, which was where her husband had said he was going. He was not there. Jill hung up, then tried again. But there was still no reply.

'I know Jill is making a tremendous effort,' Mary Hammond went on, very earnest. 'Help her, David . . . please!'

'I am trying,' he responded. 'But I don't want to pretend.' He sighed deeply. 'I do have this sort of . . . hopeless thing about Julie. I can't explain it, because I still love Jill. I know you can't possibly understand that.'

'But I do.' And as he looked surprised, 'Your father had the same weakness. The same covert need for . . . the animal attraction.'

David could hardly think of his father as a man like himself. And yet there had been the seventeen-year-long secret of Jennifer Kingsley.

'When I look at Jill,' Mary said almost to herself, 'I see myself, years, years back. When I look at you now, I see Robert. And when I talked to that woman I saw . . . only Miss Kingsley.'

'Mother—'

'It's frightening how the same pattern repeats itself . . . how the inherited things follow the inevitable course and we all seem powerless to stop them.'

He was sorry for her now, and a little remorseful. She was an old lady, still haunted by the ghosts of the past – one of them the enemy she had not even known about until the will was read. Jennifer Kingsley, the personification of wrong-doing.

Jennifer was at that moment enjoying the innocent pleasures of a walk on a gusty headland at Dover. Edward had one arm around her to help her keep her footing. They were watching the sun gilding the sea with light.

'When I was a child,' she said, 'I used to wonder why the sun didn't go out like a candle when it went down. And the sea used to fascinate me.' She looked up at him. 'I lived by the sea for the first eight years of my life.'

'I never knew that,' Edward said. He smiled. 'So living by the sea, you weren't quite such a stranger to boats as you pretended this morning.'

'No.'

'You just wanted to make me feel protective!'

'Well, why not?' she demanded teasingly.

'You're shivering. Come on. Let's go back.'

'When are you thinking of setting off for town, Edward?'
'When do you want to?'

'I don't really mind. It's been such a wonderful day.' Her eyes of clear, northland grey were soft. 'Thank you, Edward.'

She put her arms round his neck and drew him down to kiss him. His arms held her close. They stood together, for a short and blessed time completely happy.

But in David's office the telephone rang and rang – a cry of distress in a love story much less happy.

CHAPTER NINE

Jennifer's daughter Barbara was not having an easy life. The closing of Johnny's boutique and the disappearance of his partner Vince to foreign parts had left Johnny with debts of nearly six thousand pounds.

Barbara had money held in trust for her from Robert Hammond's will. So she went to see the Hammond solicitor, Mr. Cassells. She telephoned first for an appointment but all the same as she went in at the eighteenth-century door with its odour of leather-bound books and centuries of documents, she felt she had no right.

Mr. Cassells was very kind. When he had heard her request – for the use of some of the money in the Hammond estate – he took a long time explaining the situation, using words like escrow and *mutatis mutandi*. She didn't understand any of it, except the conclusion: she couldn't have the money, it was a legal impossibility until Mary Hammond's death.

Johnny wasn't damped when she told him. 'It's all right, love, I've found a way of raising the money!' He waved a magazine under her nose. 'See? "Personal Loans without Security" – and you can call in any time. Shall I ring for an appointment?'

She took the magazine and read the advertisement. It sounded straightforward enough.

But 'without security' seemed to mean something quite other than Barbara's and Johnny's expectation. Their kindly neighbourhood money-lender made a strict inquiry into their jobs, and when he heard they didn't have any, he looked perturbed and said he would have to have a guarantor.

'What's that?' Johnny inquired.

'Someone who could sign an assurance that you wouldn't fall into difficulties.'

'Oh, we won't get into difficulties,' promised Johnny.

'Of course not. It's purely a formality.' He produced a form, and put crosses where the guarantor had to sign.

Barbara thought about this point when they got home. She dismissed, one after the other: her mother, Johnny's parents, and Edward Hammond. That only seemed to leave one person.

Mary Hammond was really delighted to see her. 'How nice! It's such a long time since you were last here.'

On that occasion, Barbara had brought her husband. Mary had had no idea what to expect, but certainly not the gangling, lovable, teetotal non-smoker. Barbara had warmed to her for her complete acceptance of Johnny. She was sure Mary would help about signing the form for the loan.

'I should have rung first,' she apologized. 'But I'm a dropping-in sort of person.'

'So am I,' Mary agreed. 'In fact, I tried to do just the same to you the other day.'

'At the shop?'

'Yes, but it seemed to have closed down.'

'It has.'

'I'm sorry to hear that,' Mary said with sincerity.

'It turned out it was in the wrong position . . .' That was Johnny's explanation. She wasn't sure it was right. She plunged on. 'Mrs. Hammond, could you do me a favour?'

'Of course, Barbara.'

'It's something I need signing. A guarantor form.'

'Of course. I'd be delighted.' Mary held out her hand for it.

'I think I'd better explain first,' said Barbara. 'You may not want to do it afterwards.'

Mary frowned and looked alarmed.

'You see, it's from a private loan company.' She got it out of her shoulder-bag. 'They said they needed someone of substance.'

'A loan company?' Mary said dubiously.

'I didn't know who else to come to but you. I hope you don't think I'm a nuisance.'

'Of course not, my dear, but do you really think these people . . .?'

'Oh, they were really quite helpful, despite Mr. Cassells' dire warnings. But they did insist on guarantors.'

'Who are liable for the debt in case of default.'

'They didn't say that!' Barbara protested.

'I think, if you read the small print,' Mary said, doing so.

'Oh, I certainly wouldn't want you to have to pay anything! I thought it was just a character reference.'

'And did this loan company quote you interest rates?' asked Mary.

'I made a note of it,' Barbara said, taking out a sheet of paper. 'It's a bit complicated.'

'Barbara,' Mary said, folding the paper back into her hand, 'I know you think Mr. Cassells is a bit of a stuffed shirt, but he was quite right. You musn't have anything to do with these people. Promise me.'

Barbara's young face began to crumple. 'But Johnny's got a court order for one of the bills! If he can't pay he'll go to prison.'

'I doubt that. Magistrates don't enjoy being debt collectors. They always give time to pay.'

'But we owe so much now!'

'You mean Johnny does.'

'No. We share problems. That's the way we want this marriage to be.'

'I quite see that. But I don't think you should share your problems with a loan company charging compound interest.'

'Is compound interest very bad, then, Mrs. Hammond?'

'It certainly isn't good.' Babes in the wood, thought Mary. Poor souls. 'Now if you need to borrow money, why don't you borrow from me?'

'Oh, I couldn't! I couldn't borrow from *you*, Mrs. Hammond.'

'Why not? I've got it, you know. Not immediately to hand, but I could arrange it.'

'But it's such a lot of money—!'

'I didn't think it would be a small amount, Barbara.' Mary smiled encouragement. 'Now I want you to go home and bundle up all your bills and take them round to my bank manager. I use the branch in Lothian Street, the manager is Mr. Ardley.'

'But—'

'He will help me arrange for that amount of money to be paid into my current account, and in a few days I shall be able to write you a cheque.'

'But it's not fair on *you*, Mrs. Hammond.'

'And neither is this—' tapping the loan form – 'fair on you. Barbara, let me do this for you. I'm so very fond of you...'

Barbara hesitated. 'Who would have to know?'

'No one, except my bank manager. Why do you ask?'

'Well . . . because . . . I got married in secret, and people are just waiting to say "I told you so".'

'We needn't tell anyone,' Mary assured her.

There were a few unit trust shares and other items that could be sold quickly. She was confident of getting the child out of her financial scrape in about a week. She hoped it would be quick; the week would drag for Barbara.

For Ann Hammond, too, time was dragging. She didn't sleep well, often coming down at night to smoke and have a drink in the kitchen. Then in the morning she'd be fit for nothing.

Brian was solicitous, but that made things worse, not better. 'Is there anything I can do on the way home – shopping or anything?'

'I'm perfectly all right, Brian. Go to work.'

Pamela Graham dropped in at her request. 'I can't stay very long. You said you wanted to talk to me?'

'You're right to be curt with me. Oh, I know the truth! I've brought all this on myself. There's something missing in me. Brian bores me to tears, and yet he's concerned and kind.'

'Yes.'

'Nicholas Fox isn't kind. He's self-centred and self-seeking, like me. I don't want a kind man. If I see kindness and consideration I want to stamp on it. God knows why Brian puts up with me!'

Pamela found her talk worrying. There was an element of suppressed hysteria in it. So early in the day . . . And there was whisky in her glass already.

'Ann, you don't look at all well.'

'How can I look well when I don't sleep?'

'Have you seen a doctor?' Pamela prompted.

'I did wonder about that. Do you think I should?'

'Well, of *course*, if you can't sleep.'

It made an immediate difference, the idea of having something positive to do. But Ann did not quite get what she needed from Dr. Joan Weston. The doctor could see the stress signs, and since this was a private practice could spend time trying to get at the reasons. Ann didn't confide, because she had a feeling the other woman would sweep her emotions aside as briskly as she wrote the prescription.

'There you are, Mrs. Hammond. Those should help you

sleep but of course they won't remove the cause of your sleeplessness.'

'No,' said Ann.

'If that cause lies within your marriage . . . I could recommend someone.'

'A marriage guidance counsellor?' thought Ann. 'No thank you.'

She had the prescription filled at a High Street chemist, then did some shopping. The weather was very hot; she found it fatiguing. She reached home spent and depressed.

As she got out of her car she heard another draw up behind her, and someone tooted a horn.

'Carry your shopping bag, miss?' called the longed-for voice.

She had to hold on to the open car door to keep her balance. 'Nicholas!'

'You've been buying the shop again!' he teased.

'What are you doing here?'

He took the bag and carried it into the house, where he dropped it. As Ann stepped in, he grabbed her and kissed her. Life flowed back into her.

'I thought you were going to be away three weeks?'

'I had to come back for a meeting. It's only fifty-five minutes by plane, you know.'

'When's the meeting? This afternoon?'

'Tomorrow morning.'

It was like waking up in a new dawn of creation. He could stay all afternoon.

'Shall we stay here?' he asked. 'Or go out somewhere?'

'I don't think *here* would be a very good idea.'

'How would you like to go swimming?' he said surprisingly. 'Come on.'

They got into his car and drove to a house in a country landscape near Leith Hill. 'It's Tony Bromley's place,' he explained. 'I'll just let his wife know we're here. The pool's that way – meet you there.'

She wandered over to it. The heat of the sun was almost stupefying. She found a summerhouse in which to change into her swimsuit, then came out as Nicholas approached from beyond a rose pergola.

'I should have 'phoned,' he said. 'There's nobody in and a note for the milkman – "No Milk Today" – so clearly they're away all day.'

'Oh, then, I'll change again and we'll go.'

'No, it's all right. They've told me I can use the pool whenever I like. I know they won't mind.' And looking at him, she wondered if he had known they were away all day.

They sat down on a wooden bench in the partial shade of the pergola. A silence held them.

'If you were simply a man I fancied,' Ann said, 'it would all be very easy.'

'And isn't it? Easy?'

'No.'

'Why not?'

She smiled. 'My doctor was suggesting this morning that I ought to "seek further help". But I don't need a head-shrinker to reveal me to myself. I know what the solution is.'

' "Stop seeing him".'

'Of course.'

'But you won't.'

She hesitated. It was not in her nature to plead. But it seemed to be dragged out of her. 'I'm married with two children, Nick.'

'Wife and mother – I know. Which you find totally fulfilling.'

She gave a doleful little shake of the head.

'You're something more,' he went on. 'You're Ann, a unique person. You have one life, one chance of experiencing the things you want – no more.'

Ann said carefully: 'As we are now, I could watch you walk away, and bear it – just about. But if anything starts between us I couldn't take it.'

'I understand.' He dropped a kiss on her warm bare shoulder.

'Please let's not start anything unless you mean it, Nick!'

He would have promised her the golden apples of the sun for the sake of the next hour or two. 'Ann darling,' he whispered, 'stop worrying. There's nothing to worry about.'

And because she wanted it to be true, she accepted that.

When she reached home about seven o'clock, Brian had already come in and was talking anxiously to Pamela Graham. Pamela had dropped in, rather unwillingly, to see if Ann was all right. Her radiant arrival set Brian's mind at rest, but made Pamela even more anxious.

'Hullo darling. Hullo Pamela. Have you been waiting long? Sorry I was out.'

'You look much better, I must say,' Brian remarked thankfully, giving her a dutiful kiss.

'I feel much better. Dr. Weston gave me some sleeping pills so I took one and had a lovely snooze, so then afterwards I went round to help Molly Frazer pack – you know, darling, Tom and Molly Frazer – they're moving to St. Ives in the morning. Oh, and Nicholas Fox came round just before I went out.'

'So that's it,' thought Pamela.

'I thought he was in Brussels?' Brian said.

'He just came back for a meeting or something – goes back tomorrow mid-day. He said would you ring him.'

'Will do,' Brian smiled on her. 'It *is* nice to see you back to your old self again.'

Ann laughed. 'Why, darling? Didn't you like the new self?'

Pamela said little. She was inclined to think that this marvellous sparkle might prove to be the final glow of the supernova, the brilliant display before disintegration.

Next morning in the home of Edward Hammond and his mother, the atmosphere was cheerful though busy. Edward had overslept – the first time in years that he could remember doing so. He evaded his mother's attempts to make him eat breakfast, concentrating instead on the papers he needed to take with him to the depot. He paid little attention when the doorbell rang, nor did he listen to the muted conversation that followed in the hall between his mother and the caller.

He was struck, though, when he got outside the living-room door and practically collided with Jennifer's daughter.

'Hullo, Barbara! You're up and about early?'

She seemed flustered. 'Yes, I . . .'

'I have to go to the bank this morning and Barbara very kindly offered to drive me,' Mary explained.

'That's good,' her son said, touched at the girl's kindness. 'Well, I must dash . . .!'

The morning was hectic. At coffee time he at last had a chance to see Jennifer – not that he had anything particular to say to her, it just did him good to see her.

She looked faintly harassed. 'What time are you lunching today, Ted?'

'Is that an invitation?' he teased.

But she didn't smile. 'I've asked Barbara to come in and lunch with me. I've been thinking about her, and Johnny, and the shop . . .'

'They've gone very quiet about that, haven't they?' he commented. He'd spent a couple of hours showing Johnny round the depot some time ago, listening patiently to his waffle about men's boutiques and concessions for pop-star T-shirts, and had come to the painful conclusion that the boy was a great nit, though likeable.

He'd hinted once or twice to Jenny that she ought to keep an eye on him. But Jenny had been unwilling. She didn't want to 'interfere'. The fact that she was now proposing to have Barbara here proved that she had changed her mind. And though Edward had a mother who had brought interfering to a fine art, he felt that Jenny was right.

'I'll have a quiet word with the others,' he promised. 'I'll see you and Barbara get the boardroom to yourselves.'

'She didn't seem to *want* to see me,' Jennifer murmured. 'I've only just managed to get hold of her. I rang her before I left for work, but she was out somewhere.'

'Mm . . .' said Edward on a mouthful of coffee, remembering. 'She turned up at home.'

'Your home?'

'Uh-huh.'

'Why?'

'Don't know. Mother wanted to go to the bank or something.'

The arrival of Brian put an end to the conversation. He nodded acceptance when Jennifer offered to pour his coffee, then held out a letter, newly typed, to Edward.

'You can sign this one now, Edward.'

Edward cast his eye over it. 'You're sure it's all right?'

'I've seen the two who really matter,' Brian said importantly. 'That's to say, the bank, and our main finance house. There's a climate of confidence in Hammond Transport.'

'That's heartening. The bank—'

'They can see our cash flow for themselves. Even the hi-jack didn't slow it down much – now that's impressive to them. Our provisional interim figures helped, of course.' He smiled. 'You can sign with a clear conscience, Edward.'

David was just coming in at the boardroom door as Edward sat and with a flourish put his name at the bottom of the letter.

'David,' Brian said, making something of an occasion by his manner, 'you'll remember that I told you a few weeks ago we'd soon be in a position to release Jill's guarantee.'

'Yes,' said David, annoyed, 'and every time I raise it "soon" becomes "later." When is "later"? Never?'

'No,' said Brian. 'Now.'

He took the signed letter from his elder brother and handed it with a little bit of a bow to David.

'This is formal confirmation that, as from today, we no longer need Jill's guarantee for our loans and overdrafts.'

It was quite a tableau, Jennifer thought. The odd thing was that David, instead of looking delighted, seemed bewildered.

Edward felt it behoved him to take a part. 'But David, you will tell her how much we've appreciated it? We wouldn't be in business now if it hadn't been for Jill, and we all know it.'

'Hear, hear,' murmured Jenny and Brian.

'Thank you, I'll tell her . . .'

Jennifer saw Brian gather himself for another statesmanlike gesture.

'David,' said he, 'there's been a lot of friction between the two of us, and I want you to know that I'm sorry for my part in that. We ought to be working together instead of pulling against each other, and I'm sure from now on, we shall.'

'Thank you, Edward Heath,' thought Jennifer. It struck her that Brian could afford these demonstrations of brotherly love because he'd actually got all he wanted so far. And Edward, the big ox, quite carried away, was grinning with pleasure: it simply wouldn't occur to him that having got through Stage One, Brian was looking for an ally for Stage Two.

Julie Lane walked into the boardroom. 'The lady with the trolley told me you were having coffee in here so I hoped you wouldn't mind if I joined you.'

'Not at all. No cameras today?' Edward said.

'I'm showing a journalist round. I'm hoping he'll write the text for the brochure.'

'Fine,' said Edward, making his escape. 'Anything I can do, let me know. Brian, can I go over the rates assessment in Dover with you?'

'Coming.' Brian followed him, and with a smile and a murmur that she had work to do, Jennifer prepared to go.

'You *will* convey to Jill how very grateful we are,' she added, touching David on the sleeve as she passed.

'Yes.'

David felt Julie's inquiring eyes upon him. 'I'm sure she deserves it,' she mocked, 'but why all the gratitude?'

For answer he handed her the letter. She read it in silence. Then she said, 'You must be very pleased.'

'Yes.'

'All your problems solved.' She handed back the letter. 'Wouldn't you say so?'

'Not entirely,' he muttered.

'Don't you feel a sense of release? A feeling of new-won freedom?' She examined his wooden expression. 'No, perhaps you don't. Perhaps it just means her money will hang over you in a different money-bag.'

He walked out.

Jennifer's lunch with Barbara didn't go well. Barbara seemed uneasy and evasive from the outset, and made non-committal noises when her mother asked after the shop.

'We . . . er . . . yes, we decided to try a new area.'

'Brighton, wasn't it?'

'Oh . . . we decided against that in the end.'

'What did Vince have to say about it?'

'He's sort of dropped out of the picture,' Barbara said, pushing her salad about on her plate.

'But he's Johnny's partner . . .?'

'Not any more.'

'What happened?' Jennifer demanded, alarmed.

'It didn't work out.' Barbara advanced a foot for inspection. 'Do you like my shoes?'

'Very nice,' Jennifer replied without enthusiasm. 'When did you buy those?'

'On my way here. I needed a light-coloured pair to go with this dress . . .'

Jennifer had stopped listening. 'Barbara, did *any* of it work out?'

'What do you mean?' Barbara said, avoiding her mother's eye.

'The shop. All Johnny's plans.'

'Vince wasn't much use, and without him . . . well, Johnny couldn't manage on his own.'

'So you sold the shop as a going concern?' Jennifer insisted.

'We disposed of it, yes.'

Jennifer pushed her plate away. 'Don't lie to me,' she said.

'I'm not—'

'Barbara, I drove round once and the blinds were down. I went round again this morning and there's an estate agent's board outside. I rang the agent – they told me the shop lease was available at an advantageous price because the previous tenants were in financial difficulties.'

Her daughter hung her head. 'I said we'd disposed of everything, Mum. It wasn't Johnny's fault it went wrong. If Vince hadn't conned him—'

'Conned him? How?'

'It doesn't matter.'

'Johnny was left liable for all the debts,' Jennifer guessed aloud. 'Is that it?'

'We made a mistake,' Barbara admitted in distress, 'and we've learned something. Let's leave it at that.'

'How can we leave it? You're in debt, aren't you? No daughter of mine is going to be in debt!'

Barbara sprang up, sending her plate and cutlery shooting across the boardroom table. 'Stop interfering, Mum! It's nothing to do with you. I'm married now!'

'You're still my daughter.'

'Oh, my God, you seem to have been chanting that refrain all my life!'

'Don't speak to me like that,' Jennifer warned.

'And there's *another* refrain,' cried her daughter. 'What do you expect? *I* didn't want to come here. You didn't want to see me for a meal. You want to poke and pry into my private life!'

'Barbara, don't you understand?' begged Jennifer. 'If you've got debts you don't pay, you're liable to be sued—'

'We shan't be. It's been taken care of.'

'You've borrowed money?' Jennifer said in horror. 'Who from? A bank?'

'No.'

Jennifer took a grip on herself, thinking hard. 'You could have tried Mr. Cassells, for a loan against your father's will . . .'

'I did, as a matter of fact, but he put me off.'

'Barbara,' Jennifer said in a harsh voice, 'I want to know who you borrowed from.'

'We made private arrangements, and how it was done is our business, not yours,' Barbara replied with fragile dignity.

'With enough cash in hand to buy expensive shoes?'

'I used my credit card.'

'God in heaven! A credit card isn't a plastic Santa Claus. You still have to pay in a month's time!'

'Which I will, Mum. I'm getting a job.' She was divided between reassurance and resentment. 'Let me lead my own life, will you, please?'

'Barbara, you don't seem to see—'

But David brought Julie in at that moment for a pre-lunch sherry. With a shock Jennifer realized that her private hour with her daughter was at an end. And before she could prevent it Barbara said a hasty goodbye and practically ran out.

Jennifer could put two and two together as well as the next person – perhaps better. Half an hour later she presented herself in Edward's office.

'I'd like to take the rest of the day off. I've cleared my desk. Is that all right?'

She had herself under strict control, but Edward was developing a sixth sense where Jennifer was concerned. He could sense that she was upset.

'What's wrong, Jenny?'

'Nothing. Mr. Anderson's coming at three about the warehouse shelving, and Bill Riley left a message that he wants to see you.'

'I'll deal with it. Is it me, Jenny? Have I done something?'

'No, Edward, it's not you.'

'Only I thought . . . Sunday . . .'

'It was one of the nicest days I ever had in my life.'

'I thought we were close . . .'

'Yes.'

'Then if something's troubling you, it's my worry too.'

'I'm sorry, Edward, this is something I can't tell anyone about, not even you.'

She left, tight-lipped.

Mary Hammond ushered her in impassively. 'Sit down,' she invited, without warmth.

Jennifer took an armchair with her back to the window. Mary, unwarily, took her place on the sofa which looked towards the garden and placed her in the full light of the July afternoon.

'I wish you had telephoned me, Miss Kingsley,' she remarked. 'I'm expecting my daughter-in-law Jill to tea.'

'This won't take long,' Jennifer said.

'Well?'

'You've met Johnny Trent, my daughter's husband.'

'Yes. A very pleasant young man.'

'You know that he's had to close his shop.'

'Boutique, I think he likes to call it,' Mary corrected.

'Since he's gone out of business, it doesn't much matter what it's called.' She paused. 'Did Barbara approach you to lend her money, Mrs. Hammond?'

'No,' said Mary.

'Mrs. Hammond, I want the truth.'

'I never speak anything but the truth. Barbara did not approach me. And now,' said Mary, rising, 'if that's all, I have a great deal to do.'

Jennifer had been watching Mary carefully. She too stood up. 'Perhaps she didn't ask you,' she guessed, 'but you wormed it out of her – didn't you? And then offered to lend her money.'

Mary began to feel hunted. This was a situation she had never envisaged. Her impulse to help Barbara had been perfectly genuine but she saw now that it could not be a single act, without consequences.

'I can't imagine what makes you say all this, Miss Kingsley—'

'Everything points to you, and if I had any doubts, your face has just betrayed you. How much was it?'

'Miss Kingsley,' Mary began in a tone she'd never dreamed she would use to her, 'I don't think you quite understand.'

'Oh yes I do. Right from the start you've set out to use Barbara—'

'That's not true!'

'To use her,' Jennifer swept on, ignoring her, 'as a weapon against me. Barbara's too young and trusting to see what you've been doing, but *I* know, and so do you! I'm sure you think you're very clever, but I think you're contemptible.'

Mary was stricken. She couldn't deny that in the past she had done things which, looked at now, seemed unkind, un-Christian. But helping Barbara had been an act of pity and affection: the girl's youth and innocence had been so appealing, and after all Mary had the money and perhaps not too long to spend it.

But how was she to persuade Barbara's mother of that? She tried, but the only words she found were hopelessly inadequate. 'You're wrong, Miss Kingsley, quite wrong—'

Jennifer had taken a cheque-book and pen from her handbag. 'The amount, please.'

'If you would only listen—'

'I'd rather die than be in your debt!'

'You're not, and nor is Barbara.'

'Will you please tell me what amount I should put here?'

'Miss Kingsley, at least hear what I've got to say,' Mary said, holding out a hand in entreaty. 'Whatever you choose to believe, I've become deeply fond of Barbara. Perhaps in the beginning I did intend to use her . . .' Honesty forced the confession, and she saw Jennifer smile coldly. 'But then I realized something. I loved my husband.'

'I don't think there's any point—'

'Let me finish.' Mary sighed deeply. 'Not only is Barbara his child, she has far more of her father in her than her mother. That pleased me. I'd be lying if I said otherwise. It meant I could love her as part of him.'

Jennifer gazed past her with a face of stone. 'All I want to know is how much I owe you, so I can give you a cheque and leave.'

'Miss Kingsley, let it remain between Barbara and myself. Any help I have been able to provide has been given gladly, and without any thought of my own ends. Please,' said Mary, 'I beg you.'

'If you refuse to say,' Jennifer replied, 'I shall go to Johnny. He'll tell me.'

So it was all useless. Now, when it was much too late, Mary realized that she could have had the friendship of this quiet woman. There was a core of steel in her that Mary could have admired. They might never have become close, but they could have learned to like each other.

Now Mary had humbled herself beyond anything she had

ever imagined. And because of things she had said and done in the past, Jennifer turned deaf ears.

Mary was to blame. She acknowledged it. She must make what amends she could.

'Very well, if you insist.'

'I do,' Jennifer said, laying her cheque-book on a nearby table to write.

'In all, five thousand pounds.'

Jennifer's hand jerked. A vase of dahlias went toppling. Neither woman took any notice.

'Five thousand?'

'And twelve pounds, to be exact.'

Jennifer closed her cheque-book and put it away. 'You're cleverer than I thought, Mrs. Hammond.'

'The amount doesn't matter. It's not important,' Mary protested.

'I understand now,' said Jennifer. 'I underrated you. This is all much more subtle than I imagined.'

'There's nothing subtle about it, Miss Kingsley. The money is nothing. I'm not young. I have a heart condition. I don't know how much time I have left.'

Jennifer gave her a scornful glance. 'You can keep that sort of emotional blackmail for your family.'

'Will you please *listen*!' Mary broke out. 'I have a perfectly adequate income from the trust fund set up under Robert's will. When I die half goes to Barbara anyway. Can't you see, Miss Kingsley? Barbara's under no obligation to me, nor are you.'

'It will take me a little time to raise the money,' Jennifer said as she reached the livingroom door. 'But you shall have it back as soon as possible.'

'I don't want it back.'

'You've excelled yourself this time, Mrs. Hammond. You know that Edward and I have become very fond of each other, and you hate the idea. Well, now you've managed to end that for good. You wanted to destroy any possibility of a relationship between myself and Edward, and now you've succeeded.'

'Edward?' said Mary faintly. 'What has Edward to do with this?'

But Jennifer had nothing more to say. She went out quickly, impelled by an urgent desire to take the next step, so as to be free of this terrible woman's clutches.

Yet what could she do? She couldn't just walk into her bank and say, 'Let me have five thousand pounds, will you?'

She sent for Barbara, who came to her flat looking apprehensive. 'I want you to tell me yourself how much you've borrowed,' she said.

'Mum, I'm married now, I'm independent—'

'Independent? When you go begging to Mary Hammond? How much did you take from her?'

'Five thousand and twelve pounds. But I didn't ask. She offered. She did it out of kindness, Mum.'

'Kindness? Are you really as naive as you sound? Mary Hammond is a scheming—'

'You're wrong, Mum. I know her.'

'How could you go to her?' Jennifer cried. 'With not a word to me about it? What's happened to all your ideals about honesty and openness? First you marry on the sly, a man I'd never even seen, full of big talk but good for nothing but running into debt. Then you go behind my back to the one person in the world who really hates me. Barbara, *I'd* have helped you! Why didn't you come to me?'

'Because of all that about Johnny,' her daughter said, with a bitterness that surprised Jennifer. 'You've just had a field day, Mum, being rotten about him. At least Mrs. Hammond didn't do that.'

'I went prepared to pay her back,' said Jennifer. 'But five thousand . . . I'll have to find it somehow.'

'*You* don't have to pay her back! That's my responsibilty.'

But her mother was already planning ahead to the next move.

In the morning she went straight to Edward's office. He was on the phone, but cut the call short at sight of her face. 'Sit down,' he ordered.

She shook her head. 'Do you remember, Edward, how angry you were when your father's will was read, at not getting control of the firm?'

'That's a long time ago now, Jenny. Why?'

'You can have it now. I'm leaving the company. I'm offering you my holding in Hammond Transport Services.'

CHAPTER TEN

There was a silence in Edward's office, broken only by the ticking of the old-fashioned clock he had inherited from his father.

'Sit down, Jenny,' he said. 'Please.' He produced a packet: 'Cigarette?'

'No thanks.'

'A cup of tea? I'll order some tea.'

Despite her strung nerves, Jennifer was amused. 'Edward, will you please stop treating me like a hospital case?'

She had worked out what she had to say. She intended to keep it very calm and impersonal. Even if Edward lost his temper and shouted at her – which was not unusual when faced with something he couldn't understand – she would keep her cool.

Edward said, 'You're not making much sense, Jenny. Strolling in here first thing in the morning and offering to sell your shares as calm as you please—!'

'It's perfectly good sense. I want it all settled before I move.'

'Move where?' he demanded, almost as jolted by that as the shares offer.

'I'm not sure yet. The West Country probably.'

He sighed audibly, for effect. 'Do you mind if we start again?'

'Not at all. I've decided to leave the company and move away. I'll need to sell my shares, and I'm offering them to you.'

'Why?'

She purposely misunderstood. 'Because you were bitterly hurt when your father didn't bequeath Hammond Transport—'

'That's not what I meant and you know it. Why this sudden urge to leave?'

'It's not all that sudden, actually. I've been feeling—'

'All right. Let's forget how long the fuse has been burning. *Why*?'

Cornered, she began on her prepared excuses. 'I'm tired of perpetually being in the middle of family squabbles. David and the guarantee, Brian and the advertising scheme—'

'*Me* and what, Jenny?'

'The power struggle. If I go that will solve it. You'll have a majority holding.'

Brian walked in with a flimsy torn from a notepad. 'Edward, can you spare— Ah, Jenny, good. I talked to Nicholas Fox on the phone—'

'Who?'

'Nick. He's met a man in Brussels—'

'Brussels?' Edward echoed. His phone rang. He snatched it up. 'Hullo. Yes, David?'

'He's been in touch with this Dutchman, Van der Moewe, who—'

'Lunch?' Edward said into the phone. 'What lunch?'

'If you'll excuse me,' Jenny said.

'Hang on, Jenny.' To Dave on the phone he said, 'Brian can go. I've an appointment.' To Brian: 'It's lunch with Don Lloyd.'

'All right,' Brian nodded.

Edward hung up. Brian borrowed his phone. 'If I can just get hold of Nick so he can tell you . . .'

As he busily dialled, Edward said, 'Shall we talk over lunch, Jenny?'

'I've a busy day—'

'A snack in the pub, then. Twelve-forty-five.'

He thought she wasn't going to turn up. He'd been there over ten minutes when she came into the saloon bar looking, he thought, pale and sad. He made her sit down, brought her a gin and tonic, and ordered a ploughman's lunch for two from the barmaid.

As he took his place again at their quiet table he said, 'How did it go with Barbara?'

'Mm?' she said. She seemed unwilling to speak.

'The shop. Was I right? Are they broke?'

'Nothing that can't be sorted out.'

'So there's nothing to worry about.'

'Not now, no.'

'I always said he was a dreamer.'

'Well, Barbara seems to have taken over.'

Was he wrong, or did he detect a shade of bitterness in that?

'Shall we get down to business?' he inquired.

The barmaid waved to him that the food was ready. He

fetched it, set a plate before Jennifer, and sat down.

'You'll have to do better than those feeble excuses you trotted out this morning. I'm not buying that lot.'

'I don't have to give any reason at all.'

He frowned. 'I'd expect the courtesy of an explanation from someone I didn't like, much less from a woman I . . .'

'What?' asked Jennifer, hating her own weakness.

'I think you know,' Edward said quietly.

'Perhaps that's the reason.'

He sat back in exasperation. 'Jenny, make sense!'

He felt someone bump his arm in passing and was automatically nodding at the apology when he realized the voice was Bill Riley's.

'Hullo, Mr. Hammond, Miss Kingsley.'

'Hullo, Bill,' Jennifer said. 'Let me get you a drink.'

She was detaining him on purpose, Edward saw. He felt a desire to shake her.

He had to suffer politely while Bill was bought a drink and sat down with them. But it turned out there was method in Jenny's madness for after some aimless chat about loads and lorries, she said: 'There must be something we can do about Bill. He tells me he wants to leave.'

Riley tried to catch her eye. Jennifer refused to play. 'Surely there's something we could do? Tell us what, Bill.'

'Perhaps he doesn't want to talk about it,' Edward said. *He* certainly didn't. It was Jenny he wanted to talk to. Riley would come out with what he wanted to say when he was good and ready, because Riley was like that.

'Aye, I'd best be off,' Riley said, tossing off his half. 'I only dropped in for a jar. Lunch-hour's over.'

Edward made no attempt to detain him. When he'd gone he said to Jenny: 'For someone who wants to leave, you're still very concerned about the company's welfare.'

'I'm concerned about Bill too.'

'Never mind Bill. You've just been using him to avoid talking to me.'

'Would it be better if I put my resignation in writing?'

'It would be a damn sight better if you dropped the whole stupid subject!'

'I can't!' she said, then bit her lip. She hadn't meant to say that.

'Why not? And I want the real reason this time, Jenny.'

She hesitated. She knew she was going to hurt him.

'Remember Sunday?' she murmured. 'How good it was?'
'It could be like that all the time,' he said.
'No. That's the point,' she replied. 'It was an interlude. Time out, a few hours set aside from real life.'
'You're wrong, Jenny.'
'I don't think so.'
'If we want to – both of us, Jenny – we could be ...'
'What?'
'Together.'
'Tell me how?' she demanded.
'By deciding.'
'To live together?'
'You know I didn't mean that.'
'I don't.'
'Married,' said Edward curtly. 'Is that the word you want?'
'You know that's impossible.'
'One day—'
'Face the truth, Edward,' she cut in.
'When I look at you, I know what's true for me.'
'Yes,' she said, 'here and now ... last Sunday ... perhaps for a little while ...'
'That's what matters.'
'No. Those are just snatches when you can forget the problems from the past. But your mother never forgets for a moment.'
'She'd have to adjust,' Edward said.
'Could you really hurt her that much?' She shook her head. 'You're too nice. You couldn't live with the guilt you'd feel.'
'We could—'
'What? Escape to our own Shangri La? I can't stand any more days like Sunday, Edward. I don't want just a few hours now and then.'
'Tell me what you do want.'
'I want to get out of this trap while I still can! Get away from you and the whole Hammond family – not because I want to but because I have to!'
He studied her with concentration. 'I don't know whether I believe you or not. If there's no other reason, why haven't you said all this before?'
'Perhaps it's been building up. All I know is that I've reached the point where I want to go. There's no point in

hanging on to my shares and in any case I'll need the money so I'm asking you to buy them. I'll leave it to you to put a value on them.'

'No you won't, because you're not going to sell!'

'Edward, please—'

'You've said nothing new. All this has been the case since Dad died. I think something's upset you that you're not telling me. I don't care what it is – I'm telling you this: I'm not letting you go and that's final!'

There was no more to be said: she knew that tone of voice, that thrusting out of the stubborn jaw. Picking up her handbag, she hurried out.

She would have to go a step further.

Edward took a few short-cuts in his paper work and went home early. His mother came in from the conservatory, a pot plant in one hand and a little watering-can in the other.

'You're home early, dear.'

'It's been one of those days.' He paused, watching her. 'Jennifer Kingsley announced that she wants to leave the company.'

His mother's hand shook so that some of the water jerked from the can on to the floor.

'Oh dear,' she said. 'I'll get a cloth.'

'I'll do it,' Edward said. He went to the kitchen, picked up a cloth at random, and came back to mop up the splashes of water.

'She says she wants to sell her shares to me and go.'

'Why?' inquired Mary, feeling it was the natural question.

'I don't know.' He straightened. 'Do you?'

'Me? Good heavens, Edward. Miss Kingsley is hardly likely to confide in me.'

'But you run a one-woman intelligence service,' he said on a note of rough mockery. 'There's not much you don't get wind of.'

'I'm not sure I like the way you put that, Edward. But on this occasion I can't help you.' She very much wanted to know what had been said. 'Surely she gave you some reason?'

'Yes, and quite plausible on the face of it. Me. And the fact that you stand between us.'

Mary carefully put the plant and the watering-can down on the window-sill. 'I see,' she murmured.

'It could be the true reason, but somehow I'm not satisfied.'

'What other reason could there be?'

'I don't know,' Edward said, staring at her.

His mother moved away so as to avoid his eyes, and began to take off her protective gloves. 'Will you buy her shares?' she asked.

'No.'

'But if she wants to sell? And offers them to you?'

'I've told her she can forget it. And if you want to know why—'

'I can guess why,' she cut in, unwilling to hear him say the words.

He gave a little nod of the head. She had always known. Even before he himself had been aware of it, his mother had guessed his feelings for Jennifer.

'You may as well face up to it, Mother. It isn't going to alter.'

'But don't you see—' Mary began, then checked herself. Better not say that she found the idea abhorrent. 'It's a difficult situation . . .'

'Like father, like son, you mean?' he inquired brutally.

Mary lost colour. 'I don't know why you say things like that to me! Are you setting out to make me ill again?'

He gave her a very level, unsympathetic stare. 'Are you threatening to have another heart attack if I don't fall into line?'

'I don't know why you're attacking me,' she faltered, 'as if *I've* done something.' She put a hand up to her mouth. 'I haven't felt well this last day or two, not at all well.'

Edward took her by the elbow and helped her to a chair. 'All right, Mother, I'm sorry,' he said, although he didn't sound particularly contrite. 'Have you seen the doctor?'

'I'll ring him in the morning.'

'Shall I call him now?'

'No, no, I'll rest, have an early night.' She leaned back, closed her eyes. After a moment she said out of this comforting darkness: 'If Miss Kingsley wants to go, Edward, you can't force her to stay.'

'I could have a damn good try,' she heard him say.

Brian got home with a folder of information that Nicholas Fox had brought when he came over, about Van der Moewe

Haulage. Ann thought she recognized it; Nicholas had had it with him when she saw him.

'What is all that?'

He looked up. Ann had had her bath and was leaning in the doorway in her bath robe, a drink in her hand.

'It's about a possible European partner for us. Nick met the head of the firm in Brussels.'

She nodded and sipped. 'What will you do? Go over and see him?'

'No. He's coming to London anyway. We talked to Nick on the 'phone this morning, fixed a meeting.'

'When?'

'Wednesday. Why?' But it was asked without suspicion.

Because I want to know when Nick may be in England again, she could have replied. Instead she said, 'In case you want me to entertain them.'

'No. He's on a pretty tight schedule.'

Ann put down her drink and stretched. 'I think I'll have an early night.'

'Ann!'

She paused. What . . .?

'Ann, are you still taking sleeping pills?'

'Yes. From the doctor.'

He got up and picked up her empty glass. 'You shouldn't drink, though, should you?'

She felt quite light-hearted with relief. She'd thought he was going to challenge her about Nicholas.

'I've only had one or two, darling.'

'More than that.' He looked worried, as well he might. Ann had seemed to take a turn for the better only a few days ago, when she'd been to see the doctor. Now her malaise-illness-condition – whatever you called it – seemed even worse. 'You know alcohol and sleeping-pills don't mix.'

'No, all right. I won't in future,' she promised as she went upstairs.

Wednesday. And today was Friday. How would she live through until Wednesday?

Their time together was always so brief. Two short hours at Tony Bromley's house, and again next day – scarcely an hour – before he flew back to Brussels.

It would be the same this time. While he was in London his time would be divided chiefly between the Agency and Hammond's. All she would get were the leavings.

But it didn't matter, didn't matter! So long as she could see him, touch him, kiss him ... She would live on that, like a desert traveller on his precious canteen of water, until Nick came again. It was little, yet it was better than nothing. What would she do if she lost him?

In the darkness she put her hand over her mouth. She mustn't think things like that, or she'd begin to cry, and then Brian would ask...

Wednesday came, and with it Van der Moewe, an easy-going, slow-spoken Dutchman who impressed the directors of Hammond Transport very favourably. When they had all shaken hands and Nicholas Fox had escorted the guest away, Edward said cheerfully: 'Well, I think that concludes the meeting.'

'You haven't taken Any Other Business,' Jennifer reminded him.

'Oh.' Edward, who'd been getting to his feet, sat down again. 'Do you have something?'

'As you know,' she said, 'I want to leave the company.' She disregarded the gasps of astonishment from Brian and David, and the angry exclamation from Edward. Edward, she guessed, had thought she'd dropped the idea. 'I offered my shares to you, Mr. Chairman, but you refused to buy them. That being so, I believe I should offer them to the other directors before I try and find an outside buyer.'

Edward pulled himself together. 'I'm not taking an item like that under Any Other Business. The meeting's closed.'

'Then I demand a special meeting.'

Brian found his breath first to ask: 'Are you serious, Jenny?'

She nodded.

'Then we must discuss this, Edward,' David said.

Edward said, 'Not now. Not without notice.' He looked grey with shock.

'All right. When?' Jenny asked.

'I'll let you know.' He made for the door. 'Come on, Jenny, I want to talk to you.'

When the other two were alone they stared at each other in disbelief.

'Could she find an outside buyer?' David asked.

'Of course. Borret's would jump at the chance to buy in.'

'*That* wouldn't be a good idea!'

'No.'

'So,' said David, 'it's up to us.'

Brian got up and paced down the boardroom. 'There *are* some bridges we can cross later, David, but I think we should have that special meeting now.'

'Without Edward present?'

'Edward's ruled himself out.' He paused. 'I don't think we should talk here.'

'Where, then?'

'In the pub?'

'Right. I'll get hold of Jenny and bring her along.'

They hurried out. Nicholas Fox was in the corridor but David didn't need to stop and talk. Brian, however, had his excuse to make.

'Nick, I'm sorry, I'll have to postpone our talk. Something's come up.'

'How long will you be?'

'I don't know. Is it important?'

'It could be, yes.'

'Well, look, you go home and ask Ann to give you a drink. I'll get there as soon as I can. Okay?'

'All right,' Nick said.

Brian hurried away, unaware that Nicholas Fox was surveying his retreating back with ironic amusement.

David was already on his way across the road with Jennifer. Brian joined them, asked what they would like when they got in the bar, and bought the drinks while David escorted Jennifer to a quiet corner.

When they were all settled, Brian took up the role of convener of the meeting.

'You have already discussed this with Edward.'

'Yes.'

'Does he want you to go?'

'He tried to persuade me not to.'

'Would it be any use if we added our voice?'

'I have to leave, Brian. I can't tell you why, but I must.'

'I'm sorry,' Brian said. 'I mean that.'

'Jenny, if you're determined to go,' David said, 'there are things we ought to talk about. But as far as I'm concerned – and I'm sure I speak for Brian too – I'd much rather you stayed with the company.'

'I couldn't agree more,' said Brian.

'Thank you, both of you,' she said, rather touched, 'but for reasons I can't discuss, I have no alternative.'

Brian sipped his brandy and water. David stared down into his whisky. Each was uneasily conscious that her gratitude was somewhat misplaced: they weren't all *that* keen on changing her mind.

'Well . . .' said Brian.

'You'll be missed,' David sighed.

'Yes. Very much. But if you can't be dissuaded, there are one or two points . . .'

'Things we ought to clarify.'

'What?' Jennifer inquired.

'What did Edward say to you after the meeting?'

Jennifer's face clouded. 'He was rather upset. He thought he'd talked me out of it.'

'Did he give you indication that he might want to change his mind now and buy your shares after all?'

'We got rather heated,' she confessed. 'We didn't talk about that.'

'When did you first offer them to him?'

'Last week.'

'Well in that case,' said Brian, 'I think we could say he's had every opportunity.'

'You did give him first offer.'

'Yes,' she assented.

'Would you agree that it would be fair,' Brian said, 'to give others a chance now?'

'Well, obviously. That's one of the reasons why I raised it at the board meeting.'

'Quite rightly,' approved Brian.

'But I'm not quite sure what you're asking, Brian.'

Brian cleared his throat. 'Losing you from the board creates a different situation, which we'd like to resolve as far as possible.'

'That'll be done at the next board meeting.'

'It might be better, Jenny, to sort it out before then,' said David.

'Amongst ourselves. It would save time,' Brian added.

Jennifer looked surprised. 'Shouldn't Edward be in on it?'

'Edward had first bite at the cherry, and refused. He can't expect to be consulted every step of the way after that.'

'He's chairman and managing-director of the company,' she objected. She was beginning to think that this was not so touching after all.

'Yes, of course,' Brian said reassuringly. 'But as I mentioned, a different situation would be created. We shall be forced to re-examine several aspects of our management structure.'

She had listened with a terrible feeling that her mouth was falling open. 'Brian, you're using the most evasive kind of jargon! Can't you say what you mean?'

He smiled tolerantly. 'I can't spell it out definitively, Jenny. It's too early. There are certain fundamental questions we can't answer yet.' He glanced at David as he said this. The fundamental question: who'll get control? 'But the balance of power is bound to shift, one way or another.' Then he added, as an afterthought: 'Edward's done a good job, of course.'

'But the company's changing so fast . . . We need flair and imagination,' said David, 'and let's be honest, those are not Edward's strong points.'

'And his grasp of the financial aspect is shaky. We've seen that, time and time again.'

'We need Edward's expertise, of course, and always will do,' David admitted. 'On the day to day level of road haulage, the nuts and bolts if you like, he's first rate. That's his strength.'

'It may well be,' Brian said, 'that we could exploit his abilities more effectively, if less of his time were taken up with other responsibilities.'

'Like being chairman and managing-director,' Jennifer suggested drily.

Brian was quick to refute the charge. 'I didn't say that, Jenny. But once you've left, we shall be obliged to look at the remaining directors' functions again, that's all.'

'But you both have reservations about the way Edward is doing things.'

Brian said, 'Let me put it this way. Brakes hard on to avoid an accident – fine. But brakes on when one is trying to accelerate – that doesn't make sense.'

'And you see Edward as a brake on progress?'

'Be honest, Jenny,' urged David. 'Don't you?'

She moved her head angrily. 'Who do you see taking over his job? The one with all the flair and imagination and grasp of finance?'

'Jenny, you're over-simplifying. It's not a question who holds what titular job.'

'Then will you please try and explain it to me in terms I shall understand?'

'At present, we're four directors,' he replied, 'all with equal shares. But Ted's casting vote as Chairman in fact means that decisions are usually weighted in his favour.'

'But in future we'll be three,' David added.

'And whoever acquires your shareholding would have the opportunity to alter that weighting, which always works in Edward's favour. That's all.'

'All? That sounds like a good deal. That sounds like the real power to make decisions,' Jennifer said.

'I think we're straying from the point.'

'Yes, David, we are.'

'I don't think so,' said Jennifer.

'First of all, we wanted to persuade you not to leave. You tell us we can't do that, and we regret that. But Brian and I both feel that the shares should remain inside the family.'

'So you needn't look for an outside buyer.'

'I think I've found out,' Jennifer remarked, 'what you both want.'

Brian missed the dryness of tone. 'Good! I thought you'd understand.'

She got up. 'Which branch of the family am I supposed to deal with?'

'That's rather a premature question, Jenny.'

She inclined her head. 'Goodnight, Brian. Goodnight, David.' She went quickly.

'*Is* it a premature question?' David asked.

'As far as Jenny's concerned, yes.'

'We agreed about a great deal, Brian – about the future of the company, about Edward's future role...'

'Quite so.'

'Can we reach agreement about Jenny's shareholding?'

Brian met his bother's inquiring gaze. 'I don't know. Can we?'

'It would be silly to bid the price up.'

'Yes, it would.'

With a smile, David nodded at the barmaid for two more of the same. 'How about this, then. *You* let *me* buy her shares. Then we combine to put you in the chair.'

'The managing-director being who?'

'It would have to be Edward or me.'

'Edward combines both.'

'I don't think you should expect that, Brian.'

'With all deference to brotherly love, I don't think I much like your proposal.'

'Make a counter proposal then.'

The barmaid signalled the drinks were ready. David went to the bar for them, giving Brian time to think. When David returned, Brian spoke thoughtfully.

'I'm quite happy to go on talking, Dave. But I have an idea we may not be able to find a formula acceptable to both of us.'

'You know what that would mean,' David said slowly.

'That may be the only way in the end. Still, let's try and avoid it if we can. Come on, drink up, and I'll buy you another.'

Nicholas Fox had reached Brian's house about an hour earlier. As soon as Ann opened the door to him she put her arms round him.

'I thought you weren't coming!'

'I couldn't get out of sitting in on their wretched board meeting,' he apologized.

'I know. I 'phoned the depot.'

'And asked for me?' he said, alarmed.

'No, of course not. Don't be so apprehensive.' She led him to the settee, pulling him down beside her.

'Sorry, I should have known better. I imagine you've handled this sort of situation before.'

She let go of his hand as though it were a red hot coal.

'Obviously *you* have.'

He showed a faint amusement. 'I've said the wrong thing,' he observed. She didn't contradict him. 'Brian was going off with Jennifer and David. He didn't know how long he'd be.'

'But he's expecting to find you here, because you've something terribly important to discuss with him?'

'How did you guess?'

'No doubt you cheat at cards as well,' she said with bitterness.

He frowned. 'I think my hearing's going. I thought for one moment you had the gall to use the word cheat.'

A long silence followed. It was Ann who capitulated, because it was she who had most to lose.

'Do you think we could postpone our first row until some other time?'

'It might be more sensible. Then we could do it in style.'

She went back to the remark that had hurt her. 'For your information, Nick, I have never "handled this sort of situation before". The odd flirtation, perhaps, but not worth covering up for, because I didn't care a damn. This time I do. That's the difference.'

'I understand,' he soothed. 'It makes one edgy.'

When he used that light, caressing tone, her whole world was turned to gold. She touched his cheek with trembling fingers, and waited for his kiss.

'Glad to see me now?' he asked later.

'I am. I was.'

'It didn't seem overwhelmingly apparent!'

'I'm sorry,' she said, 'but sitting here, just waiting – it's unbearable!'

'I couldn't help being dragged into a meeting,' he protested.

'That's not what I mean.'

'What do you mean?'

She got up, impatient. 'Let me get you a drink.'

'Thank you. Scotch.'

She busied herself with the decanter. 'Where are you staying in Brussels?'

'The Palace.'

'I may 'phone you,' she said.

'I'm out most of the time – conferences and so forth.'

'Should you happen to be in,' she said drily, offering him a glass, 'I presume the switchboard would put me through.'

'They find Fox a perplexing name, odd though that may seem.' Then he relented. 'Mornings would be a good time. I have breakfast in bed and prepare for the day's meetings.'

'When are you going back?'

'I'm not sure. I have to 'phone Brussels later tonight. I'll try to drop by in the morning.'

'And so we go on,' she said with despair.

It was his turn to be impatient. 'Ann, I'm not in Brussels for long. Once I'm back, you're free all day, and a lot of the time I can arrange my work to suit myself.'

'Lunches, afternoons, and if I tell enough lies, the very occasional weekend.'

'That's the way it is,' he said, shrugging.

'Now, yes. But relationships don't stay the same.'

He paused with his glass halfway to his lips. 'You're

moving too fast, Ann.'

'Am I?'

'Even if we were both free, we'd need time to be certain.'

She suddenly flared up, her nerves giving way. 'That sounds very nice and sensible, Nicholas. But isn't it rather late. I *tried* to be wise, tried to avoid you, to have nothing to do with you – because I was afraid. I knew what would happen. But you—! You wouldn't be put off. You wouldn't leave me alone!'

Nicholas nodded. 'All right, that's true. You're the most fascinating woman I've ever met.'

'*That* was the time for you to be wise and sensible,' she cried, unheeding. 'It's too late now.'

But that displeased him. 'You see our relationship as a permanent one, do you?'

'I'm asking if you do.'

'Your marriage? Your children?'

'Those things can be worked out. Other people have done it!'

'Ann, you're rushing things. You'll spoil it before it's even begun.'

'Are you afraid to talk about it honestly?'

'No,' he said in a cold voice, 'and if we're being honest with each other, nobody has used the word "love". I certainly haven't. I'd say that was a pre-requisite for discussing drastic changes, wouldn't you?'

She moved away towards the door. 'You're quite right. You've never said you were in love with me.' She went towards the kitchen. 'I'm going to make some coffee. Would you like some?'

'Yes, please.'

After a moment he followed to watch her. It occurred to him that she kept herself turned away from him.

'Ann, are you crying?'

'No,' she said, her voice stifled.

He hesitated. If he took her in his arms to comfort her, she would take that as meaning a deeper commitment. If he did not, he would feel callous. Why did women have to get so emotional? Where was the gain in it?

He decided on a compromise, crossed, and took her by the shoulders.

'Darling, let's just take it as it comes. We've got a lot to find out about each other. Take it easy, that's all I'm saying.' He tilted her face up to him. 'All right?'

He kissed her gently. Her tears were salt on her lips. She clung to him. But in a moment she stiffened as a car came in at the drive.

'God, that's Brian! Make some excuse. I can't see him like this.'

She fled upstairs. Nicholas stood unmoving in the kitchen then took over the abandoned coffee making. He was looking for sugar when Brian came in.

'Hullo, Brian,' he said.

'Sorry to have been so long, Nick.'

'Quite all right. Ann's upstairs. Coffee?'

'Please. I'm exhausted. What a day!' Brian put his brief-case down on the nearest ledge so as to accept the coffee cup.

'But the future looks good,' he said. 'I've reason to be pleased.'

Nicholas put sugar in his coffee and stirred it.

CHAPTER ELEVEN

Jennifer had a sleepless night as a result of her talk with Brian and David. Their words kept echoing and re-echoing in her brain.

'Flair and imagination . . .. are not Edward's strong points.' 'We shall be obliged to look at the director's functions again . . .' 'On the nuts and bolts level . . . Edward's first rate.'

She had said: 'You see Edward as a brake on progress?'

And David had replied without hesitation: 'Be honest, Jenny. Don't you?'

She hadn't responded directly. If she had, her answer would have surprised him. Because she thought – she *knew* – that Edward was doing a good job.

All right, so he couldn't do tax figures in his head. He didn't have David's *élan*. He could fumble a pass, fall short of the touch line.

But Ted knew what the game was about. That was the difference.

What he wanted was to run a successful, efficient transport service. He not only did that, he enjoyed the work, took a pride in it. He wanted to build up the company – and when you examined his record on that, what was wrong with it?

He had considered the Dover depot on its merits and made a good and wise decision. He had investigated the claims of the advertising agency and given them a trial contract. He had doggedly refused to think Riley could be guilty of taking part in the hi-jack and had been proved right.

If you looked at the other two, they didn't have anything so very marvellous to show. David had mulishly obstructed everything over the past six months, simply out of a personal tantrum about his wife's money. Looking further back, it was David who had brought them Carter Express, which had nearly sent them bankrupt.

And in that débacle, where had Brian's 'grasp of financial aspects' shown up? What had he done that was so wonderful? Recently, he'd arranged for the release of Jill's guarantee, which argued that the bank had a good opinion of Hammond's financial status – but that was due to the fact that the *company* was doing well.

Why was the company doing well? Because Edward kept the lorries on the roads, nursed along new drivers, was clued up about routes and docks and loadings. Customers could rely on Hammond Transport Services – because Hammond Transport Services was Edward. Try running the lorries on Brian's bank statements or David's new-business lunches, and see how far they got!

But . . . that wasn't the real reason she continually grew hot with anger when she recalled their words. How dare they patronize him! How *dare* they! He was worth the two of them put together – ten times over, at that.

She summoned up the picture of Ted's face when at the board meeting she'd offered her shares to the others. He hadn't cared about the shares. Their importance at that moment was nil, to him. It was the realization that she really intended to go that had made him look, for a moment, like a man stricken with a deathly illness.

Jennifer walked restlessly round her livingroom, wrapping her dressing-gown closer. Though it was July, temperatures are low at three in the morning. But it wasn't the night air that made her cold.

'It's useless,' she said. 'Don't you see it's useless?' She was speaking in her mind to Edward. 'If she hates me so much that she would buy Barbara from me with five thousand pounds . . .'

However she looked at it, she could see no alternative but to pay off the debt. But there might be an alternative way of raising the money. First thing tomorrow, she'd see her bank manager.

Mr. Stevenson was a stranger to her, a replacement for her friend Mr. Ardley who had been promoted. It made things awkward, because Stevenson was not *au fait* with her account. However, at six that morning Jennifer had typed out an assessment of her assets, which he studied quickly.

Unfortunately he didn't seem to find it encouraging.

'Your flat is on lease, Miss Kingsley?'

'Yes.'

'And the lease expires at the end of the year. H'm . . . You have no property of your own?'

'No, I haven't.'

'Would you prefer a short term loan or an overdraft?'

'An overdraft would be cheaper . . .'

'Yes.' He cast his eye once more over her figures. 'Well, as always, it's a question of collateral. You're offering what against this overdraft?'

'My twenty-five per cent share in Hammond Transport Services.'

'I see.' He spoke into his desk intercom. 'Miss Mills, fetch me the Hammond current account please.' To Jennifer he said: 'I only took over this branch two weeks ago so I still have some catching up to do. My recollection is that Hammond Transport is a private company with four equal shareholders.'

'That's correct.'

'Have you thought of selling your holding?'

'Yes,' Jennifer said, trying not to sound grim. 'Two of my fellow-directors have already approached me.'

Miss Mills came in with the folder containing the Hammond trading account statements, a bulky package. She placed it before the manager, who at once began to leaf through it.

'Oh, I remember. Mr. Ardley briefed me on this one. There have been problems over the past two years—'

'The position is much healthier now.'

Stevenson did not contradict her, but he looked grave. 'There certainly has been quite a lot of credit extended, Miss Kingsley. My predecessor must have had a great deal of confidence in the company.'

'It was backed by a guarantee from Mrs. David Hammond.'

'Which has now been withdrawn,' Mr. Stevenson said, tapping the papers with his forefinger. 'That poses something of a problem, I'm afraid.'

'In what way?' she asked, with a sinking heart. She knew that tone from bank managers.

'It's a curious position. Hammond Transport Service's debts were underwritten by Mrs. David Hammond's guarantee. My predecessor allowed credit facilities beyond anything that was normal. Now that the guarantee is withdrawn, you are asking the bank to extend further credit against the collateral of a company whose credit is already extended to to the limit.'

'You mean . . . if I'd come here with Jill Hammond's

guarantee still in existence, I'd have got my overdraft?'

'I think very probably so.'

'But my shares!' Jennifer exclaimed. 'They're worth far more than the five thousand I'm asking to borrow!'

'Only if you realize them, Miss Kingsley.'

'But if I realize them I don't need your money!'

He made a pacifying gesture with his hands. 'Substantially your shares are worth only what your co-directors are willing to pay for them. Since we don't know what that sum might be, it is hard to assess it in terms of collateral security. Do you see what I mean?'

'I think we're going round in circles, Mr. Stevenson!' Jennifer said, getting up.

At the office that morning Brian and David had taken advantage of her late arrival for a further conference.

'I'd still like to know why she wants to sell,' Brian mused.

'Or why Edward's refusing to buy. Do they know something that we don't?'

'I don't think it's a commercial reason,' Brian said reassuringly. 'It's on a different level, something to do with personal confidence, perhaps. I think in the back of his mind Edward knows the company is getting too complex for him. Jennifer may feel that too, for all I know – but certainly Edward always did know his limitations.'

'Poor big brother,' said David.

'I didn't mean that disparagingly. It's a great asset to know your limitations.'

'It's no asset to admit them,' David remarked in a thoughtful tone. 'There are too many hungry people about.'

Brian met his gaze. 'If we're dealing, David, let's cut out the personalities and just deal.'

'All right,' said his brother, 'what are your stakes?'

'We'll come to that when we know how much we're talking about.'

'How much would you say Jenny's shares are worth?'

'You're asking me to assess how much this company's worth – not now, *potentially*—'

'And divide by four.'

'If you were selling,' Brian said, 'how much would you ask?'

'If you were buying,' David countered, 'how much would you pay?'

'People buy according to their resources and sell according to their need.'

'Exactly.'

'Then we ought,' said Brian, 'to try and find out Jenny's need. And how desperate it is.'

'We can probably make her a price that she'll be happy with, whatever her reason is for selling. But you haven't said anything about my proposal last night that I should buy the shares.'

'Obviously it's understood that I buy half the shares back from you.'

'Excuse my being blunt, Brian, but will you be able to do that? In cold cash?'

Brian compressed his lips. 'You'll just have to wait and see. If I can't . . .' he hesitated . . . 'you'll end up with the lot. Assuming *you* have the cold cash in the first place.'

'I can pay her price, whatever it is,' said David, his voice firm.

'Personally?'

'That's my business.'

'Since we're being blunt, David,' Brian said with irony. 'If you buy, you buy with Jill's money.'

'That doesn't have to concern you.'

'Perhaps not directly. But I think I'm entitled to know if Jill would expect a directorship out of it, since that would affect the board's balance.'

With a great effort, David controlled his expression. He was staggered by his elder brother's words. The idea hadn't occurred to him. An intoxicating prospect opened before him – himself, at a board meeting, wielding not only his own votes but Jill's as well.

'I haven't asked her yet whether she'd like a directorship,' he lied.

'Then we ought to defer our discussion until you know that.' Brian got up and headed for the door of David's office. 'I've got work to get on with.'

'Brian . . . What about coming over this evening? Then we can talk it over with Jill present.'

Brian didn't let his relief show. It would be better to be in personal contact with Jill. Trying to deal through David was tricky. 'That's a good idea. You wouldn't mind if I bring Ann?' Ann could help him handle Jill.

'Certainly,' David said. It would be a good chance to demonstrate how Jill ate out of his hand.

Brian didn't go to his desk, except to check that there were no urgent phone calls. Jenny had come in and left a note that the insurers for the hi-jacked load would be sending an investigator next week – would that suit him? There was nothing there to detain him. He hurried out.

Mr. Stevenson saw no reason to be particularly wary when the finance director of Hammond Transport Services was shown in. He came to greet him.

'Take a seat, Mr. Hammond. By a coincidence, I was looking at your company's account earlier today.'

'In what connection?' Brian said sharply.

'Oh, just familiarizing myself.'

'I'm not actually here on company business,' said Brian.

Stevenson walked round his desk, sat down, and looked questioningly at his visitor.

'I may need to ask for overdraft facilities on my personal account.'

'Oh yes?' the manager said. His antennae began a direction-finding operation.

'What's the bank policy on overdrafts at present?'

'Money's expensive at the moment, as you know.' He allowed himself a small smile. 'It would depend on your collateral.'

'I have, as you know, a twenty-five per cent share of Hammond Transport Services.'

Mr. Stevenson experienced a certain sense of *déjà vu*, which remained with him through the ensuing conversation about collateral security and the prospective value of Hammond's shares. Brian Hammond got the point quickly: since Jill Hammond had withdrawn her guarantee, Hammond Transport Services were by no means so creditworthy.

David meanwhile was clinching a deal with Jenny. 'You want the money at once?'

'Within the next few days.'

'It might involve selling of some investments, which could take a little time—'

'David, I don't want to do it this way at all,' she interrupted. 'If I have to, then the only advantage to me is if I have the money straight away.'

She was a tougher bargainer than he'd altogether given her credit for. He directed a pensive gaze at her office ceiling. What did she need the money for? How much of it did she need for whatever it was?

'How about a part payment? The rest next month?'

'What do you call a part payment?'

'Give me a figure.'

'As an immediate down payment – five thousand.'

'Got you,' he thought. He was very pleased with himself. David Hammond, our chief negotiator.

'Give me till tomorrow.'

'All right. The down payment tomorrow in cash, David. The balance in a month.'

'That's a deal.'

Brian went home, considering the pros and cons of his situation. It was quite clear from the way the bank manager had hedged that Jenny, who also kept her account at that branch, had been in to see him. Whether that was good or bad he wasn't quite sure.

He described the interview to Ann. 'It was a lovely situation. The poor man now has to decide whether to lend Jenny the money to keep the shares or lend me the money to buy them. Don't you think that's funny?'

'What?' his wife said. She began collecting dirty glasses from the drinks tray.

'The manager's dilemma. It's seldom you see so much uncertainty on a bank manager's face.'

'You should have told me you were going to the bank,' Ann said as she passed him. 'You could have cashed a cheque for me.'

He looked round at her. She looked oddly vague and dishevelled. 'Ann, have you grasped anything I've been talking about?'

'Work, as usual.'

He got up and followed, watching as she began to rinse the glasses. 'I may have the chance to become managing-director of Hammond's.'

'Oh? She paused. 'Would that increase your salary?'

He was a little hurt. 'Ann, would you stop fiddling with those glasses? I should have thought you'd be delighted. Only a short time ago you were pushing me to head the company. Well, things are panning out. Which is why I'm home at this hour of the day.'

'I did think you were early,' she said, with a glance at the kitchen clock.

'Aren't you interested in the news?'

'Of course,' she replied, making an effort. 'Congratulations. When do you start?'

He gave a little laugh. 'It isn't *quite* as straightforward as that. David has his eye on it and at the moment he's in a stronger position. We're going to hammer it out this evening at his place.'

David too was at home, explaining the problem to his wife.

'Jennifer? In debt?' Jill said. 'You know her far better than I do but she doesn't seem the kind to suddenly run into a heavy debt.'

'But she clearly has, Jill, so I'd like to seize the chance. That is, if you'll help.'

'Of course I will.'

'I know it's a bit of a cheek on my part,' he said, deeply touched by her immediate support. 'No sooner do we release your guarantee than I come begging—'

'You're not begging!'

'All right, then – asking you to invest in me . . .'

'I'll do that gladly, David, if I think it's the right thing to do.'

'You could have the shares in your own name . . . The other alternative is to make a loan to me.'

'You'd really prefer that,' she guessed.

'It would be simpler. But I don't think I have any right to ask that.'

'Why not?'

He looked at her, looked away, frowned, and shrugged. 'I haven't exactly been the perfect husband so far, have I?'

'And would you be,' she asked with a wry smile, 'if I lent you the money?'

'I wouldn't want to enter into that sort of bargain.'

'Then why mention it?' For Jill, the question was sharply voiced.

'I just meant . . . well . . .'

'You think I'd try and buy your good behaviour?'

He was a bit at a loss. This wasn't like the Jill he knew. 'No . . . I mean . . . it didn't work that way before . . .'

She held up a warning hand. 'Careful, David.'

'I just want us to understand . . .' He was floundering now.

Jill said calmly: 'Let's talk sense. At the moment my money is invested in all sort of enterprises which mean nothing to me. I know nothing of them and care less. At least I know you – and care what happens to you.'

He was totally disarmed. All the resentments that her money had caused now seemed cheap and shabby.

'Do you really still have faith in me?'

She smiled. 'So long as I think you're doing the right thing.'

When the day's work was over at the depot, Jennifer thankfully put the cover on her typewriter and picked up her bag. Outside a light rain was falling. She picked up a magazine to act as head-covering while she ran for her car.

She'd just reached it when a window in the office block opened.

'Hi!' It was Edward. 'Are you off?'

'Yes, why?'

'You didn't say goodnight, that was all.'

She busied herself unlocking the car.

'Do you have to rush home?'

'It's after six. We're the last here.'

'I just meant, could we talk?'

'Ted, I'm getting wet!'

'See you in "The Weary Traveller" in five minutes.' He banged the window shut.

'No you will *not*,' she said to herself crossly. All the same, she re-locked her car and scampered down the road in the rain to the pub. She bought a dry sherry for herself and a pint for Edward. She was just sitting down when he came in.

'Your treat, eh?'

'Neatly managed.'

He took a big swallow. She nerved herself for a new attack. He amazed her by saying: 'About Riley.'

'What about him?'

'I've found out what's wrong with him. At least, my mother has.'

She flinched. 'Really?'

'We got him to drop in this morning on his way to work. Seems his missus has been giving him a hard time.'

'What about?'

'Oh, you know . . . Kids grown up and out all the time, the walls are closing in on her . . .'

'But why should that make him want to leave?'

'New town. There's flats and jobs in the new towns.'

'You mean . . . it's all just because she wants somewhere else to live?'

'That's right. A new house. I suggested the firm could help with a mortgage. You'd have no objection to that?'

'Of course not.'

'I was going to talk to Brian and David about it—' he paused to drink – 'but they've shot off early. So I'm taking their agreement for granted.'

'I wouldn't take Brian's for granted,' she warned.

'Hard luck. I decide on staff welfare, not him. If he wants to make an issue of it, you and I can outvote him on the board.'

She made a sound of exasperation. 'Edward, I shan't be sitting on the board much longer.'

'You're not going to start that nonsense again! I scotched that at last night's board meeting.'

'You didn't,' she insisted. 'You just refused to accept it as an item of business. But you don't imagine that prevents anyone making an offer?'

Edward slowly put down his tankard. 'Has anyone?' he asked. There was disbelief in the question, as if he couldn't conceive that his brothers would have done it.

'Yes.'

'Who?'

'David.'

He stared at her. 'You haven't accepted?'

'Why shouldn't I?'

'Jenny! It means he'd own half the company!'

'That was always on the cards.'

There was a silence while the idea sank in with him. 'Does Brian know?' he queried.

'They approached me together.'

She felt almost sick as she saw him take in all the implications: the backstairs dealings, the ganging together, the opportunism.

'You realize what this means?' he said. 'They could vote me out of the chair!'

'Has that only just occurred to you?'

'Even out of the company in the long run.'

'I did give you first option, Edward,' she said defensively. 'You refused.'

'Damn right I refused! I don't want your shares – I want *you*, Jenny.'

'We've been through all that,' she said, avoiding his eyes. 'I explained—'

'You explained that you liked being with me and therefore you were about to scarper. Jenny, for the last time,' he pleaded, 'will you please tell me what's behind it all?'

It touched her deeply that even now, when he knew the danger she had put him in, his one thought was to hold on to her.

'There's no mystery,' she said. 'I've just had enough. I feel it's time to go.'

He caught her hands. 'Jenny, they're going to cut me up! Those two are going to parcel out the company Dad and I built together! You can't just walk away and let them do that.'

'You have an alternative.'

'Buy you out and get rid of you!' His voice rose in desperation.

'It's either you or them!' Jenny cried.

'There's a third alternative,' he declared. 'Tell me what the hell you're doing this for!'

Jenny became aware that all the other occupants of the bar had stopped drinking and were regarding them with interest.

'Please, Edward . . . you're making a scene!' she hissed.

'I'll wreck the place if I feel like it,' he roared, 'but you'll tell me.'

Jenny went scarlet as all eyes focused on her for her reply. The barman stopped polishing glasses and got ready to interfere in case Edward carried out his threat.

'Come on outside,' she whispered.

'Only if—'

'All right, all right! Be it on your own head! Come on.'

And that was how Edward at last found out why she was selling her shares.

Brian and David were also discussing Jennifer's shares. Brian had arrived with Ann somewhat later than he had intended because of a curious unwillingness on Ann's part to leave the house: just as he was ready to go, there was Ann, her hair wrapped in a towel, asking if he would mend her dryer for her. It almost seemed as if she wanted to stay at home. It was only when – unusually for him – Brian lost his temper that she made an effort and got ready.

Still, she looked marvellous now, her hair full of glints and her pretty pale dress setting off her summer tan. Jill, too, was a credit to the Hammond family in a long caftan in a multitude of colours. She welcomed them with genuine warmth; it was ages since she'd seen Ann.

'I've been meaning to invite you to dinner,' Ann confessed, 'but Brian's so seldom home in time.'

'What was that?' Brian asked, half-hearing.

'Ann thinks you're working too hard,' said Jill.

'Is *that* what he tells you?' David rejoined.

'David gives the same excuse,' Jill said to Ann. 'I suspect they really spend the evenings at the nearest pub!'

David dispensed drinks. He was a little surprised when Ann asked for vodka. She always used to avoid spirits, because of some theory that they were bad for the complexion.

'How are the children?' Jill queried.

'Oh . . . flourishing.'

'At least, we hope so,' Brian said. 'We haven't been to see them for weeks.'

Jill was troubled at that thought, but remarked that it must be peaceful at home without them.

'Yes. Very peaceful,' said Ann.

'Well . . .' David looked round to see everyone had a drink, then raised his glass. 'Absent friends.' He was thinking of Edward.

Ann Hammond was thinking of Nick.

CHAPTER TWELVE

The conversation soon became less social. The two men were itching to get to the important things.

David had offered originally to buy Jennifer's shares and then move Brian into the chair. But Brian found that this no longer suited his brother David.

'After all, I shall have the majority holding,' David pointed out.

'That's perfectly true, but that's such a new development that it hardly seems right . . .'

David couldn't gainsay this. The sudden acquisition of a half share of the company couldn't quite make up for a mere two year's business experience. But he wanted the chair.

'How about joint chairmanship?' Brian suggested.

'What, both trying to call a meeting to order at once?'

'Taking alternate meetings, or even alternate years.'

'Possible,' David said reluctantly. He went to the side-board for the decanter.

'Can we now deal with the question of managing-director?' Brian said as he held his glass for replenishment.

He thought Jill gave him a surprised glance, but when he looked up she was busy being a hostess, replenishing the bowls of crisps and nuts.

'You're not suggesting the managing-director's job can be done jointly!' David protested.

'It would seem rather silly, I agree. A firm of our size hardly needs two managing directors.'

'Quite.'

'So what's your suggestion?'

'Let's go back a bit. You as chairman, me as managing-director. That was my original proposal.'

'What you actually said was either yourself or Edward.'

'I think we can rule Edward out now,' David said.

Jill put down a pottery bowl with a sudden thump. 'Could I ask why, if it's not a rude question?'

'Because he'd have the minority share-holding.'

'Does that matter?'

Brian said smoothly: 'There are other reasons, Jill. We

need quite a substantial re-organization of the company, and Ted is not really the man to do it. Even if he were willing to.' He cast a glance at Ann, willing her to distract Jill's attention and let them get on.

But Ann seemed to be miles away.

'Then can we agree I take it?' David asked.

'As *well* as joint chairman?'

Ann came to. 'I thought you told me you'd be chairman, Brian.'

Oh, hell. 'I said we'd discuss it,' Brian said.

'I'm afraid I couldn't go along with that idea,' David said, secretly amused that Brian should have got such inept assistance from his clever wife.

But Ann had gathered her wits. Brian's face had told her she'd made a giant blunder.

'As a mere woman,' she said lightly, 'I don't pretend to understand these things, David, but can you tell me why Brian, as the elder brother, shouldn't have the senior post?'

'It's not a question of age.' Damn it, thought David, is it my fault I was born last?

'Then what does decide it?'

'To put it crudely, Ann – money.'

Ann directed a level glance at Jill. 'Oh, I see,' she said. Jill turned away, embarrassed. Brian, not greatly pleased at this intervention, decided on a diversion. 'I think we can safely say that Ted is going to be pretty sore about this.'

'One can hardly blame him,' said Jill.

'Sore enough,' Brian pursued, 'to want to form an alliance. His most fruitful alliance would be with me. In which case, David, you could be outvoted every time.'

He was rewarded by an approving nod from Ann.

'But exactly the same would apply if you took the managing-director's job. He'd form an alliance with me,' said David.

A pause.

'It's a stalemate,' Jill said.

Brian rubbed his chin reflectively. 'Unless,' he suggested, 'Edward becomes so outraged that he quits the company altogether.'

'I think that would be quite appalling,' Jill cried.

Ann raised her eyebrows. 'Why?'

'Why? You're all really talking about out-manoeuvring him, aren't you!'

'Brian said he might decide to go,' said Ann. 'One can hardly stop him.'

'But he's being humiliated and left with no alternative!'

Ann shrugged. 'That's business, Jill.'

'If that's business, it's immoral.'

'What's morality got to do with it?'

'Everything as far as I'm concerned, Ann!'

Ann threw up her hands at such naiveté. 'Good heavens above!'

Jill turned away, sickened. All at once she didn't like Ann. It was no wonder they had not seen each other for weeks before tonight. They had nothing in common.

'Let's examine the board structure again,' Brian suggested.

'What's the point?' his wife asked. 'It's either you in charge or David. That's all you have to settle.'

'Why don't you toss for it?' Jill demanded.

But no one paid any heed.

'It really comes down to votes,' Brian went on. 'The only reason the chairman had a casting vote as well as his own was because there were four of us. When Jenny goes, it's an odd number.'

'So Ted can stay on as chairman—'

'But with no power any more.'

'Then as Ann says, it's a straight fight for managing-director.'

The two brothers eyed each other, like circling dogs.

'We could abolish the post altogether,' Brian said. He had noticed that it was he who produced the original thinking; his brother tended to conserve most of his energy for saying yes or no to what he suggested. 'After all, what we're really talking about is a general manager to look after the depot. We could appoint someone from outside, someone young and keen but with no voting rights.'

'Then Edward really would blow his top.'

'So what?' Brian said. 'With only one vote, what could he do?'

'I'm starving,' Jill said rather loudly.

Ann nodded. The discussion had gone on so long that it was beginning to bore her. 'So am I,' she said.

'At least we can agree on something! Can I rustle up some food for you conspirators?'

'No, let's eat out,' David said.

'Fine,' Brian agreed. 'Let me take you all to The Trellis.'

'No, no, this is on me.'

'Oh, for God's sake,' cried Jill with a break in her voice, 'don't start arguing over that!'

In a similar mood of despairing anger, Edward went home from his conversation with Jennifer. When he entered the livingroom it was empty. He went back into the hall.

'Mother! Mother!' he shouted.

Mary came out of the kitchen. 'I'm not deaf, dear,' she reproved. 'Would you like steak?'

'What?'

'At last the butcher has sent some Scotch beef—'

'The only Scotch I need comes from a bottle,' he said grimly, 'and you'd better join me.'

Mary followed him into the livingroom, sensing that something was wrong but without sense enough to hold her tongue.

'I do wish you wouldn't drink on an empty stomach, Edward!' she scolded.

Ignoring her, he tossed off two fingers of Haig. Then, banging down the glass, he turned to her.

'Let's get this over quickly and cleanly. You lent Barbara Kingsley five thousand pounds—'

'Oh, not that again!'

'—without mentioning it to me but above all without consulting her mother!'

'It's nothing to do with either you or Miss Kingsley,' Mary said with dignity.

'I'm not going to repeat the things you may have heard already from Jennifer—'

'That, at least, is a blessing.'

'I just want to tell you, Mother—' he came close, glaring at her – 'that as a result of what you've done my brothers, your dear sons, are at this moment planning to squeeze me out of the company.'

Whatever Mary Hammond had expected to hear, it was not that. For a moment she thought Edward had had too much to drink, and darted a glance at the whisky bottle. But he didn't sound drunk: he sounded savagely angry.

'What on earth are you talking about?' she faltered.

'David and Brian are buying out Jennifer so that she can afford to pay you back. And do you know what happens then? They control the company and I become the office boy!'

'That's far too involved for me to understand—'

'There's *nothing* too involved for you to understand! Or to plan, or to carry out behind my back!'

Mary held up her hand. 'I lent that money to Barbara out of a simple desire to help her.'

'I'd love to believe that, Mother.' He was heavily sarcastic. 'I really would!'

'And why shouldn't you? The only reason you blame me is that you always have to have a scapegoat.'

'You are invariably behind it!'

She sighed. 'I am reluctant to say this, Edward, but you are becoming almost paranoaic these days.'

'I see!' He flung away from her. 'So none of this is happening. It's all in my imagination.'

He splashed more whisky into a glass, took a long drink to steady himself.

'When you start accusing Brian and David of plotting,' his mother reproved, 'you really have gone beyond the bounds of credence. I know my sons too well to believe such nonsense. Plotting indeed!'

The plotters were not coming too well out of the evening's work. Brian, driving his wife home, was trying to explain his difficulties.

'You told me you were going to *insist* on being managing-director,' she complained.

'I'm not in a position to "insist". Don't you understand that David can buy Jenny out by getting Jill to write a cheque? I'm going to be lucky if I scrape up enough to buy half those shares from him.'

He sounded so worried that it actually pierced the layer of self-preoccupation that had blanketed off most of the evening. 'Darling, I'm sorry. Really I am. Perhaps it'll work out.'

Brian stopped for a red light. The lamplit road was practically empty. There was no sound for a moment except the muted throbbing of the engine.

'What did you think of Jill's reaction?' he asked.

'Which one?'

'I got the impression she isn't exactly a hundred per cent behind him. I wondered how it appeared to your feminine eye.'

'Humbug,' she said crossly.

David and Jill were also having a post mortem. It began when Jill asked for Jennifer Kingsley's telephone number.

'It's on the pad,' David said. 'Why on earth do you want it?'

'I'd like to talk to her about this business, that's all.'

'But why?'

'I've heard one side of the story. I'd like to hear the other.'

'I haven't held anything back from you,' he protested. 'She's leaving, that's all.'

'Perhaps she could be persuaded to stay.'

He was astounded. 'But then there'd be nothing to—'

'Carve up? Quite.'

He came up to her anxiously as she turned the pages of the telephone pad.

'But earlier this evening you said you'd back me . . .'

'Only if I thought what you were doing was right. But now that I've listened to you both behaving like puppies over a bone, I'm not sure of that.'

He was annoyed. 'Jill, if you think that was a tough meeting tonight, then you've no idea of what goes on in the commercial world.'

'I didn't think it was "tough" at all. I thought it was simply shabby.'

'Because we were hard on Edward?'

' "Hard", "tough", all these silly schoolboy words,' she cried in contempt. 'You weren't being "hard", either of you. You were just being mean and cruel at his expense.'

'Oh, if you prefer silly schoolgirl words—!'

Jill refused to be sidetracked. 'It was particularly unpleasant because he wasn't here to defend himself—'

'He *had* his chance to buy the shares.'

'Perhaps he can't afford to?'

'I'm damn sure he can,' David said in a voice full of resentment. 'He's a bachelor, he never spends. I bet he's been tucking it away for years.'

'Then why hasn't he bought Jennifer out?'

'*I* don't know.'

'Is he in love with her?'

'Oh, they've had some sort of thing going on ever since Dad died.'

Jill stared at him. 'Then you do know the reason. He's in love with Jennifer and he doesn't want her to go. That seems to me a far better motive than any I've heard this evening.'

'Are you now trying to say,' David inquired coldly, 'that you are *not* going to lend me the money?'

'I'm sorry, David, but under the circumstances – no.'

As she made for the door, he prevented her.

'That's the way it's always going to be, isn't it?' he shouted. 'There'll always be conditions!'

'Just the one,' she replied, taking his hand from her arm. 'That you treat people with respect.'

'He's *my* brother. I can treat him how the hell I like!'

'Not with my money,' Jill said, and went out of the room.

Ann Hammond was up before Brian next morning. That wasn't difficult – she had scarcely slept. She was in the hall as soon as the letters fell on the mat.

But there was nothing from Brussels.

She went into the livingroom and quietly lifted the telephone. 'Continental exchange, please.' When she was put through she said in a low voice: 'I've tried dialling through but the connection breaks down. Could you get me Brussels 029654. Yes please. This is 246–8026.' She waited. 'All lines engaged? Then . . . would you try again later? Thank you. Goodbye.'

There had been no call by the time Brian was ready for work. Just as he was leaving he said: 'Ann . . . would you object if I took a second mortgage on the house?'

'What's wrong with the first one?' she asked innocently.

'It's just a way of raising extra money.'

'Well, I suppose it's all . . . ' She paused. 'Wait a minute, Brian. *I* own half this house.'

'But I pay the mortgage. Darling, I'm trying to bid against Jill's money—'

'Not with my property, you aren't.'

'I'm sorry,' he said tolerantly. 'You're not really awake yet—'

'I'm awake enough to know the whole business is beginning to bore me to tears,' she flared. 'I'm certainly not *paying* for it as well.'

She sounded so high-strung he decided not to pursue it. 'You're still not very well—'

The phone rang. Although she moved fast, Brian was there first. 'Hullo? What? I didn't book a call to Brussels! You must have the wrong number.'

Ann stood rooted, unable to think or speak. Brian cupped the phone. 'It's the Continental operator, insisting someone booked a call to Belgium . . .'

She summoned up a shrug of perplexity.

'What number Brussels?' Brian asked. 'I see. Well, I'm sorry, but there seems to have been some mistake. You'd better cancel it. Goodbye.' As he put the phone down he added, more to himself than Ann: 'That number rings a bell . . . Who . . .?' He snapped his fingers. 'Nick Fox, of course!'

'He was probably trying to ring *you*,' Ann said.

'She said it was booked from this end.'

'I expect she got muddled.'

'I'd better call him back,' he muttered. 'It might be urgent.'

'Do it from work,' she urged.

'I'll charge it to the firm anyway—' He began to dial.

She exclaimed: 'Don't tie that 'phone up, Brian!'

Her husband looked up in surprise.

'I . . . I have to call my doctor at home in a couple of minutes, before she leaves for surgery.'

He was at once contrite. 'Oh, I'm sorry. Of course. You should have told me . . .'

As soon as he had left for the office she tried again, but the lines were all engaged.

Brian got to the depot and almost collided with David at the top of the staircase.

'Thanks for the meal last night,' David said. 'That was a pretty good restaurant.'

'It's one of our favourites,' Brian acknowledged.

His brother moved from one foot to the other. 'I was just looking for you, actually. We're going to have to talk again . . .'

'Yes, the key problem still hasn't been settled.'

'Come along to my office.' They went in. David carefully shut the door. 'Jennifer gave me twenty-four hours to find a down payment of five thousand . . .'

'Oh?' said Brian. 'And is that now a problem?'

'There are certain difficulties.'

'Jill backing down?'

David coloured and moved to his desk. 'It may take me a little longer to persuade her.'

'Then I'll just have to see what I can do,' Brian returned in a tone of optimism. 'I'm off to the bank shortly, to see if they can—'

'Sure, sure,' David said.

'I'll let you know what they say.'

David nodded and switched on his tape-deck to check any

overnight messages. Edward's voice, firm and clear, played back.

'I'm calling a board meeting at ten this morning. I want you both to be there.'

Brian, on his way out when the tape stopped him, looked at David. 'When did he record that?' he wondered.

'And where the hell is he at the moment?' David said.

Edward was in his car, driving away from the depot and with Jennifer in his passenger seat. When she arrived in the car park and got out of her own car, he'd been there waiting. He opened his passenger door.

'Get in,' he said.

'What for?'

'Get *in*!' he said so fiercely that she obeyed at once.

After a few minutes she got up nerve enough to ask teasingly: 'Am I being abducted?'

'In a sense, yes.'

'Oh, that's nice. Can I ask where we're going?'

'To the bank.'

That took the amusement out of her. 'What for?' she asked suspiciously.

'To transfer five thousand pounds from my deposit account to your current account.'

'Are you making a down payment on my shares after all?'

'No, you're keeping them. This is a loan.'

'Oh no!' she exclaimed.

'I'm not arguing,' he told her. 'I'm also doing fifty, so keep quiet.'

'Edward, stop the car!'

He paid no attention. 'My first thought was to give a cheque to mother last night on your behalf. But then I felt you'd probably prefer to pay her back with your own cheque.'

She said, 'Edward, it's very sweet of you, but I absolutely refuse to be in your debt.'

'Then you'll stay in my mother's debt. Which would you prefer?'

'I've found a way out of that.'

'Your way would have been a disaster. For me, anyway. Jenny, I could have strangled you, when I found out what was behind it!'

She shook her head helplessly. 'I've no possible way of paying you back.'

'Let me worry about that. Concentrate on finding a parking place. Not too far from the bank – we've got to be back at the office for ten o'clock.'

When they got back they found Edward's brothers in the boardroom drinking a rather early mid-morning coffee. They both looked up in surprise as Edward said, rubbing his hands: 'Right. Ten o'clock. Take your seats.'

His exuberance was remarkable. By rights he should have been depressed. They sat down warily. Jenny took her usual place. Edward took the chair.

'Right,' he said. 'Only one item. There'll be no discussion – it's merely for your information.' He paused a moment to let that sink in. 'I know you'll be as delighted as I am to learn that Jennifer has decided she can stay with the company. Her shareholding in Hammond Transport Services is no longer for sale.'

Both Brian and David turned to look at Jennifer. She stared impassively back.

'I know,' Edward went on with conscious pomposity, 'that you will both wish to congratulate Jennifer on making a very wise decision. May I record that in the minutes?'

There was a fractional pause. David suddenly woke up to the fact that his brother was gazing at him, waiting for a reply.

'Yes, of course,' he stammered.

'Brian?'

'Oh, yes, indeed.'

'Good. Now the following will *not* be recorded in the minutes . . .'

Jennifer got to her feet in haste. 'If that's the only item I'd prefer to leave.'

'All right, as you wish, Jenny,' the chairman said.

An awful silence accompanied her to the door. Then it closed behind her.

'Now,' said Edward. 'For the past forty-eight hours you two, without my knowledge and behind my back, have been huddled together like crows over a carcase, plotting your disreputable and, in the end, pathetic moves to take over this company.'

David got up. 'I don't think we have to stay and listen to this—'

Edward hit the table with his fist. 'You'll sit down and hear me out!' David hesitated. 'I said, sit down!'

David subsided into his chair. He had never seen his eldest brother so furious. Brian didn't dare move.

'I don't know the sordid details, and I don't want to,' Edward resumed. 'I don't know who fancied himself in the chair or who preened himself with the thought of "Managing-Director" across his door. All I know is that both of you – both my brothers – were ready and eager to take advantage of Jenny's problems without a single thought but how you could profit from it. And kick me in the face at the same time!'

He leaned forward on the table. 'I came up the hard way. Let me tell you this: neither of you – scheme and plot as you may – will ever take this company away from me! I'd sooner burn it to the ground.'

Neither dared to speak in the ensuing pause.

Then Brian said: 'Have you finished?'

'I've finished. Now get out of my sight, the pair of you!'

They left the boardroom in silence. Brian was feeling that nothing worse could ever happen to him in this world.

He might have changed his mind if he could have been outside his house just then. A taxi had just drawn up outside his front door.

The door opened. Ann came out of the house.

'London Airport,' she said to the driver, and got in.

CHAPTER THIRTEEN

Ann could not have explained what she hoped to achieve by her action. It was now ten-thirty in the morning. If she caught the next plane it would be about noon when she got to Brussels, and about one by the time she reached the Palace Hotel.

In all probability Nicholas Fox would have a lunch engagement with his business associates. Even if he was in the hotel, he would probably not be pleased – she shivered as she imagined his surprised annoyance. She would explain that she intended to fly back at mid-afternoon, in plenty of time to be at home when Brian came in. She would tell him that she couldn't exist any longer without seeing him, even if only for ten minutes.

Some vestige of normality told her she was behaving wildly. It didn't seem to matter. She *had* to see him.

Easier said than done. An earlier flight to Belgium had been cancelled and the next one was packed out with the extra passengers. She asked to be put on standby. But she had no luck. Neither that flight nor the next had room for her. She waited hours – centuries. Then at last she realized that even if they found a place for her, it would be too late: once she reached Brussels she would have to turn round and come straight back.

At nine-thirty next morning when Brian had safely left the house, she went straight to the telephone to dial the number of the Palace Hotel. By a miracle, she got through immediately – the first time since Nicholas had gone there.

'Room 221, please.'

'I am sorry, madame. The line is engaged.'

'Look, I'm calling from England. It's very important. Would you be so kind as to break the call going on now? Thank you so much.'

There was a series of clicks. Her heart was hammering. She began to drum nervously with her fingers on the telephone table.

'Hullo? Room 221?'

'Yes. Mr. Fox's room.' It was a girl's voice.

Ann was so surprised that she couldn't speak.

She put back the receiver with an unsteady hand. She stood for a long moment with her head back. Then she dialled another number.

'Pageant Advertising,' said a brisk voice.

'Good afternoon,' she said. 'Is it worth putting some papers in the post to Mr. Fox's secretary in Brussels, or will she be back soon?'

'One moment please.' A moment later another voice came on. 'Mr. Fox's office. Can I help you?'

'Is that his secretary?'

'Yes, it is. Who's speaking?'

Ann put the phone down.

By and by she began to go across to the stairs, unbuttoning her suit jacket. She took it off and folded it over her arm. She went slowly upstairs. When she reached the fifth step, she slowly crumpled forward with her face hidden in the folds of the jacket.

She felt the soft wool against her cheek, and the dampness where her tears began to soak into it. She was aware of a strange sound. She did not know it was her sobs.

The phone rang. It took a moment for the noise to penetrate. When she realized what it was she dragged herself to her feet and went to it. She had to summon all her strength to pick it up. It might be Nicholas – and if it was, she couldn't bear it.

And if it was not, she couldn't bear that either.

The caller was Brian. 'Hullo, darling, how are you?'

'Fine, thanks.'

'Did you get through to your doctor?'

'Yes.'

'Was it to make an appointment?'

'Yes.'

'Well, when is it for, darling?'

'Tomorrow.'

'I see. In the meantime you're all right?'

'Of course I'm all right.'

'You sure? You sound strange.'

'Brian, I am perfectly all right!'

'Very well, Ann. I'll ring again later.'

'No, don't,' she cried.

'Why not?'

'I'm – I'm going out. To have my hair done. For heaven's sake, do I have to report my every move?'

'Oh. I'm sorry, dear . . . Well, 'bye for now.'
'Goodbye.'
She slammed down the receiver, breathing hard, furious with Brian and his inane concern for her. Why did he have to keep forcing her to tell lies? Why couldn't he leave her alone?
But the call had put adrenalin back into her blood supply. It gave her the impetus to make some attempt at helping herself. With trembling fingers she dialled the number of Pamela Graham's school.
Ten minutes later Pamela was on her doorstep. There was actually chalk still on her fingers – she must have come straight out of the classroom.
'Pamela!' Ann took hold of her arm with both hands and pulled her indoors. 'I wouldn't have rung you if I hadn't been desperate!'
Pamela surveyed her with anxiety. She looked flushed and dishevelled. Her eyes had a strange expression – too bright, as if she had a fever. 'Have you seen your doctor?' she asked.
'What could I say to her?'
'She'd be more help than I, Ann. I can only make sympathetic noises.'
Ann wasn't listening. 'I tried to go and see him yesterday. To Brussels.'
'Ann!'
'I thought I could just hop on a plane, be over there in an hour, just *talk* to him. I'd have been back by six. But all the planes were full.' Her voice was like a forlorn child's.
'Would that have solved anything?'
'I suppose not. I just wanted so badly to see him.' She looked down at her hands. 'As it turns out, it was lucky I didn't go.'
Pamela watched her in alarm.
'I managed to get through on the telephone. Through to his room. A woman answered. Used a sort of secretary voice.'
'How do you know she wasn't a secretary?' Pamela said.
'His secretary's in London. I checked.'
'Perhaps the hotel provided one, Ann?'
'No.' She shook her head from side to side. 'It explains everything. Why he never rings, why he's never available when I ring him.'

'It very well might be a secretary,' Pamela said. 'But assuming you're right – what made you think you had an exclusive option on him?'

'The things he said . . . led me to believe . . .' She stopped, confused. 'Pamela, I don't know what I'm saying any more.'

'You realize,' Pamela said in a voice that came out very schoolmarmish, 'that you've got yourself into a very familiar trap.'

'I suppose so.'

'You fell for him because he represented an escape from all this.' She indicated the pretty suburban house with a wave of her hand. 'The more remote he becomes, the more you want him – and the less likelihood you have of getting him.'

'That's the diagnosis,' Ann said with a glint of humour. 'What's the cure?'

Pamela sighed. 'We've discussed that endlessly. *Forget him.*'

'I read somewhere,' Ann murmured, 'that doctors can put people into a very deep sleep that lasts for weeks . . . and when you wake up everything is new again.'

'That's a new remedy for a love affair.'

'No, but wouldn't it be marvellous . . . just to sleep it all off.'

'Why don't you go upstairs and lie down,' Pamela suggested. 'You look worn out.'

'I'd only lie and think.'

'But I can't leave you like this,' said Pamela, feeling hunted, 'and I *must* get back. I'm taking detention class today.'

Ann got up. 'Yes. Of course. I'll see you out.' As she was about to open the door she said suddenly: 'Did you bring your car?'

'My car? Why?'

'Could you drop me off at a taxi rank?'

'You're *not* going to try for a plane again?'

'No, a train. I want to see the children.'

'The children?' Pamela was startled. 'Why suddenly, the children?'

'I just have to see them. That's all.' She picked up her handbag.

Pamela was very perturbed at this sudden change of mood. Instead of the confused lethargy of a moment ago, now there was purpose and determination – but still no logic.

Ann seemed to sense her hesitation. 'Didn't you once say to me that children are a stabilizing influence? I was rude and said how could you know since you'd never had any, but you were right. It's what I need now. To see them, to talk to them, to make me feel I belong . . . somewhere.'

Pamela was still dubious – for the children's sake, if not for Ann's. It was unfair for young children to have to cope with a distraught mother. Yet what right had she to forbid it? And – she smiled to herself – what notice would Ann take if she did?

She saw her on to a train and scuttled back to school just in time to count her ten naughty children into the classroom where they were sentenced to half an hour's extra French verbs.

Ann reached Carol's school as the girls were sitting down to tea. There was an air of excitement and indiscipline – end-of-term was near. The headmistress was a little surprised to see a parent on a visit so close to the time when she would have her daughter home, but made no comment: parents were always welcome.

Carol looked quite pleased to be taken out for a walk. 'Why didn't Daddy come?' she asked.

'He's working, darling.'

'Will he come at the week-end?'

'I expect so. What have you been doing this afternoon?'

'Games. Stupid basketball.' She looked up at her mother. 'Where are we going?'

'Oh, I don't know. Along the tow-path?'

'All right.'

'Carol, do you like it here?'

'It's all right.'

'And you've made lots of friends?'

'Yes.'

'Tell me their names.'

'Sylvia and Jean.'

'Oh.' That seemed rather few. 'And the teachers?'

'They're all right.'

'Just . . . all right?'

'Except Miss Mavor. She's not.'

'But you like it better here than at the other school?' Ann persisted.

'It's about the same.'

'You liked Miss Graham at the other school, didn't you?'

'Yes,' said Carol, her face lighting up.

Ann felt the warm, unresponsive hand in her own. Was this her child, her flesh and blood? If they were mother and daughter, why did no current run between them? She'd seen children greet their mothers outside school at the end of classes, running, school bags banging, arms open wide for a sticky hug. And she'd thought, 'How droll.' But now she understood that she had missed something, and so had Carol, through no fault of her own.

'Do you miss us?' she asked.

'Who?'

'Daddy and me.'

'You ask me that every time,' Carol said in a vaguely resentful tone.

'And you say no. Is that the truth?'

'I don't know what you *want* me to say!'

'Carol . . . if I was away when you came home at the end of term, would it upset you?'

'Away where, Mummy?'

'Just away. Not at home,' Ann murmured.

'Would Daddy be home? And Nigel?'

'Oh yes. So that would be all right, wouldn't it? If Daddy was there and I wasn't?'

'Who'd do the cooking? Daddy can't even fry an egg.'

'So the only thing that would worry you,' Ann said with a bitterness she couldn't prevent, 'is who would do the cooking.'

'Could I sleep in your bed?' Carol inquired, beginning to see possibilities.

'Carol, I am trying to find out if you would miss me if I wasn't there.'

'Are you going off with another husband then?'

Ann gasped. 'What on earth made you ask that?' she said.

'Well, Helen Palmer's mother went off with another husband. She's in my class,' confided her daughter.

'And what did Helen Palmer think of that?'

'She cried at first,' said Carol. 'But then her father came to see her with her new mother and she likes her better.'

'I see,' Ann said.

'Mummy, I must get back. I've got choir practice. I'll be in trouble if I'm late.'

'All right, Carol.'

They walked rather silently back the way they had come. The river slipped by, and on it a pair of white swans and two brownish cygnets. Carol seemed more interested in them than in her mother.

When they reached the school Carol politely offered her hand. 'Goodbye Mummy.'

'Goodbye.'

But all at once she swept the little girl up into her arms and kissed her eagerly. Carol accepted the embrace, far too polite to say that her blouse had been pulled adrift from her skirt.

'Be good,' Ann whispered. 'Work hard, be brave . . . all those things. Goodbye.'

She let the child go. Without a backward glance she ran into the hall.

'Goodbye, Carol,' Ann said, though there was no one there to hear.

There was another mother-and-daughter confrontation a little earlier that day. Jennifer rang Barbara and told her to come to the depot.

'I don't know if I can, Mum. Johnny and I are going to see a man—'

'I'm not inviting you, Barbara, I'm telling you. Be here! Twelve-thirty!'

So Barbara arrived, looking part-depressed and part-apprehensive. 'I'm here in response to your summons,' she said.

'No need to put it that way.' Jennifer looked up from her desk and waved her in.

'You were jolly peremptory on the phone. What's it about?'

'Your debt to Mrs. Hammond.'

'Oh,' her daughter groaned. 'Am I going to get another lecture?'

'No, Barbara. As from this morning we can drop the subject . . .' She reached into her desk drawer and produced an envelope. 'Here is the counterfoil of a paying-in slip. Five thousand pounds was paid into her account by me this morning.'

'*You* paid it?'

'That's right.'

'You had no right, Mum,' Barbara said feebly. 'It was *my* debt . . .'

'Well, it's done now,' her mother said with cheerful briskness. 'Off you go.'

'But where did you get five thousand pounds?'

'That's my business.'

'Then I owe it to *you* now.'

'There's no hurry to pay it back,' Jennifer said. Her expression softened as she said the words. No hurry at all: her creditor was not the kind of man who would ever send the bailiffs in. She pulled herself together. 'You'd better get round there and give it to her in case she's going out for the afternoon.'

'Why didn't you post it to her?' asked Barbara with real curiosity.

'That would have been very impersonal.'

'Or take it yourself?'

'I thought you would prefer to. As you say – it's *your* debt.'

'Are you trying to humiliate me, Mum?' her daughter said, slowly trying to work out the implications.

Jennifer got up and went to the coat rack where her coat was hanging. 'Barbara, I was the one who was humiliated. Far more than you may have realized. But if you find this embarrassing, I'll go with you.'

Barbara was nonplussed. The older generation were a peculiar bunch! Here was her mother, who had wiped the floor with her about borrowing from Mrs. Hammond and talked as if they were mortal enemies, now quite calmly offering to go with her into the enemy camp because sending the money by post was 'too impersonal'. What went on behind those busy, conventional lives? Were their thought processes as entirely divorced from instinct and emotion as she had supposed?

Her hesitation was brought to an end by the abrupt entrance of Edward Hammond. 'Jenny, have you a minute—' He broke off. 'Oh, hullo, Barbara.'

'Hullo,' Barbara said.

Edward realized Jennifer had her hand on her coat. 'Sorry, are you going out?'

'No, she's not,' Barbara replied for her. She picked up the envelope from the desk. 'I'll go.'

Looking disconsolate, she went out slowly.

Edward occupied a few minutes with the business queries he had used as an excuse to drop in. Finally Jennifer said, hiding a smile: 'Edward, you didn't need my help with those schedules, nor is it important that there's fog on the East coast. Now what did you come in here for?'

He grinned. 'Ah . . . Well, now you've raised it . . . I was thinking of taking a holiday.'

'Yes?'

'I thought . . . next week perhaps.'

'August is a busy time. Where did you think of going?'

'What I'd really enjoy . . . just get in the car . . . drive into the country . . . stop overnight at some little pub and move on next day . . . or not.' He gave Jenny a slow smile. 'Would that sort of thing appeal to you?'

'It might,' she said, returning the smile.

'You're due for a holiday, you know. You haven't had more than a day off since Christmas.'

'True.' She felt all sorts of trickles of emotion going out to her nerve ends – pleasure, affection, gratitude . . . 'Do you think the firm could spare us both at the same time?'

He made a grimace in which there was grimness as well as humour. 'Brian and David fancied they could run it on their own. Now let them try it for a week. That should take the wind out of their sails.'

'Can I let you know later?'

'What is there to decide?' he countered, a shade anxious.

'A lot of things, Edward. We're getting close again. Perhaps too close.' She looked down at the work on her desk, seeking escape there. 'I have to decide,' she murmured, 'whether I want to go through all that again.'

Barbara was already on her way to Mary's house by bus, anxiously rehearsing openings to the forthcoming conversation. 'Thank you, Mrs. Hammond, for lending me the money, and here is the repayment.' 'Mrs. Hammond, you were so kind to help me when I was in a jam . . .' Or even: 'It is with great gratitude and affection, Mrs. Hammond, that I hereby repay . . .'

What she actually said was: 'Mother's sent me with this. You will accept, won't you?'

Mary Hammond opened the envelope and took out the paying-in slip. She felt her heart give a big throb of pain. So much rejection, so much determination not to be in her debt.

She woke up to the fact that the child was watching her

anxiously. 'Since your mother has already paid it into my account, I don't have much alternative, do I?'

Barbara shook her head.

'Well,' said Mary, dropping the slip on her bureau, 'I suppose I would have done the same.'

'I'm sorry it caused . . . all this trouble.'

'You weren't to blame. I was.'

'No, no! You were being kind.'

Mary produced a wan smile. 'People don't always see it that way.'

'By "people" she means Mum,' Barbara thought. 'It's awful the way things have gone between them. I mean, why do they waste time disliking each other? Life's too short.' It struck her that this was literally true where Mrs. Hammond was concerned. She must be really old. After all, Edward was . . . what? . . . fortyish. So his mother must be sixtyish, and these days looked older. *Really* old.

'I know I shouldn't say this,' she blurted out, 'but I wish you and Mum could be friends.'

'Do you, Barbara?' sighed Mary.

'I mean . . . does it really matter what happened years ago?'

'It conditions us,' Mary replied.

'I had a boy friend once,' Barbara said, 'who had this marvellous philosophy. He used to say – when you wake up every morning, pretend you've just been born. Nothing's ever happened to you before, so everything you do, you do for the first time. And everyone you meet, you meet for the first time.'

'What a lovely idea! And did he carry it through?'

'Yes,' Barbara replied ruefully. 'I rang him up one day and he said, "Who are you?"'

Mary laughed. The child was so uncomplicated! What it was to be young . . . 'If I could live my life again,' she thought, 'could I live by that philosophy? "Nothing's ever happened to you . . . everyone you meet, you meet for the first time." If I were to meet my husband's former mistress for the first time tomorrow – would I dislike her?'

Aloud she said: 'Barbara, I'm going to pour us both a sherry.' Everything you do, you do for the first time. It was the first time she had ever drunk sherry at two o'clock in the afternoon.

During the afternoon her sons David and Brian were

doing something for the hundredth time – conferring about Edward. They were in the boardroom for afternoon tea.

'He's just been in my office, laying down the law about Riley,' David said.

'Oh, yes, I had that bit. Provide him with a mortgage.'

'I've nothing against helping Bill out of a spot, but I think it's a dodgy precedent. They'll all think they can come to us for mortgages.'

'Exactly my reaction,' Brian agreed, putting a sliver of lemon in his tea. 'But he more or less said I could get knotted!'

'He's cock a hoop at having quashed the insurrection.' David crunched a ginger biscuit. 'I hope it doesn't last!'

'We both know Edward too well,' Brian said blandly. 'When did his self-confidence last more than a day?'

The door burst open and Julie Lane came in, tall and handsome in skin tight jeans and a carefully-faded denim shirt. 'I've just shot the most beautiful boiler in your yard,' she announced, waving a Rollei.

'I *beg* your pardon?'

'The ship's boiler for Southampton,' David explained.

Brian laughed. 'I thought you were talking about chickens!'

'Boiler, not broiler. It'll look super in colour in your new brochure.' She sauntered to the tea trolley. 'Pour me a cup, David?'

As he obeyed, she caught his wrist. 'Oh . . . they're super in colour too.'

He was wearing gold and onyx cufflinks. 'What? Oh . . .'

'Present?' she queried.

'Yes.'

'Been having a good birthday?'

'My God!' said Brian, clapping a hand to his forehead. 'It's today, isn't it! In the midst of all the crisis, I forgot!'

'Jill remembered,' said David, 'I didn't.'

Edward came in with a sheaf of papers.

'And what's Edward brought you?' said Julie.

'A message,' Edward remarked. 'Thames Grinding want you on the 'phone.'

'Now *there's* excitement for you,' she cried. As David went to the door she added: 'Are you having a party?'

'No.'

'Then we'll organize one for you.'

He shrugged and hurried out. 'If you'll make a small contribution, Brian,' she went on, 'I'll get some bottles in.'

Edward directed a surprised glance at her. Who the hell did she think she was? 'In where?' he asked.

'What's wrong with here?'

'This happens to be a boardroom. It's not licensed for singing and dancing. Now perhaps you'll get on with your snapshots? Brian and I have business to discuss.'

'Get him,' thought Julie. 'What's come over him?'

She organized David's party in 'The Weary Traveller'. He was a bit reluctant, she felt: it seemed that awful mother of his had got something laid on for the family at her house that evening. Jill was to be there, and Ann was expected.

'I can only stay half an hour,' he insisted.

With the help of his brother, Jennifer Kingsley, and one or two others, she managed to prolong the affair for nearly an hour. But then the men began to make definite moving-on noises.

'I really must ring Ann,' Brian said, looking at his watch.

'Thought you'd done that,' Edward said.

'I tried from the office. There seems to be no one in.' He looked uncertain. 'She may be taking a nap, of course. She has bad nights, recently.' He went off to use the pub's phone-booth.

Julie said to David: 'Am I invited to this shindig at your mother's?'

He smiled wryly. 'I hardly think so.'

'Then invite me.'

'It's not up to me. It's my mother's party.'

'Supposing I just tag along?' she countered, leaning close to him along the bar.

He stiffened. 'You're drunk, Julie.'

'Have you ever known me get drunk?'

'Then what would be the point, apart from embarrassing everybody?'

'I feel like an interesting evening.'

'Then have it at someone else's expense,' he replied.

Stung by his tone, she straightened and picked up her glass. 'Oh well . . . If your idea of fun is to sit around with your mother drinking sherry, go ahead.'

Brian rejoined the group. 'Strange,' he murmured. 'There's still no answer.'

The three men decanted themselves at their mother's

house about twenty minutes later. They weren't drunk, but they were decidedly merry. The remains of an interminable shaggy-dog story reached Jill where she was laying out buffet snacks on Mary's sideboard.

'The revellers have finally arrived,' she called.

Mary joined her from the next room. 'Oh dear, they do sound noisy . . .'

'Sorry, Mother,' David said as he came in to kiss her. 'We meant to be earlier.' He kissed Jill too, with warmth. 'Have you been waiting long, darling?'

'Yes,' she said, but without resentment.

'Where is Brian?' Mary asked, looking round for him.

'In the hall, phoning, Mother. He's trying to raise Ann to tell her she's expected here.' That was Edward, throwing his briefcase behind the sofa.

'You certainly seem to have got a good start on the festivities,' Jill said to David.

'We had a bit of a party. With Jenny. I could hardly refuse once it was arranged.'

'Arranged by Julie, I hear.'

'How did you hear?' he demanded, ready to be angry if she was checking up.

'Brian rang here, to ask if Ann had arrived. He mentioned it.'

'Oh . . . well . . . I thanked Julie nicely and sent her home.'

'There's champagne in the fridge, Edward,' Mary announced. 'Will you see to it?'

There was general, though unexpressed, surprise. Mary Hammond offering champagne at a more or less impromptu party? Edward went out to get it, and on the way passed Brian, who still looked perplexed.

'Still no luck?'

He shook his head. 'Maybe I ought to go home . . .'

'Oh, stay a bit. Just for a glass of champers.'

'Champagne?'

'Yes, quite a fiesta, eh?' Edward strolled in, feeling relaxed and happy. Partly it was the drink, but partly it was the sensation that his world was beginning to come right. The awkwardness left by his angry speech to his brothers had dissolved in the birthday goodwill. There was only one hurdle left – and he was going to take that at the first opportunity.

His chance came when, glass in hand, his mother made a

speech for David. 'Now that I've got you all here, I just want to say . . . I know there has been some friction between you, and that has distressed me very much—'

'Mother, that's been resolved,' he put in.

'Then I'm delighted. May I appeal to you not to allow rancour to remain in your minds. I was told today that one should live one's life as if born anew every morning. I think it's something we might all find helpful. And now . . . happy birthday, David.'

They all drank. Edward, after the chatter of birthday congratulations had died, seized his chance. 'I'm thinking of being born anew to the extent of taking a few days holiday, Mother.'

'That's the first *we've* heard of it,' said David.

'Then I'll send you a sober memo about it tomorrow.'

'It really is about time, Edward,' his mother commented. 'How long will you take? A fortnight?'

'Leave the firm in their hands for a fortnight?' he replied, only half-joking. 'Much though I appreciated your little speech, Mother, I'm not *that* daft.'

'I thought I might take some time off,' Brian said. 'I think a holiday would do Ann good.'

'That's all right,' David said cheerfully. 'Jenny and I can look after the depot.'

Edward took a careful breath. 'Jenny is probably going to have time off too.'

A pause. 'The same week as you?' asked Mary.

'Yes, Mother.'

After the others left, Mary began clearing up the remains of the party. He watched her. Where had he ever got the idea she was indomitable? She looked tired, and somehow smaller.

'I'll do that, Mother. You go up to bed.'

'No, it's all right.' Her voice was still the same, though – cool and competent.

'Did you enjoy the evening?'

'For the most part.'

'Until I mentioned that Jenny was going on holiday with me, you mean.'

She sighed. 'You didn't actually say that, Edward, but it did seem implicit.'

'I think it's fairly certain.'

'Oh well. I've no doubt you'll enjoy yourselves.'

She was turning away but he took her by the shoulders and made her face him. 'Mother, it was my idea, so if you want to think badly of anyone, think badly of me.'

She looked up at him with a strange composure. 'Edward, I am trying very hard to keep in mind something that Barbara said to me this afternoon. Easier, perhaps, for the young than the old. But I *am* trying. Goodnight, Edward.'

He couldn't quite understand her attitude. He'd expected either a big row or several days in Coventry. Well, be thankful for mercies small and large, he told himself, and set about carrying the dirty dishes into the kitchen.

His brother, on reaching home, found his house less than welcoming. There were no lights, and when he switched them on he saw used glasses on the livingroom drinks table, unwashed breakfast things in the kitchen, and a general air of neglect.

'She must be really ill,' he thought with sudden fear. Ann had always been so fastidious . . .

He ran upstairs calling her name, but there was no response. The bedroom was in darkness, but in the moonlight coming in at the window he could see a shape in the bed.

On the bed. Fully dressed except for shoes.

He switched on the bedside lamp. 'Ann,' he said.

She didn't move.

'Ann. *Ann.*' He shook her, without effect. 'Ann, darling!' In a moment of panic he knelt at the bedside and slapped her cheek. 'Ann, wake up!'

But she did not. And after a moment he saw out of the corner of his eye the half-empty bottle of sleeping pills on the bedside table.

CHAPTER FOURTEEN

The ambulance was very prompt, the ambulance men brisk and efficient. He had carried Ann downstairs by the time they arrived: they wrapped her in red blankets and carried her out in a stretcher.

'She's still breathing,' he told them.

'Very shallow.'

'It was all right to move her, wasn't it?'

The senior man gave a non-committal nod. 'What is it – pills?' he said, in a voice that betrayed the fact he'd seen it all many times before.

'She'd taken some. I don't know how many.'

'Barbiturates?'

'I'm not sure . . .'

'Got the box?'

'A bottle. Upstairs.'

'Fetch it, will you? It'll help the doc.'

Brian raced upstairs. When he came down and hurried out, the ambulance man was closing up the vehicle from inside.

'I'm coming!' he protested. 'There's room, isn't there?'

'I'd sooner you didn't,' was the reply. 'I've got work to do.'

'I won't get in the way—'

The man looked at him kindly. Poor bastard, didn't know what had hit him. But he'd get in the way of the resuscitator. 'We've got to keep her alive, sir. You get in your car and follow on.'

Everything after that was totally unreal. He was left in a corridor where there were some benches. People came and went. Now and again he would catch a nurse or a sister by the elbow, and after a few times he began to know which of them was dealing with Ann. All they could say was: 'She's still in a coma.'

By and by a man in a white coat approached him. He had the pill bottle in his hand. 'Mr. Hammond?'

'Yes. How is she?'

'We're still working on her.' He held up the bottle. 'How many sleeping pills does she normally take?'

'Normally . . .? She's only had them a week or two.' He thought about it. 'One a night, I think.'

'You think.'

'Sometimes she'd take one later, if the first didn't work.'

'Say two. This prescription was filled the day before yesterday – the doctor prescribed another thirty pills. There should be twenty-six pills left. There were only fifteen in the bottle.'

Brian stared at it. 'She took eleven in one go?'

He was appalled. Eleven? How could she swallow eleven accidentally?

'Has she tried this before?' inquired the doctor.

'Tried what?'

'To take an overdose.'

He drew back. 'Suicide? Of course not! This was an accident.'

'How do you know if you weren't there?'

'She . . . she probably got fuddled . . . She's been drinking a bit . . . She just didn't remember she'd already taken one.'

'Eleven times?' said Dr. Johnstone wrily.

A sister appeared at the swing doors of the casualty ward, beckoning him. He turned to go, but Brian detained him.

'Could that number be fatal?'

'Depends on the person,' Johnstone said. 'And the drink doesn't help.' He walked off, too hard-pressed to have time for conversation.

Edward heard the news in the middle of the night. He came downstairs in his pyjamas to answer the phone, and was startled to find Brian on the other end.

'What?' he said, only half-awake. 'You're where?'

His mother came down behind him. 'What is it, Edward?'

'Ann – she's in hospital.' To Brian he said: 'What exactly happened?'

'We're not actually sure yet,' Brian said. It wasn't a conscious evasion, he had something else on his mind. A terrible thought had struck him as he sat in the hospital corridor, taking him hotfoot to the pay-phone. 'Edward, the reason I rang is – I left the house in a hurry – I'm not even sure if I closed the front door. Would you—'

'Let me speak to him,' Mary said, taking the phone out of her son's hand. 'Brian, this is terrible news! What do the doctors say?'

'Nothing much at the moment, Mother—'

'They must have some idea. Look, Brian, I'll get dressed and come over straight away.'

'No, Mother!' Brian was horrified at the idea. 'It's quite unnecessary – they're doing all they can and—'

'It's always as well to take a firm line, Brian, otherwise they tell you nothing.'

'Mother, I don't need any help! Will you put me back to Edward, please?'

This was said so loudly that Edward heard it and retrieved the phone. He understood exactly what his brother felt.

'Hullo, Edward? Will you keep Mother *out* of this!'

'Calm down, calm down. I'll see to it.'

'I only rang,' Brian said in a more normal voice, 'because my briefcase . . . I left it in the livingroom. The cashier's away sick so I've got all the wages sheets in it. You'll need them today for making-up. Could you . . .?'

'Leave it to me, Brian.'

'And keep Mother off!'

'I will, I will.'

And he did, for the first day or two. A fable was established that Ann was suffering from 'toxicity', which was not exactly untrue and sounded authentic. Such feminine things as Ann needed when she began to regain strength were brought from home for her by Pamela Graham, without need to call in help from Mary Hammond. When the day came that 'toxicity' had to be explained, Edward and Brian decided to translate it into 'food poisoning'. She could certainly never be allowed to know that Ann had taken an overdose.

Gradually the crisis passed. Ann was out of danger.

But the talk had begun.

David became aware of it through Julie Lane. She was laying out photos for his inspection on the boardroom table. One, of Bill Riley looking like a walrus, made him laugh.

'If Edward sees that in print he'll cancel the advertising contract!'

Julie shrugged. 'I don't suppose the agency would lose much sleep over that.'

'They worked hard enough to get it.'

'You mean Nick Fox did,' Julie said. 'But hardly for commercial reasons.'

'No? Then why?' David said, puzzled.

'Nick has a secretary with a runaway tongue,' Julie explained. 'But you always pretend you don't like my little bits of gossip . . .' She smiled slyly.

'I don't. Neither do I like the way you dangle them in front of my nose.' He was frowning now, trying to catch the overtones of her words. 'If there's anything you know that affects this firm, I'd like to hear it.'

'Down, Rover!' she mocked. 'It'll cost you a dinner . . . with champagne.'

'I doubt if it's worth it.'

She gave him a wide smile as she passed him on the way to the door. 'Did I ever sell you short, David?' Seeing him hesitate, she finished swiftly: 'Ring Jill, tell her you have Brian's work to do as well as your own – so you'll be working very late tonight.'

'All right,' he agreed, seeming to make up his mind suddenly. 'Eight o'clock at the Trellis?'

'You're on,' she said, and went out before he could have second thoughts.

That was the day that Brian, who had practically been camping out at the hospital, was allowed into the ward to see Ann.

She was propped up in a semi-reclining position with pillows. As he walked down the long room he could tell she was unable to focus on him.

'Darling,' he said, his voice very low. 'It's me . . . Brian.'

She made a little sound. It might have been a welcome.

'How do you feel now?'

'Tired,' she mumbled.

'You're going to be all right.'

'Am I?'

She seemed so listless that he wondered if she was quite awake.

'You're in hospital, Ann.'

'I did gather that,' she said, with a flash of herself.

'There's nothing to worry about now.' He began to be aware he was talking in clichés, but couldn't seem to help it.

She turned her head away. 'Is there any water?'

'Yes of course.' He poured some from the carafe on the bedside cabinet.

'What time is it?'

'Don't bother about that.'

'I want to know the time!'

'Just after eleven o'clock.'

'And the day?'

'Thursday.'

'Oh.'

He helped her to sit up, and gave her the glass. She drank deeply.

'Better now?' he asked, retrieving the glass.

'Why not?' she murmured. She put a hand to her head as if to stop the ache. 'What did they do to me?'

Brian was uncertain. 'Some sort of injections, I think. Carbohydrates, I believe they said. They washed out your stomach.'

Ann made a shuddering gesture. 'I'm sorry about this . . .'

'It's all right. It wasn't your fault, was it?'

'No,' she said. And then, as if it was torn out of her: 'Oh God, what a mess . . .!'

Brian put it all down to weakness brought on by the drugs.

When he rang Edward that evening he was able to report that Ann seemed not too bad.

'Glad to hear it, Brian. Now when is it okay to visit?'

'Perhaps tomorrow, Edward. I think she needs a bit more rest.'

'I quite understand. But *you* were allowed in twice?'

'Yes, about tea-time the second time. Mother wanted to come in, but—'

'Oh, yes, sorry about that,' he said ruefully. 'I did try to stop her. But at least Jill went with her as a restraining influence.'

'It had to happen eventually, Edward.'

'Is she still there? Oh—' Edward broke off. 'I think I hear her now.'

'Right – then I'll go now, Edward.'

'You do that. Go home and get some sleep.'

When he turned to greet his mother he could see she was very pleased with herself.

'I'm sorry to be so late, Edward,' she said. 'I did leave something in the oven.'

'Yes, thanks, I've had it.' He waved a welcome to Jill as she followed his mother in.

'Hullo, Edward. Nice to see you.'

His mother said, 'It's been quite a day.'

'I bet it has,' Edward joked. 'That hospital will never be the same again!'

'I was most restrained, wasn't I, Jill?'

'A model of diplomacy,' Jill agreed, smiling.

'I've just spoken to Brian—'

'He wanted me to thank you for the flowers, Edward,' Mary said. 'Oh, and I insisted Ann should be moved to the private wing . . . it's much nicer.'

'I suppose so.'

'Apparently Brian had asked about a private room but they said it would have to wait till tomorrow. Quite ridiculous! She was supposed to stay under observation until the psychiatrist had seen her.'

'And he only comes round every Tuesday,' Jill added.

'Psychiatrist?' Edward said.

'Oh yes,' his mother swept on. 'We finally discovered what was wrong. For some reason her doctor had prescribed pills that were far too strong for her . . .'

'And she accidentally took too many,' said Jill.

'I see.'

Mary said rather hastily: 'They expect to discharge her on Sunday. I've suggested to Brian that he takes her immediately away for convalescence. Jill knows a marvellous hotel by the sea.'

'I was planning to start my holiday from Monday,' Edward said with regret.

'That's no problem. We've just had a word with David on the phone. *He's* going to look after things while you're both away.'

'*Three* of us will be away, Mother.' He felt Jill give him a sympathetic look.

'Can't Miss Kingsley wait another week? After all this is an emergency.'

'Don't be silly, Mother. If Jennifer doesn't go, I don't go.'

When he rang Jennifer to discuss it, she said unprompted that it would be more sensible to postpone their trip. But when she passed on this idea to David, he was quite indignant.

'Don't you think I'm capable of handling the situation?'

'Of course,' she soothed, 'but there's all my work, as well as Edward's and Brian's.'

He took her by the shoulders and gave her a little shake. 'Jenny, anything I can't deal with, I'll just leave over till the following week.'

'Perhaps we could discuss it at tomorrow's board meeting—?'

'There's nothing to discuss. I shall hold the fort. You two go on holiday and enjoy yourselves . . .'

'But your mother—'

'Never mind Mother. *I* decide what I can do.'

The phone on his desk rang. 'Excuse me,' he said, and picked it up. Jennifer nodded goodnight, then went out.

It was Julie, ringing to check their date. 'Yes, see you there,' he said. 'Eight o'clock.'

She was perhaps three minutes late at the restaurant. She was looking very attractive in a low-cut dress of dark velvet, her hair caught up from her neck in a heavy silver clasp.

'So what was this story about Nicholas Fox?' he asked, when they were settled at table.

'Oh, it's quite a habit with him, apparently.'

'What, exactly?'

'Loving and leaving. He's afraid that if he lingers they'll see through his façade.'

David frowned. 'You mean he didn't linger around Ann.'

'Well, he didn't, did he? Seen him recently?'

He disregarded that. 'Why did you feel it necessary to tell me all this, Julie?'

'I thought there was a lesson in it for us.'

'And all for the price of a meal?'

She made a little moue. 'I'll pick up the tab, darling, if you're feeling mean.'

'Actually, I'm charging it to the Pageant Agency. For research.'

'*I* did the research, darling. *You're* getting the report.'

'And what lesson did the research teach you?'

'That a marriage only comes to grief over an affair if one of the couple behaves stupidly.'

'You surprise me.'

'And that even in this case, no real harm's been done.'

'No harm?' David said, thinking of Brian's desperate anxiety, Ann's defeat.

'I hear they're going off on a second honeymoon. By the time they come back he'll be falling over backwards to please her. He'll have decided it was all his fault.'

'You predict?'

'I'm never wrong.'

'I wouldn't bet on it, Julie. For the first time since I've known you you're beginning to sound a little at a loss.'

'Never let it be said . . .!' she parried. 'We're two of a kind in that respect, David – we always take a firm line. Why, I even hear you're going to be left in charge of the depot next week.'

'Assuming that the board approves the idea . . . and I think they will.'

'Will you spend the time reorganizing everything while they're away?'

'I'm not in a position to. But there are one or two things I shall be taking a hard look at.'

'Such as the employees of your advertising agency?'

'That contract has a few months to run yet. But I'll bear in mind what you've told me tonight when it comes up for renewal, particularly with regard to Nicholas Fox.'

She looked cross. 'Don't forget *I'm* an employee too. You'll put me out of a job.'

'You can go back to free-lancing,' he said coldly.

His tone made her look at him in surprise but she recovered at once. Then she said, 'I didn't intend to stay much longer anyway.'

'Oh?'

'Do you want to know why?'

'You're going to tell me.'

'Yes,' she said. 'All of a sudden I want to.' She looked unlike herself, confused and troubled. 'If you recall any of this afterwards, put it down to the drinks. All right?'

'All right.'

She studiously avoided his glance as she went on. 'It started as a game. You . . . wanted me. I didn't particularly want you. It was just . . . fun. And then . . . it became a silly sort of challenge.'

'A challenge? From whom?'

'From Jill, of course! Oh, not consciously. It was that . . . that irritating calmness of hers. It was almost smug! I wanted to shatter it, to see her fly to pieces . . . if only for a moment.'

She had formed her words with difficulty. Now they came even more slowly.

'But the only games worth playing are the dangerous ones. Sooner or later, I suppose I was bound to fall in love with you.' She gave a little shrug. 'End of game.'

David was deeply embarrassed. It had never occurred to him that he would ever hear the bright, brittle Julie speak like that.

'Julie, I don't know what to say . . .'

She looked up despairingly. 'You don't want me any more?'

He shook his head.

'No . . . It never matches up, does it? You want me – I don't care. I care – you don't want me.'

'I'm sorry.'

'That's all I really wanted to tell you tonight. The stuff about Nicholas Fox was just ground bait.'

David could think of no way of ending the painful scene, or preventing what was to come next. He didn't even dare look at his watch. He knew it was zero hour.

Right on time, Jill walked in.

She had never looked more beautiful. She threaded her way between the tables with the grace of a dancer.

'I'm sorry I'm late, darling.' She arrived at their table with a hand held out in greeting. 'I got held up on the 'phone.' She touched David's cheek, then leaned down to kiss him.

Then she spared a glance for the other girl. 'Hullo, Julie.'

Julie ignored her. She sat while one might have counted up to five, staring at David. 'You bastard,' she said.

And then she got up and walked out.

CHAPTER FIFTEEN

Edward and Jennifer set out on Saturday morning in search of the peaceful countryside that he had known in days gone by. Strangely enough it still existed: all you had to do was leave the motorway and follow the yellow lines on the map, the lines that delineated roads so narrow that sometimes you had to back up for a hundred yards to find a place for another car to pass.

The weather was perfect. August had come, and with it a clear blue sky under which the trees along the roadside seemed to dream in a summer haze.

The rapport between them was perfect too. He discovered again the Jenny he had nearly got engaged to a year ago, and it seemed to him that the twelve months since then had been a waste of his life, because he had spent them estranged from Jenny.

That had been his mother's doing. What a hold she had gained over him since his father's death! Thank God for Jenny, who had given him the incentive to break free, because without her he might have dwindled into a middle-aged mother's boy.

Jennifer must have been in telepathic communication, because just at that moment she inquired, 'How was your mother when you set out?'

'Putting a brave face on it – since her last manoeuvre failed!'

'I suppose,' Jennifer said without malice, 'she'll be sitting at home now planning the next move.'

He smiled at her tolerant tone. 'I don't think she really expects them to succeed any more. She just does it to keep her end up.'

'Do you really believe that, Edward?'

'Yes, I do. I'm more than half persuaded she's on the verge of accepting things.'

'What sort of things?'

'You and me.'

She half-closed her eyes, in pretended thought. 'And you and I are—?'

'In love.'

The holiday of Brian and Ann was less idyllic. The hotel recommended by Jill was superbly positioned. They would breakfast late, on the terrace in the sun, and Brian would tell Ann that she was looking better and she would say she felt all right.

Sometimes they would go for a walk. Not far, because walking tired and bored her. She urged Brian to go on his own, but he refused.

'Don't be silly,' she said. 'You go. I shan't have any more . . . accidents.'

'I didn't mean that. I just want to be with you.'

'What on earth for? I don't imagine I'm very good company, so what pleasure do you get out of it?'

'To see you get well,' he said.

Her mouth curved in scorn. 'You'd really sooner be at work.'

'Then why aren't I?' he challenged.

'Because your mother told you it was your duty to park the kids with my parents and bring your wife away for a week!'

'Duty? Nonsense! Listen, Ann, supposing I'd been ill and convalescing, wouldn't you want to come with me?'

'If that's what *you* wanted. But you might prefer to be alone.'

'I see,' he said, hurt. 'You'd have preferred to be alone.'

'I might. But you never asked me.'

Suddenly he seized her hand and blurted out: 'Ann, why is it that everything I try to do for you is wrong?'

'Because you try too hard! And that puts an impossible burden on me. Do what *you* want to do, Brian. If you want to go back to the office, go back to the office!'

'I never mentioned it,' he protested. 'You did.'

'It doesn't have to be put into words. It's always there – the firm.'

'No, you're wrong. I don't think of it. It's you that matters!'

But she looked sardonically unconvinced.

When he came back from his stroll she was lying on a chaise-longue with a magazine over her face. He was frightened – but she sat up on hearing his footsteps. 'Had a nice walk?' she inquired.

'I was looking at the oyster-catchers.'

'They fish for oysters here?'

'It's a bird, Ann . . . Oh, never mind.'

The waiter came with a tray of tea. She busied herself pouring it. Then she said, 'Brian . . . while I was ill . . . were there any 'phone calls for me?'

'Mm? I don't know. Were you expecting some? Who from?'

'Oh . . . I thought . . . the children . . .'

'But I didn't let them know you were in hospital.'

'No, but I just wondered . . . there was some problem about a Scout uniform for Nigel. You're sure no one . . .?'

He looked at a loss. 'I don't really know, Ann. You must realize I was at the hospital, and when I wasn't, I was at the depot. So the 'phone could have been ringing.'

'Could have been ringing . . .' she repeated in a whisper.

Brian didn't hear. He was gazing out to sea. A moment later he murmured, half to himself, 'I wonder how David's coping?'

David reckoned he would have got on pretty well if only Bill Riley would stop being so bloody-minded. Everything he suggested was met with: 'That's not how Mr. Edward does it.' When the union wanted a consultation: 'Oh, we'll wait till Mr. Edward gets back.' After his re-organization of the parking: 'I should change that back afore Mr. Edward sees it.'

On the Thursday, driven beyond endurance, he lost his temper and told Riley to keep his place.

Which caused Bill Riley to say sourly to one of the drivers: 'Never let the bosses lend you money to buy a house. From then on, they think they own you!'

But untouched by any such irritations, Edward and Jennifer conducted their grand tour of rural England, ending at last at a little village called Bargate. 'My retirement spot,' Edward announced when he saw it. It was certainly a pretty, unspoiled place, and the village pub where they put up was delightfully rural.

Next morning, rather subdued, Jenny said as they drove away: 'Our last day.'

'It's gone quickly.'

'Too quickly.'

'Well, it's not over yet. We've still got today, Jenny. Let's make the most of it.'

'All right. Where are we going to spend today, Edward?'

'Wait and see.'

'Oh,' she said, pleased, 'a mystery tour!'

They went on for about half an hour through winding lanes. Then Edward pulled up on the grass verge by a bridle path.

'Where now?' Jennifer asked.

'We stretch our legs.'

They both got out and wandered to the beginning of the path.

'Shall we see where it goes?' he asked.

'Why not?'

'Probably to a field with a bull in it!'

But there was no bull. They sauntered through a wood of oak and beech, where a squirrel darted away, scolding. Suddenly Jennifer paused.

'Look over there!' she said, pointing through a gap in the trees. 'What a lovely farm house!'

Edward looked. 'Seems a bit broken-down to me.'

'Nonsense. Come on, let's go and look.' She took his hand and urged him on. He seemed quite unwilling. When they had crossed the field to reach it he shook his head while she exclaimed rapturously about its gables.

'I'll go and look round the back,' he muttered.

Jenny struggled through a bed of neglected garden flowers to peer through a ground floor window. All at once a face appeared. She nearly died of fright. But it was Edward. He pointed to his right, towards the front door.

When she got there, he had it open.

'Good afternoon, madam, would you care to look around?'

'Edward, you frightened the life out of me!' she scolded. 'How did you get in there?'

'With the key.'

'How come you've got the key?'

'Strange as it may seem,' he informed her, 'I got it from the estate agent. They keep large supplies of them.'

'Oh, Edward!'

'Anyway, come in.'

She followed him in. The livingroom was big, with a stone floor and an enormous fireplace with inglenooks. The kitchen was relatively modern, but needed repainting. There were two rooms upstairs plus a bathroom and a huge walk-in cupboard.

'What do you think?' Edward asked.

'Oh, Edward, it's gorgeous. But when did you get hold of the key?'

'This morning, while you were getting yourself packed, I saw the ad. in the paper. The agent's office was only a few doors from the pub, so I nipped out and asked for the key.'

'But why did you want to look at it?'

'I thought I might want to live in it. And I find I do.'

'Edward, are you serious?' she demanded.

'Yes, on the whole, I am. It's quiet and peaceful. And when you've spent your life working with lorries, that's no small advantage.'

'And would you be happy here? Away from the noise and the lorries?'

'That depends,' he said seriously.

'On what?'

'On . . . whether you'd be happy here. Jenny, that's the real reason I wanted to come here. To see if you felt the same. Do you, Jenny?'

She met his steady gaze with one as steady. 'Yes, I do.'

'Will you marry me, Jenny?'

'Yes, I will, Edward.'

The drive home was taken up with planning what needed doing to the house and how soon they could move in.

Home in the Hammonds' house, Jill was saying goodbye after a cosy chat and a cup of coffee. 'Have you heard from Edward?' she inquired.

'No.' Mary was quite curt. 'Mind you, he never writes,' she added. 'But Brian's sent a card. "Weather still holding. Tell Jill hotel lovely. Ann much better".'

'Oh, that's good!'

'I'm almost tempted,' Mary went on, 'to take a week at that hotel myself.'

'Why don't you?' Jill urged.

'Oh, I don't think I'd like to be on my own. Not at the moment.' She put Brian's card back on her mantelpiece. 'How's David been getting on?'

'Oh, he's in his element, poor darling!'

'Jill, is everything all right now between you two?'

'Yes, everything's fine.'

'I'm so glad.' Mary turned to her armchair, but somehow seemed to miss her step and had to clutch the arm for support.

'Are you all right?' Jill asked, moving quickly to help her.

'Yes . . . fine . . . just my legs . . .'

'You really don't look well. Let me help you upstairs to lie down.'

'No, dear, you run along. I'll just sit here quietly for a minute and then I'll do some gardening.'

'Are you sure?' Jill hesitated. 'If you want me for anything, you will ring?'

'Yes, I promise.'

'All right then.' Jill dropped a kiss on her cheek. 'God bless,' she said – a phrase she never used.

A long time after she had left, Edward nosed his car into the space in front of the house. He and Jennifer got out and hurried indoors, holding each other by the hand – he in pride of achievement, she in apprehension. They went through the hall.

'Mother!' Edward called.

No reply.

'Mother! I'm back!'

But Mary Hammond could not reply to her son's call. She lay silent amongst shards of pottery and broken plants.

When Edward saw her, for one terrible moment his own life seemed to come to a stop. He felt as if he'd been smashed by some huge sledge hammer. Even when he tried to call her name again, it wouldn't come: he was sure she was dead.

So the sledge hammer hit him another blow. Guilt . . . He'd gone away, pursuing his own happiness, while all the time she was ill, really ill.

He got down beside her, carefully clearing away the scattered soil from about her head. Under his fingers it felt like the earth he'd thrown on his father's coffin. It wasn't time yet to do that for his mother. He wouldn't let it be time, not yet!

'Mother,' he said in a hoarse, pleading voice. He leaned forward to listen for a heartbeat. If he had been praying, he could not have been in an attitude of more humble supplication.

Jennifer stood watching him in stricken silence. Though she owed Mary Hammond nothing, she couldn't evade a sense of having done wrong, somehow – of taking her eldest son, her main support, away from her when she needed him.

Yet . . . if she were dead, how many problems it would solve.

As soon as the thought formed, Jennifer thrust it away and stifled a gasp of horror at her own callousness. She got down beside Edward. 'Is she still breathing?' she asked.

'I don't know! Oh, God, I just don't know! Jennifer, get to the 'phone – the doctor's number is on the pad—'

'Yes, of course!'

Just as she was scrambling up, her eye caught the faintest movement of Mary's hand – a tremor of the fingers as minute as the flutter of a strand of thistledown.

'Edward!' she whispered.

He didn't hear her. His ears were strained for a sound that was more important to him than Jennifer's voice.

His mother was breathing. Only just, but breathing.

'Quick,' he ordered, straightening. 'What're you hanging about for, for God's sake? Get the doctor!'

She ran to the telephone. A thousand feelings were fighting for supremacy inside her. First of all, they must save Mrs. Hammond's life. Of course they must! She couldn't live with her conscience if any neglect or stupidity on her part caused her death.

Yet even as she dialled the doctor's number with trembling fingers she was beginning to admit a dreary sense of defeat.

It was wrong even to think this – but wasn't it strange that Mary Hammond should have a heart attack *now*, of all times? People didn't want to be struck down: it would be monstrous to suggest such a thing. Yet somehow these disasters often seemed to strike when they'd have the greatest effect.

'Dear heaven,' she said to herself as she listened to the ringing tone, 'what's the matter with me? Am I inhuman or something?'

She didn't want to make judgements or assessments at the moment. She gave all her attention to explaining, in a dozen terse words, what had happened and what was needed. The doctor said he would be there in less than five minutes, and ordered her to call an ambulance. She replaced the receiver then lifted it again to dial 999.

When she got back to the conservatory Edward was gently chafing his mother's hand. His palm made a whispering sound as it passed over the knuckles and the skin of her wrist. He turned his head as Jennifer came in, without speaking but asking his question.

'He's coming,' she said, 'and an ambulance.'

'Good. You hear that, Mother? You're going to be all right . . . all right . . .'

'But what about us, Edward?' Jennifer asked silently. And knew the answer without having to hear it.

All the happy plans of this morning would come to nothing. She and Edward would never live in the farm house. Why had she ever allowed herself to believe it? Hadn't she learned yet that life was never going to relent? The dream would have been difficult to achieve with Mary Hammond hale and hearty. But with Mary lying in a hospital bed, a rival who need not so much as speak a word or raise a finger, the dream would disintegrate.

Jennifer stood watching Edward as he in turn watched Mary struggle to draw each faint and painful breath. All around them was strewn the wreckage of the plants Mary had been caring for.

The plants might in time renew themselves. It was possible that Mary too would cling to life, would even recover.

But invisible wreckage was scattered at their feet – the broken pieces of Jennifer's hopes. And Edward wasn't even aware of it. Sick at heart, she acknowledged that the future looked empty for her. There was nothing to fill it now. Barbara was talking about going so far away, and the firm to which she'd given her loyalty was changing out of all recognition.

She had thought that Edward was going to give new meaning to her existence, but it was no use denying facts: so long as his mother lived and took first place, Jennifer would have to be satisfied with the leavings.

Bitterly she turned away. She'd have to find the courage to start again, to build something for herself in which Edward was not a cornerstone. But even as she summoned up that little fragment of courage from among the ruins, she knew that the road ahead would be cruelly difficult – and not less so because now she had admitted to Edward that she loved him. It was an added burden she'd have to shoulder.

She would have to learn not to look back on what might have been. That was the only way – to walk forward, looking neither to right nor left, ready to meet anything that life might have in store.

But it wasn't going to be easy.